THE GARDEN OF A
DesertRose

THE GARDEN OF A

DesertRose

A Spiritual Mystery

DEBORAH L. KELLEY

BALBOA
PRESS

A DIVISION OF HAY HOUSE

Balboa Press books may be ordered through booksellers or by contacting:

Balboa Press
A Division of Hay House
1663 Liberty Drive
Bloomington, IN 47403
www.balboapress.com
1-(877) 407-4847

Because of the dynamic nature of the Internet, any web addresses or links contained in this book may have changed since publication and may no longer be valid. The views expressed in this work are solely those of the author and do not necessarily reflect the views of the publisher, and the publisher hereby disclaims any responsibility for them.

The author of this book does not dispense medical advice or prescribe the use of any technique as a form of treatment for physical, emotional, or medical problems without the advice of a physician, either directly or indirectly. The intent of the author is only to offer information of a general nature to help you in your quest for emotional and spiritual well-being. In the event you use any of the information in this book for yourself, which is your constitutional right, the author and the publisher assume no responsibility for your actions.

Any people depicted in stock imagery provided by Thinkstock are models, and such images are being used for illustrative purposes only.
Certain stock imagery © Thinkstock.

ISBN: 978-1-4525-3591-3 (e)
ISBN: 978-1-4525-3590-6 (sc)
ISBN: 978-1-4525-3592-0 (hc)

Library of Congress Control Number: 2011910643

Printed in the United States of America

Balboa Press rev. date: 7/27/2011

DEDICATION

May this offering awaken within you a conscious movement away from ego's story recognizing your true center as a Being of which we are each a shining star.

ACKNOWLEDGEMENTS

I acknowledge with joyous heartfelt thanks:

My husband, John, for support and encouragement during the early stages of writing this book.

My children, Danny and Julie, for becoming the true masterpiece I always longed to paint.

My beloved grandchildren and the many children of my heart for the constant joy they bring into my life.

My parents, siblings, extended family and friends who help me daily by their loving kindness and support.

My editor, Katy, who cut through my work with a sharp editor's sword helping me to uncover what I really wanted to say.

My lovely friend, Eshan, for his insightful help as I struggled to understand my dreams of sacred geometry.

All my teachers, known and others yet to come, thank you in advance for your light and truth which help lead me from the unreal to the Real.

CONTENTS

PREFACE

I dream wondrously! And often when I do, I find myself in conversation with deceased loved ones. I firmly believe in the angelic kingdom, and many times those who loved us in life and still love us on the other side stop by for visits. One such happening shook me to the core, uprooting false perceptions of who I am—or rather, who I thought I was. And the message gifted to me in that encounter rests at the very heart of this novel, my personal myth.

My teacher in spirit on that long ago dark night of my soul was my maternal grandmother. I did not see her, but without doubt, I heard her loud and clear. It has been said when the student is ready, the teacher appears. At some level, beyond my conscious awareness, I must have been ready to push aside my mind-created clutter and move on to a new level of awareness.

My Granny, as I call her in this novel, knew about patterns. She was a skilled seamstress and quilt maker. And I like to think she took a quick glance from heaven and, as she often did in my teenage years, threw up her hands in frustration as she witnessed my self-destructive thought patterns. It was little wonder she was upset, for as spiritual masters often say, every thought received as truth and acted upon comes to be. At the time of Granny's visit, I was completely sabotaging my life with a multitude of unloving thoughts, mostly pointed inward but with some boomeranging outward and then coming home to rest heavy on my heart.

During one of her visits, my Granny referred to me as a Desert Rose and commanded me to grow. She spoke not to my physical self, but to my inner child—my ever-innocent, created Self. In my mind, this Self is a barefoot mountain girl with her head in the clouds and her arms wrapped around the nearest tree. Why, I pondered, did Granny metaphorically shove me into the desert?

At first, I didn't see that before I could grow spiritually and manifest a happier life, I needed to take out the garbage. I had to clear out everything in my conscious and unconscious mind that hindered me from expanding into great self-love and appreciating the unique place only I hold in the great mystery of creation. I needed to stop judging and comparing myself to others. At the time, I thought I was a wild, unruly weed, not a rose seeking her season in which to blossom. But as I gradually began to realize how necessary it was to shift my perception to one of unconditional love, I could see that I was the one who had shoved me into the desert! Granny was reminding me that even if my seed had been planted in a harsh place that I indeed had something beautiful to offer, as do we all. And it was time to cultivate that.

I wasn't exactly sure how to begin, but as I distanced myself from my ego, I became flooded with undiscovered aspects of myself. Remembering how someone wrote that Carl Jung looked at his own soul with a magnifying glass, I thought how fun it might be to look at my soul with a child's kaleidoscope instead. So I began to pry open old wounds, looking at what came up in creative and playful ways.

As I did so, many of this novel's characters as well as archetypes and animal guides started showing up in the middle of the night. For several years, I sporadically felt inspired to write, draw, and record these images that I felt might link my outer life with my inner inspirations. Once, on a road trip to visit a girlfriend, I began to have imaginary conversations with my inner child. I had to pull off the road several times to write down what she said.

Like my Granny, I'm cut from artisan cloth and am almost entirely right-brained. As these mystical experiences continued to unfold, I realized that on some level, the *truest* way for me to tell my story would be to use fiction instead of strictly following the facts, which would undoubtedly read like a poorly scripted soap opera. (That's why I could never write a memoir. I would surely lie.) And the longer I played with writing my life as fiction, the more I felt my novel was writing itself. While I was certainly a player, the universal theme of self-appreciation and love was for everyone.

It also felt natural to plant my myth inside a holiday where trees and stars are central. Jesus Christ had His star, and so do we, hidden within our inner space, shining forth when we become empty of all we are not. During Christmastime, our inner child often steps forward, free and unafraid to be herself or himself. Such innocence can have the power to move what was previously immovable, allowing a space to open within our heart.

It is my wish that as you read this truthful novel (or perhaps this novel truth) that you will also be able to read your own story between the lines.

Love, light, and laughter,
Deborah (Lenny) Kelley

Within each of us is a garden, a place of magnificent beauty and peace.
We just need to sing and dance and imagine it to the surface.
This is our true home and making it manifest is our calling.
—heart mantra by an unknown author

GRANNY'S VISIT

Even in our sleep, pain that cannot forget falls drop by drop upon the heart, and in our despair, against our will, comes wisdom through the awful grace of God.
—Aeschylus (525–456 BC)

The unseen visitor noticed a current 1982 calendar dishrag, reeking of mildew, carelessly tossed atop a pile of dirty white undershirts. She tried to kick it off with her foot. It didn't work, but she really didn't care. She was focused on delivering a message to a young woman, her granddaughter, who was in grave danger. The visitor would do the best she could to address the sleeping woman's inner child and lift her limited awareness into a vaster awareness of the Light-Soul within.

She had to work fast, and yet she needed to wait for just the right moment. She watched for signs that Lenny was between conscious and unconscious awareness. As she watched Lenny's eyes roll just a certain way, she zapped the top of her head with electrifying nonphysical fingers. The touch of her hands sent patterns of energy into Lenny's inner decoding system. The visitor smiled, looking down at her pink, flowered, cow creamer, sitting on the nightstand next to the bed. While she had been on Earth, the creamer had been one of many treasures given to her by her husband. Now it belonged to Lenny. Then she looked down at the darn dishrag and kicked it once again. It didn't budge.

"Maybe next time," she whispered. She thought of her Light-Soul, and then, she was home.

"I just heard Granny," Lenny whispered to empty space. But Granny was dead. No question about it. Yet, there was not a single doubt in Lenny's mind she had just heard her Granny's voice. "A center stays where it is," she'd said. "You are a Desert Rose. Now grrrrooow!"

The last word sounded more like the growl of a tiger. It could also have been, "Now go," or, "Now glow." She wasn't sure. She reached up to rub the gummy mascara and sand from the corners of her eyes. With one arm, she swept heavy bedclothes off the top of her warm body. The air felt chilly. Lenny's feet were on the floor before she realized she was standing.

She stood silent as a statue until her brain wrapped around what she thought she'd just heard. Standing, confused and more than a little disoriented, she looked around the bedroom for Granny's ghost. She had seen her before in a lucid dream. It wasn't that spirit communication was something new to Lenny. It was ingrained into the tapestry of who she was, because she'd experienced it firsthand. Otherwise, like many other people, she'd probably think it was hogwash.

She got up, walked toward her dressing table, and plopped down, Indian-style. Her pink-and-green-striped satin vanity bench felt cold pressing against her ankles. She surveyed the landscape of her pale complexion. Her eyes were red from too little sleep, and too much wine. And tearfulgirl-talk whining had left her senses dulled.

Yet, Lenny still sensed Granny's presence. Her room suddenly felt too dark and lonely. On her vanity sat two tall lamps with tiny fringed shades. She switched one on and then the other. Together they cast a warm, golden glow over her chilly bedroom. But her body still felt cold, covered in goose bumps from her encounter.

Was the voice really Granny's? It *was* forceful and scolding, firmly fixed on the conviction her words must be obeyed. If not, punishment was certain. Although, if it *had* been Granny's ghost, she didn't bother to wallop Lenny on the head with one of her whipping Bible verses. The voice didn't sound happy with her. And Lenny knew she wasn't happy with herself. Was her unconscious mind mirroring her own inner anxieties and frustrations with her life? She didn't know.

A sob welled up in her throat. Lenny picked up a half-empty glass of water and took a big gulp. She looked into the mirror and sighed as she set down the glass, which had left a white ring on the dark surface of her vanity. As she did so, a Bible proverb, once her favorite, drifted up, like a balloon tied to an almost forgotten dream. She closed her eyes and let the ancient wisdom speak aloud through her lips. *"Hope deferred makes the heart sick, but a longing fulfilled is the tree of life."*

All Lenny really wanted was to grow a different past. And since that was impossible, she felt too worn out and emotionally drained to hope for anything. No doubt, her Granny knew this on the other side.

She looked over at her half-closed drapes. She planned to offer them to Goodwill as soon as she could afford to buy new material. They were much too masculine for her taste. She had chosen the dreary brown and beige abstract fabric while married to husband number two, Dick. Before their marriage, her room had been a soft pastel mauve, a color he insisted was too pink for comfort. Beyond these hated drapes, a foggy gray morning was trying to smother whatever was left of the night.

Lenny stared back at her reflection in the mirror. Her eyes were puffy. She dipped a snowy white cotton ball into a jar of cold cream. It smelled like her mother's cheeks. Her mother had been a raven-haired Scarlet O'Hara type in her day. Lenny succeeded in inheriting only her green eyes and fair complexion. Her own naturally reddish-brown hair was currently completely void of naturalness. She'd gone chemically Marilyn Monroe following her divorce. It felt bold and sexy at the time. But not this morning.

Granny had been like a second mother to Lenny. She'd moved in right after Lenny's parents divorced. Her mother had gone back to school, and Granny took over the household chores, which included raising Lenny and her two siblings. She and her older sister had both been preteens. Their younger brother was not yet old enough for school. The arrangement had worked well for Lenny's mother, who had felt swallowed up by what she considered to be the sin of all sins. In the early sixties, this sin was called *divorce*. Now, like it or not (which Lenny didn't), she seemed to be carrying on a family tradition of non-perennial unions. Her love affairs were bright and beautiful, one season, maybe two. And then they faded.

If Lenny didn't feel so tired most of the time, she'd probably try to figure out why she was such a failure at the marriage game. But not today. She'd just been called a Desert Rose by her Granny, and the mystery of what she had heard and what it might mean was much more compelling. The phrase "Desert Rose" seemed to be a startling proclamation of possible soul identity. What else could it be? But Lenny was a born and raised East Tennessee mountain girl. Granny should have called her a pink lady slipper. No mystery in that name: Lenny was a shoe-aholic, and she missed her sheer pink bedroom draperies and the fernlike green lace bedcovers she quickly disposed of following her first marriage. A wildflower like herself could easily grow in such a feminine bedroom. Now she felt hopelessly stuck in beige. The color might be appropriate for a desert, but it was definitely not to her liking.

Lenny reached up and patted down her over processed hair, which was a tangled mess. But she had to admit, she didn't look bad for a thirty-two-year-old, divorced mother of two. She suddenly felt vain. She could almost hear Granny's ghostly voice saying, "Pretty is as pretty does."

Lenny didn't know if that phrase was biblical, but she felt certain it wasn't one of Moses' top-ten commandments. Her second marriage, a mistake from the beginning, had ended, leaving her bitter and battle-scared. She'd always tried to smile when her heart was breaking and to put on a happy face for the children. However, the mask she had been wearing was slipping.

A beauty herself, Granny wasn't prissy like Lenny and her mother. She was solidly built, with square cheekbones befitting her Cherokee bloodline. She feared vanity like a rattlesnake bite. She once admitted to Lenny that her own creamy white complexion was the envy of many a girl. She had never, ever sunbathed. Oddly, it was the only kind thing she'd ever said about herself to Lenny. Just thinking about her Granny's bashful, yet proud, evaluation of herself almost made Lenny cry.

Granny died when Lenny was seventeen. She was sixty-four years old, without a single wrinkle on her face. She loved nature with a passion, as did Lenny. Granny never went outdoors without wearing a hat or a modest, long-sleeved shirt worn over her cotton, waist-clenching, one-piece dress.

Lenny glanced at her alarm clock. It wasn't even six o'clock. She'd gone to bed later than usual. Feeling exhausted from tension the night before, she'd reluctantly gone to a nightclub with two of her girlfriends. Actually, Mitzi and Dawn had forced her out of the house.

Dawn was part Japanese and part African American. She was large-boned and tall, like her father. But she had her mother's almond-shaped eyes. She straightened her hair, but it often looked over processed, like Lenny's hair did now. She worked for her brother's insurance company, while also studying for her MBA at the University of Tennessee in Knoxville.

Mitzi was a true blonde. She wore her hair in a short pixie cut, feathered toward her round face. She had pale blue eyes, deep dimples, and naturally large breasts. She worked at the University of Tennessee Hospital, where Lenny once worked as a medical records clerk before transferring to a secretarial job in the university's football office.

Suddenly, Lenny felt the needle-like pain of her foot trying to go to sleep. She got up and started walking out the tiny needles that were stinging her toes. Her bedroom floor was a wreck. Her children, Mack and Elizabeth, had used it for their gift-wrapping table, and they had not cleaned up their mess.

Something sharp stung the bottom of Lenny's left foot. It was the heel of one of her red snakeskin shoes. She'd worn them the night before. They'd looked perfect with her equally hot red sweater. The sweater had not been on sale, but Lenny's mother said it looked so nice on her that she'd buy it as an early Christmas gift. At the time, this extravagant purchase helped chase away Lenny's holiday blues. But that joy had faded too quickly.

She picked up the shoe she'd stepped on, held it in her hand, and smiled. She'd never seen a snake the color of a cherry-red tomato. But the black lightning-bolt streaks looked authentic. The shoes had a narrow ankle strap she believed made her thick ankles less noticeable. They did not match the outfit she'd decided to wear today, so she tossed

DEBORAH L. KELLEY

the shoe in the direction of her open closet. It missed by inches and landed next to a chair.

Then she noticed the equally bright red Christmas sweater lying at the foot of her bed. Before picking it up, she smelled a stale, smoky fragrance. Knowing her sweater was dry-clean only, she cracked open her bedroom window. A cold December breeze might help, she thought. She picked up a hanger from the floor and hung the sweater between her hated draperies.

Making her way across the clutter strewn floor, Lenny walked into a small, adjoining half-bath. While brushing her teeth, she wondered what in the world she could possibly do with her starchy stiff hair. The night before, she'd piled it high on her head in a French twist. She'd overdone the hairspray, but still, her up-do had made her feel sophisticated and thin at the time. Now, it was a hopeless mess.

She'd laid out clothes for today the night before. She'd opted for her favorite peasant skirt and a hand-me-down blouse from her mother. It had a mock Victorian collar with fancy lace cuffs. As she thought about getting dressed, she was surprised at how awake she felt. Lenny wasn't much of a morning person and usually spent the first hour or so after she woke up feeling half asleep. But Granny's morning message was as chilling as it was penetrating—and much more effective than her alarm clock. She figured she had better stop piddling and write down Granny's words before they slipped forever from her memory.

Granny had never discouraged Lenny from talking about her dreams. She herself was a natural intuitive. However, she discouraged Lenny from talking too much about her vivid imagination. She warned people might think her crazy. But Lenny, always the class artist, felt it her calling to be considered a little odd. It didn't bother her at all.

Granny's Cherokee blood filled Lenny with as much pride as it filled Granny with shame. The Indian tribe linked to her family was driven out of the North Georgia hills against their will. The Trail of Tears was a horror not easily forgotten. All Lenny knew was her early ancestors had previously been members of the Owl Clan in North Carolina. She longed to know more about their customs and traditions. It drove Granny crazy when Lenny begged her to tell her about their

Indian heritage. Lenny's mother told her to stop bugging Granny. She'd been scared as a little girl hearing her brothers called half-breeds while working in the coal mines of Kentucky.

Lenny's family kept lots of secrets while she was growing up, but Lenny didn't follow suit. If a thought crossed her mind, she said it out loud. She knew this wasn't smart, and she often regretted words she spoke in haste or anger. Granny never liked this about Lenny. She scolded her often about her temper. But calling her a Desert Rose still didn't make sense to Lenny.

Her thoughts became quiet as she stood near the bedroom door, listening to an odd sound drifting down the hallway. It was coming from her seven-year-old daughter's bedroom. She knew immediately it was Steve, her daughter's pet mouse, scratching on the screen covering his tank. Lenny loved all animal and plant life—with the exception of poison ivy, snakes, and wild mice in the house. Steve was okay, as long as he stayed in his cage.

After getting dressed and zipping up a pair of stylish black stovetop boots, Lenny pulled her shoulder length hair back into a neck-hugging ponytail. No need for hairspray. It wasn't going anywhere.

By the time the radio alarm went off, Lenny realized she had still not recorded Granny's message. She needed to write it down before she forgot. But first she had to wake up the children, so she walked out into the hall, calling out, "Elizabeth! Mack! Time to get up!" Elizabeth always got up easy. But Mack, her eleven-year-old son, was not a morning person. He was either still sound asleep, or he was simply ignoring her. She figured it was the latter.

She yelled louder. Then she tapped on their bedroom doors before walking back into her bedroom. She bent down and picked up several items of clothing. As she did, she discovered several newly wrapped Christmas packages. They were addressed to her from both children. She knew they'd recently gone shopping with a meager allowance. It didn't matter what was in the boxes. Unwrapping love mattered, not the gift.

Piling the boxes into her arms, she carried them into the living room and placed them in an empty corner. Today was payday. She and the children would go shopping for a tree when she got off work. She stacked up her children's packages, and then smiled down at them. Without reading the tags, she knew which present Mack had wrapped. His paper corners were wadded and sealed with what looked like half a roll of tape per package. She remembered seeing an empty tape dispenser in her bedroom. She made a mental note to buy another roll at the campus bookstore during her lunch break.

Lassie, their Shetland sheep dog, ran out of Mack's bedroom. She greeted Lenny with a happy wag of her tail. Lenny bent down, patted her nose, and let her out the front door. She stood and watched her furry friend sniff several bushes before finding just the right spot. As she let her back in, she remembered she still hadn't recorded Granny's message.

"Damn," she mumbled as she closed the door. She hurried down the hallway with Lassie fast on her heels.

"Time to get up sleepy heads," she said turning on the overhead lights in Elizabeth's room first, and then in Mack's. Both children looked startled and sleepy. Because Lenny had stayed out late, their babysitter let her children stay up late as well. Lenny didn't mind since it was so close to the holidays. They both grumbled as they stumbled out of their beds.

"Mom, did you just say a potty word?" Elizabeth asked still half asleep.

"How did you hear me? I thought you were asleep."

Elizabeth just giggled. Lenny helped her pull her nightgown over her head and walked back into her bedroom. She surveyed the cluttered floor. To clear some walking room she stuffed unused rolls of candy cane paper under her bed. The three bedrooms of her house were so small even the little bit of room under the beds was treasured storage space. She stuffed unused ribbons and scissors into an empty shoebox and shoved it under her bed.

Looking for something to write on, Lenny stuck her hand inside the mouth of a popcorn tin filled with gift tags and scraps of paper. She fished out a red ballpoint pen, and a square of snowman paper. She began writing.

You are a Desert Rose.

No, that wasn't exactly it. She marked through it.

You need to find center.

No, that wasn't quite right. How could she have forgotten so quickly? Determined, she took several deep breaths and closed her eyes. Her cluttered outer world clearly reflected her cluttered inner world. Perhaps if she cleaned her room up a little it would come back to her.

She wadded the snowman paper into a ball and tossed it into a pink, flowered trashcan hidden behind her vanity bench. She walked to her bed and smoothed out the wrinkles of her bedcovers. As her hands fluffed up her bed pillows it came back to her.

She hurried and picked up her red pen. She put her hand back into the popcorn tin and pulled out a large blank gift card with red-and-white candy-cane edging.

"Perfect!" she exclaimed, thinking Granny's visit and message definitely felt like a gift. She wrote as neatly as possible: A center stays where it is. You are a Desert Rose—now grow.

Or was it "go"? Or maybe "glow"? She pondered, second-guessing herself.

What she heard actually sounded more like a growl than a word. But perhaps it only sounded like a growl because Lenny awoke so suddenly from a deep sleep. Her children had that same startled look when she turned the lights on in their bedrooms to wake them up.

"I'll try to grow," she whispered to her unseen grandmother's spirit. But she would definitely need some help figuring out the Desert Rose part of her message. She stuck the gift tag into her nearby wooden decoupage purse. Then, realizing the late hour, she hurriedly checked on the children. She poured cereal into two bowls and yelled out their names, imploring them to come and eat.

Her breakfast was a piece of dry toast and instant coffee overloaded with thick cream. It tasted bitter. But it was hot. Later, she would enjoy a real cup of fresh brew once she got to her office. For now, this would have to do because she hated to be late. Rushed as she was, her thoughts still drifted to Granny.

The night Granny died, Lenny had been out on a date. She arrived at the hospital late—after normal visiting hours. Her grandmother's departure was eminent. But at seventeen, Lenny believed her Granny too strong willed, and bossy, to allow cancer to win. But it did.

That night, she watched several relatives exit her Granny's hospital room wiping away tears. Her mother looked tired and complained about Lenny arriving so late. She scolded Lenny and told her that her grandmother had been asking to see her. Lenny promised her mother she would visit Granny first thing in the morning. But Granny passed away during the night. Lenny's grief mixed with guilt went unresolved for many years.

Then, when Mack was three months old, Granny showed up at Lenny's bedroom door, as real as real could be. She remembered jumping out of bed and running into Granny's open arms. She felt her soft body pressed against her own. She looked into her eyes and they seemed to wordlessly scold her.

"Granny, Granny, where have you been?" she pleaded. "I thought you were dead!"

"Honey," she whispered, "I've come to tell you to get over it! I know why you didn't come to the hospital. You were just scared."

Lenny started crying into her grandmother's loving embrace. The shock of seeing this familiar ghostly silhouette did not cause Lenny to awake startled and confused. Instead, she hungered to stay in the dream. Her Granny was alive. And it felt wonderful to think Granny's death had been a mistake. She awoke to find her pillow wet with tears as she pulled herself out of what felt like a thick, heavy fog. Her Granny had never come to visit again, until last night.

As Lenny put her empty coffee cup into the sink, she noticed her children seemed extra quiet at the breakfast table. They, too, seemed miles away, caught in their own secret thoughts.

She opened a nearby drawer and found a rubber band. She pulled Elizabeth's hair into a ponytail as she ate her cereal.

"Mack, since you're still eating, I'll take Lassie for a quick walk."

"Thanks," he mumbled with a mouth full of cereal.

She put on her coat, attached Lassie's leash to her collar, and walked outside.

2
REACHING FOR CENTER

Center is not a narrow tightrope through life requiring stern effort. Center is a spacious field of consciousness where the flowering of feelings is honored.
—Thomas E. Crum

As she walked Lassie, Lenny thought about a center staying put. She had no idea what a concept like this had to do with her life. She'd taken yoga classes where thinking only of your breath was important when meditating or relaxing. Privately, she knew it would take a bulldozer to remove her runaway thoughts from inside her head. She was never able to focus on her breath for more than a few seconds. Could this be her problem and the unmovable center Granny was talking about?

If it was, Lenny certainly didn't feel relaxed and centered this morning. Her life had too many unsolvable mysteries for that. When she was younger and she turned things over and over in her head like this, Granny would say, 'just let things be. You climbed on this bad feeling, now climb off.' But Lenny could never seem to climb off anything. Her raging thoughts stirred up unwanted emotions and she habitually replayed them over and over. Granny's thoughts were obviously not as wild as her own. She seemed to have an answer for everything. But Lenny's life wasn't that simple. Her emotions were like riding on the backs of wild horses. She didn't control them, they controlled her. Lenny craved answers that would make the unbearable - bearable. She couldn't just let things be. When life tossed her a puzzling bit of intuitive information, she felt compelled to figure out its meaning. In her mind, the spontaneity and synchronicity of every moment deserved serious, awakened attention. And she was determined to ride this mystery until it was tamed and named.

Once, when Lenny was sixteen, she had a strange experience she couldn't quite make sense of, and Granny spoke similar words of advice. After sharing her rather odd experience, Granny scolded her about being too serious. "You try so hard to understand life, you're going to miss the fun of being a child," she warned

Earlier that long-ago morning, Lenny and a few friends agreed to meet at a local diner for lunch. It was a hot August day, and Lenny had worn a mini-dress she'd just finished sewing the night before. As she'd entered the restaurant, she passed a table of three men. Two looked to be the age of her father. The third looked much older, with white hair, and ocean-blue eyes. He smiled and nodded. Lenny returned his smile.

"Miss, can you come here please?" he'd called out. Feeling slightly embarrassed, Lenny walked toward him.

"I'm sorry, but I'm not your waitress," she'd said. "But I'll be happy to find you one," she responded, smiling.

"I know you're not my waitress," he'd replied, suddenly sounding defensive. "Has anyone ever told you how lovely you smile?"

"Not since I got these hideous braces," Lenny answered. "Well, not really before that either. Thank you."

"I didn't mean to embarrass you in front of your friends."

"No bother," she said as she walked toward her friends. They had all been watching her. She sat down at their table with her back toward her admirer, and they'd teased her unmercifully. Before long, they'd changed the subject, and by the time their food arrived, Lenny all but forgot the overtly friendly stranger. But just as she'd finished eating the last bit of her grilled cheese sandwich, he'd approached their table.

Initially startled by his compliments, and captivated by his blue eyes, she hadn't noticed his odd attire. Much like her grandmother, he was wearing a long-sleeved shirt on a blistery hot August day. His white hair was thin on top and his short mustache was trim and dashing. He smiled with his eyes more than his lips. In his hand he held a paper placemat, and he'd handed it to Lenny. Apparently, while she'd been eating, he'd been drawing. His drawing was a rustic-looking cabin scene drawn with a ballpoint pen. Probably, the same pen that now peeped out of his left breast pocket. Beside the cabin was a tree with long bare limbs. A buck deer drank from a stream in the foreground.

As Lenny took the drawing, he whispered into her ear, "I know something about you. You'll marry young."

"Never," Lenny answered. "I don't even have a boyfriend, and for that matter, I'm not sure I even like boys."

Her stranger just chuckled and shook his head.

"Well, if I do marry young, will I be happy?" She asked, smiling back at him.

"Don't try so hard," he said with a more serious look on his face. Lenny suddenly didn't want to know any more predictions. She looked away from his intense stare and tried not to blush. Lowering her head, she noticed his hands. His fingernails were perfectly manicured. Although, he was dressed like a local farmer or common laborer, it was obvious to Lenny this man was neither. He patted her shoulder, turned, and then hesitated.

Not sure what to say, Lenny told him she was an artist and she, too, loved to sketch with black ballpoint pens.

"I know," he said. "We're a lot alike."

Lenny longed to know why he seemed to see through her so clearly. For weeks, his words dangled inside her head like newly discovered puzzle pieces. Back then, she didn't know how they fit into the whole of her life. Yet, reflecting back on these memories, Lenny did marry young. She also worked hard to be happy. In fact, she was still working hard at it. But the key to happiness wasn't in her pocket, or in her head. Maybe happiness wasn't written into her life plan, if she had one.

Since her friends easily overheard her stranger's words to her, they, like Lenny, assumed he was a fortuneteller or a psychic. They began bombarding the poor man with questions about their own futures. He laughed and said kind words to each of them. He told one of her girlfriends she was smarter than she wanted the others to think. Another friend, he said, was too honest with her words. And Lenny's poet friend, a boy new to their group, recited one of his poems to the man about life flowing generously, lovingly, wondrously, and continuously. The stranger clapped his hands, applauding the boy's brilliant writing skills.

They all marveled at his knowing intuitions. When he finally left their table, Lenny rolled up his drawing and stuck it into her open pocketbook. Soon, they called the waitress to their table and asked for their bill.

"That white-haired man paid your lunch tab" she said, swirling a piece of chewing gum round and round in her mouth.

They all looked over at the table where Lenny's stranger had been sitting, but he was gone.

"He paid tip and all. Ya'll don't owe me a dime. Now you darlin's have a nice day," the waitress said as she stacked up their plates.

When she got home, Lenny told Granny the whole story. But by the time she told it, the stranger had grown into a psychic millionaire as well as an artist who had told her they had a lot in common. Maybe, she'd be a rich artist someday who could tell fortunes, she said to Granny excitedly. Granny told her nobody could tell the future because God gave man free will. Everything is cause and effect she said. It's in the Bible. You reap what you sow, she warned.

Then, another thought come to her and her eyes suddenly widened. Maybe, she said in awe, the man was really an *angel in disguise*. Granny shook her head and laughed. She was an excellent listener. Lenny remembered their conversation ended as usual with Granny saying, "Just let it be."

Today, though, Lenny wasn't about to just let Granny's visit be. She turned and walked Lassie back into her yard. As she reflected on the truth of her stranger's prediction about her marriage, she wondered if anything ever happened by chance or if a pattern or plan was already in motion from the time a person was born. How much control *did* Lenny have over her life? She wondered. She simply wanted to understand her Granny's strange message and heed her curious advice.

Lassie barked, and the sound brought Lenny's attention back to the present moment. She looked down and then up. The sunrise was hidden behind pink cotton-candy clouds, and the sky was so beautiful Lenny caught her breath. She silently thanked Lassie for shifting her focus, but the dog was caught in her own moment. Whiskers, her neighbor's golden-haired tabby, had crossed the street into their yard. The over-fed cat jumped atop the hood of Lenny's Tweety-Bird yellow Chevette. Lenny didn't mind. She'd bought the car used from her brother, and it was already christened with multiple dents. What were a few added cat prints?

"Go home, Whiskers," she warned as Lassie jumped up, barking to encourage the cat's departure. As the tabby jumped off the car, she hissed at the dog. Lassie wagged her tail, thinking it was a compliment.

Ms. Tallulah, Lenny's next-door neighbor, was now backing out of her driveway. She and her neighbor were not on speaking terms. Ms. Tallulah made it obvious she did not like children or pets invading her property.

Mack walked outside and put Lassie inside their fenced-in back yard. School was within walking distance from the house, but both Lenny's children liked Lenny to drive them in the mornings since they had to walk home after school.

On the drive, Mack talked about his upcoming birthday. Lenny thought how handsome he looked as he talked. He had reddish-brown hair and pale blue eyes like his father. On Mack, this shade of blue looked less icy than it did against his father's darker complexion. Elizabeth's hair was blonde like her mother's, and her eyes were a shade darker than Lenny's blue-green eyes.

Lenny waited in front of the school in her car, making sure her children got into the building safely. Elizabeth turned and waved goodbye at the entrance. Mack didn't give her a backward glance. Waving at one's mother wasn't cool at his age.

Before starting out on her twenty-minute commute, from the small town of Maryville, to where she worked on the UT campus in Knoxville, Lenny pulled out a round compact mirror from her purse. She applied lipstick and powdered her nose. The compact's mirror was broken. Spider-web cracks radiated out from a single point of contact. Lenny accidently stepped on the compact in high-heeled shoes. Staring into her reflection, she had a flash of insight into what her elusive center might look like. All she could see in the round mirror was her face. As her arm moved the mirror, the small circular spot that was the point of impact moved with her arm. But her face did not change because of her arm's movement. That stayed the same.

She put the mirror away and prayed traffic would move as quickly as her thoughts had raced all morning. She glanced at the radio, which she turned off while talking with the children. Lenny loved music, and it seemed to help her think less and enjoy the ride to work more. If only she would learn to enjoy her ride through life. At times she had. But most of the time, she had not.

As she twisted the radio dial to on, Elvis was singing "Blue Christmas." She joined him. It didn't cheer her, but it did make her feel less lonely. Elvis was a beautiful soul who was loved by the entire world, but deep in his eyes, there was undeniable loneliness. Thinking of his blue days, and also her own, she was reminded of a summer day when she rescued a bright yellow butterfly.

Sitting in the kitchen, peeling and cleaning husks from a basket of corn, picked from her father's garden, Lenny saw something flash atop a nearby crepe myrtle bush. When she looked out the window to see what it was, she saw a yellow butterfly helplessly stuck to a large spider web. Lenny thought how the poor little creature had once been a caterpillar crawling on its belly. Now, finally transformed, she wasn't going to stand by and watch it become a spider's dinner. She ran outside to rescue it. But the branch was too high. She hurried to the water hose and sprayed the web, releasing the beautiful creature from its prison. Although, a little startled, it flew straight for the nearest blossom.

Lenny knew metaphorically the imagery of a butterfly was often symbolic of a new beginning on a higher plane. She'd read of saints and sages experiencing transformative times of rebirth and deeper spiritual awareness. Her heart longed for such an experience. But she felt trapped mentally in a much stronger spider web. Looking out heaven's window, Granny must have witnessed Lenny's troubled state of mind. Lenny had long been able to hide her mental depression and confusion from the rest of the world. But heaven sees the unseen. Even psychics, like her stranger of yesteryear, were able to see she was trapped like this little yellow insect. If Lenny's metaphoric center remained ever the same, it was the place within her where her Creator resided.

A Being that stayed perfect, just the way it was created. Thinking some aspect of herself remained ever perfect helped her feel slightly less disturbed. But it was only a thought. Could it be real? All she had created in her life was a mess. After all, not a single friend she knew was twice divorced. She had no idea how to get the heavy sense of failure off her back. Her overactive mind was never still. The best she could hope for was the slim possibility that Granny's message was like the rushing water that set her little butterfly free.

When she reached dead-end thinking, unable to figure things out for herself, she often turned to books. Beneath her purse, she'd tucked one such helpmate, a birthday gift from her friend Dawn. *The Game of Life & How To Play It* was a magic book. It was a self-help book that included lots of quotations from the Bible, and for the first time in a long time, Lenny enjoyed reading them. Whenever Granny had quoted scripture, you knew you were in trouble. When Florence Scovel Shinn, the author of this book, quoted scripture, the same words turned into magic wands of immense power. Lenny had been reading it every night for weeks. She talked so much about it at work, Katy, one of her coworkers, wanted to borrow it over Christmas break.

The book became a topic of conversation last night during happy hour (which, Lenny thought, wasn't really all that happy). Lenny wasn't in a dancing mood that night, but Dawn and Mitzi went crazy wild on the dance floor. They called Lenny a wallflower, but she didn't care. She wanted to be a wallflower. She had a terrible headache, and her mood, unlike Elvis' song, wasn't blue, it was gray. Blue said, "I miss someone." Gray said, "I'm so out of focus, I don't know who I am, where I'm going, or what I want."

Lenny used to think the world was black and white. If you did this, that happened. If you didn't do this, then this happened instead. But life didn't exactly work like she once dreamed. It wasn't black and white. In between birth and death, there was a vast array of grays.

Several men asked her out following her divorce, but she had declined. She'd never before feared opening her heart and entering into a new relationship. She simply followed where her heart led her to go. But that had changed. She had changed. Last night, Dawn asked her why she turned down every man who asked her to dance. She told Dawn she was afraid she'd end up agreeing to marry the guy before the darn song was even finished.

"You're crazy!" Dawn said, giggling so hard she almost spit out her Pink Chablis.

"Right now, my thoughts are too stuck on what I should have, what I could have, and what I wish I'd not done," Lenny tried to explain. "I'm constantly frustrated with myself. My body feels tired and heavy, and I feel old. I know thirty-two isn't really old, but I feel old. I guess because old people like to sit and re-live the past, hoping somehow their thinking can change it or make it seem more acceptable."

"Don't be so hard on yourself!" Dawn scolded. "Act more like Florence tells you to act in her book. Affirm you've already met Mister Right and give thanks you hear him knocking at your door."

"No! *Hell no!*" Lenny exclaimed.

That kind of thinking had dropped her into two emotional hurricanes. The first blush of love always felt exciting, calm and peaceful with both men. But each time, with the ink barely dry on her marriage certificates, she'd discovered the full furry of frantic, possessive relationships. What part she played in creating these storms still weighed heavy on Lenny's mind. She instinctively knew she needed to examine her role in these two disasters before victimizing or being victimized ever again. Besides, something about really nice guys never appealed to her.

"I've always been attracted to the bad-boy, Clint Eastwood types," she admitted to Dawn, laughing.

"But Lenny, Clint plays the good guy in his movies," Dawn had countered, laughing right back.

"I know," Lenny laughed. "But Clint possesses a very appealing sort of bad just beneath the surface. You can see it in his eyes. That look makes him sizzle. And that's exactly what I'm afraid of attracting—

except the guy I'll end up attracting really will be the bad-guy type. It won't just be his natural sex-appeal."

"Hmmmm," Dawn sighed with a far-away look in her eyes. "I think you're right about Clint."

The two friends sat in silence for what seemed a long time before Mitzi returned to their table with her dancing partner. Mitzi was petite, and her new companion looked like a giant standing next to her.

"Mitzi," Dawn giggled with a sly look on her face. "Help me push our buddy onto the dance floor." The DJ was calling everyone to dance *Cotton Eyed Joe*. The entire bar crowded onto the dance floor for this popular line dance. Lenny didn't try to argue.

Shortly, into the dance, Mitzi accidentally kicked off one of her shoes. Her giant boyfriend rushed over to pick it up. A drunk accidently kicked him in the back of his leg and he tumbled over, knocking into two strangers plus Mitzi. They all ended up in a heap, piled on top of one another. Mitzi's underpants had been clearly visible as she fell to the floor. Lenny had sideswiped someone's cowboy boot in the fracas and tore a large hole in her pantyhose. Everyone around them exploded in laugher. Lenny laughed again, just thinking about it.

Her thoughts shifted back to the present as she drove into the employee parking lot at the University of Tennessee. Lenny loved her secretarial job, and her recent transfer from the university hospital to the football office had been like a dream come true. Because she worked around a lot of boy-like men who passionately loved their career in football, she found the excitement of this competitive sport contagious and fun. She often felt she was getting paid to work and play at the same time.

Arriving only a few minutes late, Lenny didn't need to start the coffee brewing. Several of the office staff sat huddled around a circular table in what was considered their break room. A fresh pot of coffee was bubbling and burping in the noisy coffee maker. It was an inviting aroma, a warm and welcoming hello. And it seemed to put an end to Lenny's morning long search for an ever-elusive center. A hidden key she'd hoped might unlock her Earthly purpose, her master plan of unfolding into the best she could possibly become.

NATURE'S CLUES

Life has always seemed to me like a plant that lives on its rhizome. Its true life is invisible, hidden in the rhizome. The part that appears above ground lasts only a single summer.... What we see is blossom, which passes. The rhizome remains.

—Carl G. Jung

Lenny poured a cup of coffee and sat beside a secretary who worked in another office. The room was buzzing with planned trips to the Citrus Bowl. The head coach had invited all the administrative staff, including secretaries, to the Florida bowl game.

Lenny's first husband, Bob, along with his new wife and baby, had planned to visit during the holidays. And some of the days of his proposed visit matched the dates of the bowl game. But, when Lenny asked Bob to babysit so she could go on the trip, he sounded put out by her request. He wouldn't promise. Bob was a retail store manager, and he reminded her January was inventory season. Lenny doubted he would actually even visit, although she tried to stay optimistic in front of her children.

This year marked Lenny's first bowl season in the office. She sipped her coffee as she listened to her coworkers telling stories of their previous bowl trips. They spoke of fans going wild, tossing ice and beverages on each other. It sounded terrible, but wonderfully exciting at the same time.

Lenny had married young, just as the stranger she'd met at the diner when she was sixteen had predicted. She'd often felt she missed out on the excitement of going off to college. But now, working for the university, she felt as if she were making up for a lost opportunity—at least in terms of school spirit. Although Lenny had never even watched much football on television before this job, now she attended as many home games as possible, cheering loudly and enthusiastically with the rest of the fans. Her blood was definitely running orange (the university's color), as they said in this part of the country.

As the coaches arrived at the office, the secretaries scattered toward their desks like chickens. Lenny walked to hers, opened her purse, and pulled out a small gift-wrapped ornament. She placed it under a plastic, orange Christmas tree strangled by long stands of fluffy white tinsel. It was the ugliest Christmas tree she'd ever seen.

The wrapped ornament was for one of the office's four secretaries. Every year at Christmas, the secretaries drew names for gift giving, each of them keeping the name they had drawn a secret. This year, Lenny had drawn Katy's name.

Lenny had purchased Katy's ornament in a little craft store near downtown Maryville. It was a crystal-clear plastic ball with a silver, flower-shaped lid, and it looked like a snow globe. She'd attached orange and white ribbons around its neck. When it was turned upside down, tiny silver stars danced gently in the fluid inside the ball. Across the belly of the ornament were three words: love, light, and laughter.

Lenny's heart yearned for all three, so she almost loved the ornament too much to give it away. But that's exactly why it felt like the perfect gift for Katy, Lenny's favorite coworker, and newly acquired friend. Katy was ten years older than Lenny. She had taken Lenny under her wing from Lenny's very first day at work. Katy also helped Lenny with her shorthand and always took the time to proofread Lenny's letters. Sometimes her coaches wanted practice plays typed and ready to hand out in a matter of minutes. One day, the defense head coach, teased Lenny about misspelling one of their important plays. He warned her if they lost the football game that Saturday, it would be because of her typo. But when the team won the next game, he laughingly gave her credit. After that, Lenny always asked Katy to help her proofread the plays, too. Lenny so appreciated Katy she really wanted to gift her with something special, so she hoped Katy would love the ornament as much as Lenny did.

Soon it was 10:30—time for Lenny's morning break. She called Mitzi, and her friend answered on the second ring.

"I had a dream last night," Lenny said without waiting for Mitzi's *hello.*

"Lenny?" Mitzi asked in response. "Well, I don't know why I asked if it was you. Who else would have a crazy dream they needed to tell me about? I was sitting here by the phone, waiting on a ring back from the emergency room. I may have to pull someone's chart if they call back."

"Want me to call you at a better time?"

"No. Tell me your dream. You can't just hang up now that you've piqued my curiosity."

"Well, it wasn't exactly a dream," Lenny said, trying to find words to describe Granny's visit. "I'm pretty sure I've told you my maternal grandmother who helped raise me died when I was seventeen. Well, last night she came into my room and spoke to me. She gave me a very important message, but it's coded and mysterious."

"And you're calling *me?*"

"Yes! Nancy Drew always worked out mysteries with her two best friends. And you are, after all, one of my dearest and closest friends."

"So, you've also got Dawn working on this mystery? What did she say?"

"I haven't called her yet. She's working on her grandmother's rock garden this morning, and she won't be near a phone until later this afternoon."

"Well, Nancy, which of her two best friends do you see me playing?"

Lenny laughed. "Who do you want to be? There is Bess, the pretty blonde, or George, the girl with a boy's name?"

"I'm definitely Bess," Mitzi answered. "Dawn is more masculine and self-reliant. She'd make a perfect George."

"I'll tell her you said that," Lenny said teasingly.

"You better not! But if you did, she'd agree. She thinks we're both too sissy and prissy anyway."

"Look, I know you can't talk but a minute. But I really wanted your input on my dream."

"I thought you said it wasn't a dream."

"I meant to say visitation. It was like a spiritual wake-up call that I need to figure out, because if I do, my life will be better. I will blossom."

"Wow, this does sound intriguing. Keep talking," Mitzi said.

"I'm taking it out of my pocket right now. I believe I've copied her words exactly as I heard them. Here it is: *A center stays where it is. You are a Desert Rose—now grow.*"

"A *what*?" Mitzi asked.

"I know," Lenny said. "I'm just as confused as you are. But isn't the symbolism fascinating?"

"Lord, Lenny!" Mitzi exclaimed. "You had me expecting something truly profound! I simply don't understand what you just said."

"But it *is* profound. Well, to me it is. It's definitely some sort of coded message and I intend to figure it out. Mitzi, these words did not originate inside my head. That's why I know they must be from some higher plane of consciousness. I didn't imagine my Granny's energy. I can't swear it was her, because I didn't see her. But it was feminine and bossy, exactly like my Granny. She would not ask me nicely to grow. She would order me to get on with it and toss a few scriptures at me to make me feel guilty if I didn't obey. I *know* it was her."

"I guess you're right about that," Mitzi laughed.

"Why would anyone, Granny or not, call me a cactus plant? And most puzzling is the part about a center staying where it is. How can I figure that out?. I have been tossing this around in my head all morning. Granny was always telling me to let things be, to concentrate and stay focused on what was in front of me. But my mind has always been like a butterfly flitting about here and there, enjoying one moment and then regretting it two months or ten years down the road."

"Was that what was wrong with you last night? You sure were moody. But wasn't if funny when I lost my shoe? That made even you laugh."

"I laughed because I saw London and France and your underpants," Lenny said, laughing all over again.

"Okay, okay, lets not get started on that again," she giggled. "Let's get back to Nancy. Did her friend Bess ever help her solve a case or was it strictly up to Nancy's intuitive detective skills?"

"I don't remember," Lenny answered. "But you're the psychology major. How do you think Carl Jung would analyze my dream?"

"He'd sit you down and ask you a lot of questions. Then after you pay him a lot of money, he'd make you figure it out for yourself."

"Not true!" Lenny exclaimed. In spirit, I ask for Jung's help all the time. So don't spoil my dream of our father-daughter mental bonding. I adore his genius. I've read almost everything he has written. I don't always understand it, but I know he possessed a knowing I can only hope and dream of someday achieving."

"He is awesome," Mitzi agreed. "Well, this Bess is too puzzled to help her Nancy. Maybe Dawn, or George, will do better. Whatever you find out, Cactus Rose, keep me updated."

"*Desert* Rose," Lenny corrected, laughing again.

"Well, you *were* prickly last night," Mitzi responded.

"I'm newly divorced for the second time and can barely pay my bills," Lenny said, sounding a bit defensive. "You and Dawn don't have children. I have two who need me to be happy, and I'm a terrible actress. It's exhausting pretending I don't feel the way I feel."

"Okay, calm down. I'm just trying to be silly and get you out of this moody phase of thinking bad things about yourself. I'm sure your Granny was doing exactly the same thing last night."

"Sorry, Mitzi, I know you're just trying to help. I hope to feel more enlightened about roses that grow in the desert after I drop by the library on my lunch hour. Finding my center, however, is probably going to be harder to define."

"Lenny, you are very blessed. I wish I had dreams like you do."

"Sometimes I wish I didn't. Some of my visions are unpleasant or maddeningly difficult to understand—like this one."

"That reminds me," Mitzi said. "I took a dream workshop several years back. I'll see if I can find some of the handouts and bring them to you when I see you at Dawn's party. You're still going, aren't you?"

"Wouldn't miss it," Lenny answered. "Thanks for taking the time to find those sheets. They may help me a great deal. I have a dream dictionary, but it isn't always helpful."

"Belly button!" Mitzi suddenly exclaimed. "I think center would definitely be located inside the belly button. Hey, I've gotta go. My supervisor just walked in."

Lenny hung up the phone.

"Belly button?" She whispered to herself as she walked back to her desk.

When Lenny returned to her desk, Katy (who only worked part-time) had arrived. Lenny opened her bottom desk drawer and pulled out Florence Scovel Shinn's book for her co-worker, who eagerly took the book and immediately started reading a few passages.

Katy noticed the book was crammed with lots of Bible scripture. She loved scripture, like Lenny's Granny, but she wasn't preachy about it. Katy had once given Lenny a beautiful calendar with daily inspirational readings. This morning, Lenny had forgotten to turn the calendar to the next day. So, after handing Katy the book, she walked back to her desk and flipped the spiraled page to December twenty-second.

"I don't believe it!" Lenny exclaimed. "I just don't believe it!"

"What don't you believe?" Katy asked rushing over to examine the words beneath Lenny's pointing finger.

"Look at this picture. I don't believe it!"

"You don't believe a picture of a cabin in the woods? Have you been to this cabin before?"

"No, you don't understand," Lenny tried to explain. "This morning, in my head, an almost-lost memory resurfaced of a picture someone drew for me when I was sixteen. This photograph looks just like that picture. It even has a big naked tree and a deer with antlers standing by a stream. I don't believe it! It's spooky! It is so spooky!"

"Okay, dear," Katy responded. "I'm sure it's just a coincidence." She put her arm around Lenny. "This sort of thing happens to me all the time. I never think anything about it."

"Yeah, but I'm not sure I believe in an accidental coincident. The author of the book I just loaned you doesn't. Do you?" Lenny asked.

"Yes, I do." Katy said, laughing. "But I'm very interested in what this author has to say about such strange phenomena. Maybe you just need a vacation. We've all been working hard this past week."

"You're so sweet. I know you think I'm going nuts. But how can I go nuts when I've been a nut all my life?" Lenny teased, watching Katy's warm, motherly smile turn into a chuckle.

Lenny's phone rang, and she was glad. She needed to ponder her picture before she spoke of it further. Lenny's Granny would tell her to let it be, to stop questioning everything that happened. But that was not who Lenny was. Carl Jung questioned everything, and it seemed he lived a long and good life. He didn't sit back and let things be. He lived a life that was heavily influenced from the start by early childhood visions and dreams. Years ago, in a psychology class, Lenny watched an interviewer ask Mr. Jung if he believed in God. He answered, he didn't believe in God, he *knew* God. And as he spoke, his eyes twinkled as if he'd discovered a secret and could barely keep it quiet. He spent his life looking within his Soul as if looking through a telescope, and reading his work, one knew he had discovered hidden worlds within worlds all hungry to be explored by everyone. She wanted to know herself, know God. If one man could experience the process of individuation, acquiring a true sense of wholeness and oneness with his Creator, then so could she. But to know her God-Self, she must first come to a clearer understanding of the symbolic imagery of a Desert Rose. She could worry about staying put and finding center later.

Lenny made a feeble effort to listen to the voice on the other end of the telephone line. She was relieved the caller only needed directions to the ticket office. Pressing a button, she transferred the call. As she hung up, she read the inspiration of the day beneath the cabin picture. It was Matthew 13:31-32: *The kingdom of heaven is like a mustard seed, which a man took and planted in his field. Though it is the smallest of all your seeds, yet when it grows, it is the largest of garden plants and becomes a tree, so that the birds of the air come and perch in its branches.*

Lenny couldn't believe her eyes. Here she was wondering why she'd been called a rose that blossomed in the desert. Jesus metaphorically spoke of the kingdom of heaven being like seeds, plants, and trees. As she stared at the picture, she noticed a red bird perched on a branch above the deer. Like a heavenly messenger, the bird was looking down on the scene, observing.

Suddenly, the phone rang bringing Lenny back to earth. Still deep in thought, she picked up the receiver and pretended to listen. Her mind was full of unanswered questions. Why hadn't Granny showed up warning her not to marry her second husband? She was so ashamed of her failed marriages. Her mother and sister tried to warn her about rushing into a second marriage soon after her first one ended. But stubbornly she followed her heart's desire. She desperately wanted family again. Because of this compelling need, she overlooked warning signs the man she loved was not the forever-after kind. He adored Lenny as much as he adored all women. *"You're mine,"* he would tell her. And if she didn't do as he said, there was war.

Lenny responded to the caller's request almost without thinking. But now the man was asking something else and Lenny didn't know what to say because she hadn't really been paying attention.

"Excuse me, sir," she responded, "Could you please repeat that?"

"I asked to speak to your head coach and you told me he wasn't available. So then I asked you to let me speak to your offensive line coach, and you didn't respond," he huffed.

"Sorry, I was checking to see if his secretary was available," Lenny lied.

"I don't want to speak to his secretary. I want to speak to the coach."

"Just a moment please," Lenny said. She was more than happy to transfer the call to the offensive secretary.

The phone rang for the third time. This time, Lenny focused on her caller. It was a local fan Lenny knew by name who often dropped by the office. He had questions about the upcoming bowl game and Lenny was happy to discuss all she knew with him. Sometimes fans thought she knew a lot about football just because she worked in the football office. She tried to fake it and sometimes it actually worked. Her caller seemed happy when she hung up the phone.

This morning, everything she dealt with, including simple phone calls, seemed like a bothersome distraction. When Lenny's lunch hour finally arrived at one o'clock, it was more than welcome. She reviewed her lunch plan. First she'd walk to the bank. Then she'd make a quick trip to the nearby university bookstore before heading to the library. She'd eat her lunch as she walked.

As she stepped out into the street, the wind whipped past her. Fortunately, Lenny's hair was too plastered with hairspray to move. She'd been pinching pennies to save money for Christmas gifts by brown bagging her lunch. She'd forgotten to pack anything to eat this morning, but she had half a cheese and pickle sandwich that was left over from the day before. Lenny ate as she walked, and the half-sandwich disappeared in two bites. As she hurried from the bank to the bookstore, her ankle-length skirt got caught in a blast of wind and bellowed upward.

The skirt's belt dipped down in a v-shape over her stomach. She loved the waist-cinching style because it seemed to flatten her belly. Thinking about her belly button, Lenny laughed at Mitzi saying it was her center. Perhaps Mitzi was right, but if Lenny had to assign a body part to the concept of a center, it would be the heart. Not because it was centrally located, but because to Lenny, the heart was the home of one's soul. It was a place where she could imagine God residing.

Suddenly, a shock of cold air alerted Lenny to the embarrassing fact the back of her skirt had bellowed upward way too far. She tugged it back down as she hurried across the street. She wasn't as worried about showing off her underpants as she was about exposing the exceptionally large runner that ran up the back of her panty hose.

Inside the bookstore, Lenny bought a roll of scotch tape, a pair of stockings, a football for her son, and a bright orange notebook for taking notes at the library. Her package seemed a little heavy as she walked up the steep hill toward the library.

Once inside, she found an empty seat and hooked her package onto the back of the chair. She took the tape out of her shopping bag and taped her Granny's message, written on the candy-cane gift tag, to the top of the first page of her orange notebook. Then she located a book on exotic and tropical plants and picked up an oversized encyclopedia before returning to her seat.

She found a cactus-like plant that was indeed called a Desert Rose. But there were many different species. In the encyclopedia, she also found a Desert Rose that wasn't even a plant—it was a rock made of crystallized sand. The picture of the rock formation showed odd blossom-like characteristics that fascinated Lenny. *Gypsum Rosette* was its official name. Apparently it formed under arid and sandy conditions.

During happy hour with her friends, Lenny felt hard and cold as a stone. She had struggled to rise above her emotions. This left her feeling cold and numb to the world. This couldn't be the right way to live one's life. And Mitzi was right, she was acting prickly. She easily saw herself in both species of Desert Rose.

Feeling the urge to draw, Lenny pulled a black ballpoint pen out of her purse. She made two sketches of the fancy rock formations in her notebook before copying, in abbreviated shorthand, key words that seemed like possible clues.

Desert Rose, Adenium obesum / Hybrid…Grown from seeds…numerous varieties…some are tree-like…green fleshy bark…blossoms vary…waxy rounded leaves…some have star-shaped blossoms…fungus is its only enemy…needs good drainage.

Tree-like hit Lenny in the gut. She suddenly knew this was indeed the Desert Rose she had been searching for. If the soul of God was expressing itself through her physical body, she liked imagining it as a tree that blossomed. A wave of emotion rolled through her and she almost cried. Trees were more evolved than rocks, weren't they? But the earth, being symbolic of the whole, still needed her rocks and prickly things. Yet, it was much easier for Lenny to imagine the sap running through trees, much like the God essence flowing throughout her physical body.

Trees were ancient symbols rich with meaning. And the scriptures were full of references to trees, such as the two growing in the Garden of Eden. The Bible also said a man, like a tree, was known by his good or bad fruit. Lenny supposed that as a tree-like Desert Rose, her fruit would be a rose blossom—a pleasant thought. For the first time in a long time, it felt good to be Lenny. Could she really learn to love herself again, she wondered? And most important, could she silence the tormenting blamer that lurked inside. She'd once read a seeker must become empty of self before God can enter. But maybe, this was half true. Maybe, God was already inside the heart like a seed. Once empty of self-blame, and other rampaging, obstructive thinking, the God sap could freely flow.

Now, solving what it might mean to be a Desert Rose, she was ready to take the next step. She'd locate center, stay put, and try to find some way to grow. And grow *now*! This part wouldn't be easy.

Lenny turned the pages of the book to the picture of the *Gypsum Rosette*. She studied the pictures of the cactus and the Desert Rose tree. Indeed, depending on her mood of the moment, she was capable of being all three. Perhaps when she was stuck in the depression over her misfortunate past, she was like a stone. A rock had life within, but it was a very dense vibration. The God-sap that flowed through it could not be seen with the naked eye. The desert cactus sap could be touched and seen. And when she was in a bad mood or sick, she was definitely a cactus. Her friends were holding a mirror to her face saying, this is you – *now*.

Lenny picked up her pen to make a quick sketch. She didn't really like thinking of herself as a cactus, so she decided not to draw it. She was, however, glad she saw herself in this image. It felt so unpleasant, she definitely wanted to change. And there was no better time than right now. She felt ready to blossom. But just as she began to sketch the tree, her pen ran out of ink.

"*Damn!*" she exclaimed a little too loudly. She glanced around the room. The only person who seemed to notice her outburst was a female student with ruddy skin and red hair. The young woman rose up from her chair and hurriedly walked in the direction of the ladies' room, leaving behind, in the crack of her open notebook, a yellow highlighter and a number-two pencil.

Surely she wouldn't mind if I borrowed it for just a second, Lenny thought. Like a tiger sneaking up on its prey, she walked over to where Ms. Red had been sitting and snatched up the pencil. Returning to her seat, Lenny drew a rough sketch of the squatty tree with clusters of open five-petal flowers. The tree's rounded leaves were hard to capture. She tried to darken the inner edges to emphasizing a little shadowing. That's when the lead of the pencil snapped and rolled to the floor. Now, Lenny was not only a thief but a vandal.

She decided to confess as soon as Ms. Red returned. She couldn't just put the pencil back without saying anything. As soon as Ms. Red got back to her seat, she'd walk over and apologize for borrowing, without asking and show her the broken pencil.

Ms. Red walked exceptionally slow as she returned to her seat. She held her head low, no eye contact. Lenny got up and walked toward her, waving the broken pencil in the air to get her attention. Ms. Red continued to ignore her as Lenny moved closer.

"I stole something from you," Lenny whispered, bending close to the woman's ear. Ms. Red's mouth dropped open, looking much like a dark silent cave. Her eyes were bloodshot and she appeared to have been crying. She slammed her notebook closed as if trying to guard a top-secret document.

It was just a pencil, Lenny thought, confused by the response. Immediately, without responding to Lenny's confession, Ms. Red collected her things, got up, and walked away. Shocked, Lenny dropped the pencil and had to stop and pick it up before she chased after her, hoping to explain.

Her high-heeled boots made a loud clacking noise against the oiled hardwood floors of the library. And then, as suddenly as Ms. Red had run away, she stopped. Lenny almost ran over her. She couldn't help noticing the woman's face appeared white as a sheet, as though she'd seen a ghost.

"Look, if you're Professor Brown's wife, stop following me," she pleaded as if begging for her life.

"*Who?*" Lenny asked, bewildered. "I'm just the person who stole, well actually just borrowed, your pencil. I'm just trying to give it back to you. I'm sorry, but I broke the lead. I should have asked you first. I didn't read your notes or look at anything in your notebook. Honest!"

"You did *what?*" Ms. Red whispered in response.

"I took the liberty, wrong I'm sure, of borrowing your pencil when you went to the ladies' room. I didn't read your notes or whatever it was you were trying to hide in your notebook. You see, I'm here on a mission. My Granny, long passed, woke me up this morning. She gave me a strange message that has worried me all day. I was trying to research some of the things she said, and my pen stopped working, and I saw your pencil, and…"

Ms. Red just stared at Lenny with squinting eyes that could barely control her anger.

"When you said 'Damn,' I thought you recognized…Forget it," she said shaking her head.

"Well, I'm usually nice. I'm normally not rude to strangers. And I didn't mean to tell you my whole life drama. Please take your pencil back before I embarrass myself even worse."

"Look," the woman said. "I don't want my pencil back. You can have the damn thing. Just stop following me!"

Lenny stood speechless as she watched her victim walk away. A silly thought entered her mind. She wondered if there were degrees or classifications of sin in heaven's accounting system. Dismissing the thought as quickly as it came, she walked back to her library table. She put her stolen pencil inside her purse and stuck her notebook in her shopping bag. She took her belongings and moved toward the exit, but when she was only inches away from the front door, someone tapped her on the shoulder.

Surprised, Lenny turned and faced her next-door neighbor, Ms. Tallulah. Lenny took a deep breath and tried not to stare at the librarian's hideous purple-black hair.

"You can't grow *Adenium obesum* in East Tennessee. They hate cold climates and it's much too humid here. I do not recommend you purchase one and try to keep it as a houseplant."

Lenny stared at Ms. Tallulah. Her mouth must have looked like Ms. Red's dark open cave. Her research book was tucked awkwardly under her not-so-friendly neighbor's arm.

"Let me put my package down and I'll return my book to the reference desk," Lenny said, feeling guilty.

"I've already taken this task in hand. That won't be necessary," Ms. Tallulah responded crisply.

Lenny noticed the corners of the librarian's mouth dipped downward as she spoke. She had never noticed this before. She looked much like a starving bulldog, and Lenny felt like her next meal. She wasn't sure what to say. She thought about sharing her story about Granny, but she'd already made a fool of herself more than once this morning.

Ms. Tallulah tilted her head down to peer above her reading glasses into Lenny's eyes with an ice-cold glare. "Carelessly, not returning your book to its proper place is not what I wanted to talk to you about," she said in a snippy voice. "Have - you - any - idea - the - damage - your - dog - has - done - to - my - azalea - bushes?" Being a good librarian, Ms. Tallulah kept her voice so low Lenny could barely make out what she said.

"Excuse me?" Lenny responded sheepishly.

Ms. Tallulah pointed toward the door and motioned for Lenny to step outside so they could talk. Lenny did, followed closely by Ms. Tallulah, whose voice then became much more audible.

"I put a note in your box last week," the librarian scolded.

"You did? Well, I didn't get it," Lenny answered, feeling more than a little surprised. "It must have blown away. You could have called me. My number's in the phonebook."

"Your dog has killed one of my prize azalea bushes. I don't ask much from my neighbors. But if you don't take responsibility for your pet, I will take matters into my own hands. I believe you call the creature Lassie—an original name, by the way," she commented sarcastically.

"My son was three when he named our dog. *Lassie* was one of his favorite movies," Lenny shot back defensively. "And had I received your note, I would have responded. What did it say?"

"I just told you. Your dog has killed one of my prize azalea bushes. I want to know what you plan to do about it."

"My dog is a female. She squats. She didn't kill your azalea bush. Were I to guess, I would say it was Goober. He's the Miller's dog down the street. He's all over the neighborhood peeing on everyone's bushes."

"I've more sense than you think, missy," Ms. Tallulah hissed. "I've already taken the liberty to examine the sex of your dog. I'm fully aware she's a bitch. When she relieves herself in my yard, it attracts every male dog in the neighborhood. I'm sick and tired of it!"

Lenny's mouth dropped open for the second time during the conversation, not in shock this time but in horror. The witch of the neighborhood, the snoopy shadow behind half-closed drapes, this horrible mean-spirited old woman who delighted in watching her every move, who was unable to communicate without frowning, had picked up her Lassie with unkind hands and examined her sex.

"Ms. Tallulah, *you're* the bitch!" Lenny exclaimed, raising her voice. Tears filled her eyes. This caught Lenny by surprise, she turned away from her neighbor, and hurriedly walked away.

"How dare you!" Ms. Tallulah called after Lenny before storming back into the library.

Fortunately, the "walk" light was lit when Lenny reached the first intersection on her way back to her office. She walked as fast as her high heels allowed. Suddenly, a car sped past out of nowhere, missing her by inches. She almost dropped her shopping bag. Her face felt hot and flushed. Was this how her first step toward blossoming would begin? If so, it was a bad first step. A brick from out of nowhere had landed on her heart. Much like the car that barely missed running over her. She had just hurt two people without even trying. In a matter of seconds, she had gone from loving herself to despising herself once again. Throwing rocks at others turned her right back into one.

"Better thank your lucky stars," said an elderly man with a starched priestly collar. "Or maybe you've got an angel in your pocket."

"Just a candy wrapper," Lenny said with a sigh. She pulled out a nutty bar wrapper and made a sad face.

Having felt run over by her neighbor and almost hit by a car, Lenny was suddenly rather emotional. In *The Game of Life*, Florence warned her readers about being careful with their words because they were like boomerangs that eventually come home. She wondered about her angry altercation with Ms. Tallulah. Maybe calling her a bitch wasn't such a good idea after all. Since the priest was walking beside her, Lenny decided to ask for some advice.

"Father, may I ask you a question?" Lenny asked as they both waited for a second traffic light to change. "Is anger a sin?"

"Not in my book," he answered. "We all get angry sometimes. We wouldn't be normal human beings if we didn't occasionally lose our tempers. There is a lot of injustice in the world, after all. I myself can get very angry. Even Jesus got angry. But he didn't stay angry, and that's the secret. You've got to let it go."

"Thank you," Lenny said, smiling. "I needed to hear that. I was very angry a few minutes ago but almost getting hit by that car knocked it right out of my head. I don't have an angel in my pocket. But I think you might be one."

"That's awfully sweet of you to say," the man said with a wink. "I'll tell you a little secret about anger. If you bottle it up, keep it hidden, and pretend it's not there, then it will grow into a mighty mean-looking creature. However, keep in mind, controlling or restraining harmful impulses that hurt others isn't easy, but your own happiness depends on it. Yet, I've seen it happen more than once. At the moment of our greatest darkness, light will come shining through. Don't give up. You watch out, okay?"

"Yes, I will," she promised. "Thank you, again."

The light changed and they walked across the street in silence. As the priest got to his car, he turned around and bowed low as if Lenny were a queen. She smiled and waved. Her morning's quick emotional shifts from startled confusion, guilt, anger, sudden fright, followed by sincere gratitude for unexpected kindness, for being alive and unharmed, made Lenny feel as if she'd just gotten off an emotional rollercoaster ride. This see-sawing back and forth made her feel unbalanced and weary. Had she put logic on the shelf, exchanging it for an overactive, terminally serious imagination? Maybe Mitzi was right. Maybe she did need a vacation. But right now, all she wanted was to get back to work so she could relax.

A DAMAGED ROSE

O Rose, thou art sick! The invisible worm
That flies in the night, in the howling storm,
Has found out thy bed of crimson joy:
And his dark secret love does thy life destroy.

—William Blake

Thankfully, the rest of the day flew by without further drama, or trauma. Lenny felt so tired; once again, she drove home with a silence radio. She'd never understood the value of getting into the breath, the body during meditative silence. This realization came to her shortly after she started practicing yoga and breathing on a regular basis. Her yoga teacher told her that in order to become like an antenna to the Cosmic Consciousness, one had to clear the mind of unwanted discord and static. This made a lot of sense to Lenny. She often tried to sit in silent meditation. But her antennae squealed with noisy mind chatter all the time. It didn't have an off switch. If it did, Lenny hadn't discovered how to turn it off.

As she found herself pulling into her driveway, without really remembering most of the drive, Nikki and Elizabeth were sitting on the porch. Nikki was the teenage babysitter she'd hired to watch the children for the two hours between school and Lenny's return from work. She was a tall brunette, with a heart-shaped face, and a cute nose covered in freckles. Nikki always seemed extra shy around Lenny. But Elizabeth said they talked a lot when Lenny wasn't around.

Nikki was an only child. She looked a lot like one of Lenny's elementary school friends who was also an only child. Nikki's parents were both in their fifties, so the girl had no hope for siblings. Lenny suspected this was probably why Nikki acted thrilled to accept babysitting jobs.

As Lenny walked toward the girls, she noticed they weren't wearing their coats or shoes. They were busy shaking loose glitter off of paper fans they'd made from colorful construction paper. Elizabeth's socks were covered in both silver and gold sparkles. Like her mother, Elizabeth loved drawing and creating things with her hands. Lenny always kept lots of crafts materials around the house for both of them to use.

Elizabeth's and Nikki's fans were stapled at the bottom, and then wrapped with matching ribbons. Lenny discovered the pattern in a woman's magazine the week before. She'd hoped to decorate a small artificial tree in her bedroom with nothing but fans. However, her recent depression, the one she tried to hide from everyone, was putting an unaccustomed drain on her creative energy. This thought made her feel a little guilty. She needed to release, cleanse away the old; but how? She knew she couldn't turn outward, only inward for her answer.

"Look what we made today!" Elizabeth squealed, beaming as Lenny walked onto the porch.

"They're beautiful!" Lenny exclaimed.

By the time Lenny sat her package down and took off her coat, Nikki had slipped on her shoes and was getting ready to go. Mack was lying on the couch watching cartoons. Lassie curled up in Mack's lap, jumped down and looked up at Lenny with begging eyes.

"Mack, take your dog for a walk," Lenny said as she waved goodbye to the babysitter. "And absolutely, positively, do *not* let her go *near* Ms. Tallulah's yard. In fact, put her on her leash."

"But mom, she *hates* her leash," Mack protested.

"Well, I don't care. Ms. Tallulah hates dogs. And after today, I'm sure she hates me even worse. Please don't argue. Just do as I say. I need to get supper started. Today was payday, remember? Tonight, we're going shopping for our Christmas tree."

That got Mack excited. Once he got Lassie on her leash, dog and boy ran out the door.

Lenny washed her hands, peeled the potatoes, and greased up her heavy frying pan. Mack wanted fried potatoes almost every night, and Elizabeth loved vegetables. She took a frozen bag of green peas out of the freezer and tuned the stove on high. She had cooked hamburger patties the night before and decided to reheat the leftovers. When the potatoes were nice and crisp, she tossed the leftover meat into the pan.

After supper, she and the kids drove across town to the Big K. A year before enrolling in an evening secretarial course, Lenny worked there as a hardware manager. A girlfriend from high school helped her get the job. It didn't seem to matter to the store's supervisor that Lenny didn't know a thing about tools. If you were dependable and came to work on time, that seemed to be good enough for him.

Every year, in the corner of the Big K parking lot, a local farmer sold reasonably priced Christmas trees. Lenny let the children pick out a tall, skinny one that barely fit on the top of her small car. While Mack and the farmer tied the tree to the roof, Lenny and Elizabeth went into the super-saver store to buy popcorn, candy sprinkles, and some food coloring for making sugar cookies.

While they were shopping, she ran into a coworker from her days at the Big K. Bonnie, a sales clerk in the dry goods department, was marking down damaged Christmas ornaments and chipped pottery. She and Lenny hugged and shared the latest gossip. Lenny had left her hardware manager job at the Big K because her second husband didn't want her to work. Not working felt like a treasured luxury at first. But later on, it felt more like a prison sentence.

"Don't wander off," Lenny warned Elizabeth. But for the moment, her daughter seemed quite content to rummage through a large pile of unpackaged and somewhat damaged tree trimmings. Elizabeth spotted a porcelain angel tree-topper that had also caught Lenny's eye. From head to toe, the angel was white as snow. Her hair, beneath a starry crown, was long and crimped like the style Lenny's Granny wore in the 1920s. In fact, Lenny thought she looked very Art Deco. Her dress hung in folds like a bride's white veil. Around her waist was a thick satin ribbon with a long unraveled sash that trailed behind her long dress.

"Look, Mom!" Elizabeth exclaimed. "She has real feather wings. Can we buy her?"

Lenny took the angel and examined her price tag. A blob of glue was stuck to the top of her head, and she was missing a star from her crown. She also had a cracked foot.

"How do you attach her to the top of the tree?" Lenny wondered aloud.

Elizabeth helped her mother examine the ornament. The ribbon at the back of the angel's dress could be undone so the angel could then be tied with a pretty bow to a tree spire. Her skirt opened in the back as the ribbon was untied.

"You better grab her if you want her," Bonnie said with a smile. "She's damaged goods, but aren't we all? Her original price was $19.99."

"That's pricy for Big K," Lenny laughed.

"Let me see what's wrong with her and I'll see if I can give you a good deal," Bonnie smiled giving Lenny a little wink.

Elizabeth handed Bonnie the angel. She was already begging for the new tree-topper, regardless of what the price would be.

The sales clerk took note of the angel's cracked foot as well as her crown's missing star. "Well," she said, looking down at Elizabeth's eager eyes, "How about three dollars?"

"Mom, can we get her? Can we? Pleeeease?" Elizabeth pleaded.

"Sold!" Lenny declared, smiling down at her daughter. All the way to the check out, Elizabeth cradled and comforted the wounded angel.

On the way home, Lenny prayed their Christmas tree wouldn't slide off the top of the car. Once they got it inside the house, Mack untangled the lights while Lenny popped popcorn. Elizabeth had insisted on stringing popcorn garlands this year.

They hung the ornaments on the tree, and the last to go up was their new tree-topper. Elizabeth brushed a strand of the angel's cotton-candy-spun hair over her missing star. This made her look as if her hair was blowing in the wind, and they all agreed it suited her well.

Trying to defer any further damage, Lenny repaired the angel's foot with a piece of tape. She was glad she'd remembered to buy some extra today. As she caressed the cracked foot in her hand, she couldn't help but think how glad she was that the angel was not perfect. After all, who was?

But more than feeling merely imperfect, Lenny felt damaged, too—just like the angel. Was she beyond fixing? She needed much more than a strip of tape to defer further damage to her life with her negative thinking. She still didn't feel comfortable dating, for example. She didn't trust men. She didn't even trust herself. She'd more than once known the bliss of overpowering, thrilling attraction. This kind of love felt like an emotional storm. She began to wonder if she was even capable of attracting *real* love.

After she and the children decorated the tree, they watched the Charlie Brown Christmas special on television. It seemed metaphorically a forest of trees had come her way today. They were everywhere! Charlie Brown's little tree was almost bare of needles, yet like magic, love brought it to life. As the program ended, the characters marveled at the transformation of Charlie Brown's sad little tree. Lenny thought about how wonderful it felt to sit down with her children and hear them laugh.

Chasing fun hadn't worked the other night at happy hour. But watching Mitzi laughing heartily at herself in the line dance pileup was indeed a happy moment. Maybe her white-haired stranger of yesteryear was right. Maybe she did try too hard to find lasting happiness in places where lasting happiness could not be found.

Lenny thought about some words of wisdom her yoga instructor had once shared during class. She'd been so captivated by what he said she'd expressed the concept in an oil painting. "Happiness is like a butterfly within your reach, you can catch it with diligence," he said. "Become still, and it may land upon you. Attention is a mental reaching."

Maybe that was the same message the stranger in the diner had been trying to tell her. Lenny's mind was never still. It was always caught up in a past drama she kept trying to rewrite without success. A large part of Lenny wanted to be still, to stay in the moment. But a stronger, more reactive part, exploded in fear, frustration and judgment at the drop of a hat… or pencil. Simply pretending she was happy when she wasn't felt like a slow death.

Lenny got up and turned off the television. Her favorite part of the evening had arrived – story time. Mack ran down the hall toward his room to retrieve a book, with Elizabeth close behind. Lenny had long created a space in which they could share each other's thoughts about what they'd just read. It was a tradition she treasured.

Lenny looked up at her grandfather clock to see its shortest arm resting on the number eight, and the long arm on the number five. Then she glanced down at her wristwatch. It read 8:35. Lately, it had been running five minutes fast. Now, it was ten minutes faster than the grandfather clock. Maybe her clock radio had the correct time.

"Mack, check my alarm clock in the bedroom," she called down the hall. "I think my wrist watch is running fast."

"It's exactly 8:30," he yelled back. So her watch was still five minutes fast, but now the grandfather clock was five minutes slow. Lenny got up, opened the clock's glass face and pushed the minute hand forward.

Elizabeth beat her brother back into the living room. She handed Lenny a childhood classic, *The Velveteen Rabbit or How Toys Become Real.* But Lenny shook her head.

"Elizabeth," Lenny sighed, "its Mack's turn to pick out a story tonight. And tomorrow we're going to a holiday party. We'll have to skip reading your book until Christmas Eve."

"I know," her daughter said with a sigh. "I'm just putting it in the living room so you won't forget."

"Why would you think I'd forget?" Lenny asked before deciding she didn't want to hear the answer. "Never mind," she whispered patting her daughter's leg.

She put her feet atop a wobbly marble-top coffee table. One of the legs was slightly longer than the others. She figured if it broke it wasn't a great loss. Elizabeth cuddled up to Lenny on one side, while Mack returned with his book and started to snuggle in on the other.

"No nursery fairies tonight," the boy said teasingly to his sister, looking straight into her eyes, with a sly grin on his face. "Tonight, we're going to take an adventure trip with *The Arabian Nights!*"

"Oh boy!" Elizabeth squealed as Mack presented the book to his mother. Lenny was shocked he chose a book his sister also loved. Lenny loved it, too. She'd always dreamed of traveling to exotic and foreign places, and books seemed a great place to start.

She opened the book to the sliver of paper that served as a bookmark. The next story was entitled, *"The Enchanted Horse."* It was the story of an artificial magic horse that had the ability to fly anywhere in the universe. The king of Persia did not believe the poor Hindu when he said it was magic. To prove his story, the Hindu flew far away and from atop a mountain, he discovered a palm tree. He returned to the king with a single palm branch as proof.

"A mountain palm tree," Lenny said in halting tones.

"Do we have palm trees in our mountains?" Elizabeth asked.

"No. But today has been a tree day for your mother. I dreamed about one, thought about one, looked at several tree pictures, watched one on television, trimmed one, and now we're reading about one. I'm deep in a forest of tree symbols tonight," Lenny said shaking her head. Elizabeth giggled.

"Think it means something, Mom?" Mack asked.

"Maybe, but it would hurt my brain too much to think about it right now," Lenny answered.

"Pretty interesting," Mack said with a faraway look in his eyes.

Lassie was snoring in his lap by the time the prince of Persia and the princess of Bengal got married. It was written they lived happily ever after, but Lenny doubted it very seriously.

"Bah humbug!" Lenny cried out. "That happy ending just shot an arrow into my butt. I need to kick it off. Let's get crazy and dance to a little Merle!"

Mack turned on their boom box and pulled out an old eight-track cassette. He and Elizabeth proceeded to help their mother kick off the wedding bell blues. Legs went flying as Lassie, ever the good herder, circled them into a tight ring and nipped at their ankles. As they danced, she prayed someday she might be able to control her negative thoughts about herself, like her gentle, little sheepdog now controlled their movements.

In the middle of Merle Haggard singing about a man who was "serving life without parole," the phone rang.

OUR ARROWS

Your children are not your children... They come through you but not from you. And though they are with you, yet they belong not to you...You are the bows from which your children as living arrows are sent forth. The archer sees the mark upon the path of the infinite, and He bends you with His might that His arrows may go swift and far. Let your bending in the archer's hand be for gladness; For even as He loves the arrow that flies, so He loves also the bow that is stable.

—Kahlil Gibran

Lenny suddenly felt a fight-or-flight sensation. She and the children were so happy. She feared the call was from her ex-husband. She wanted a total departure from old ways of dealing with him. She never considered herself psychic. But when a sick feeling hit her stomach, she knew something was coming. She ran to switch off the music, while Mack ran to get the phone. When he did, his foot got tangled in the long extension cord. He fell to his knees but still managed to pick up the receiver before the third ring. He'd been anxiously waiting all week to hear from his father about when he and Mack's baby brother were arriving, and Mack hoped this would be the call.

Lenny failed to move out of his way as Mack lunged toward the phone. She saved herself by grabbing the arm of the couch.

"Hello," Mack whispered into the phone, out of breath. He lay with his back on the floor and his feet against the hallway wall. For a while, he just listened without saying a word.

Elizabeth slipped past her brother to go play in her bedroom, awaiting her turn to talk. Lenny circled the coffee table. Inner conflict began to rise up against her strongest desire to remain tranquil and at peace. Mack was being too quiet. Mentally, she began preparing what to say to the children if he canceled his visit. She only hoped her ex would not insist on talking to her.

She stopped circling and sat back down on the coach. She thought of the altercation she had with her neighbor, Ms. Tallulah. Lenny had left the library in a rage, but a priestly stranger had helped her with his words. She tried to remember exactly what he'd said. *Everyone gets angry*, she remembered him saying. *It wasn't a sin.* He'd said something else about anger. But at the moment, she couldn't remember. Entangled in fiery anger with Ms. Tallulah had left Lenny even more reluctant to fight with her ex-husband. Chances were, they would never resolve their conflicts. They both would end up hurting their children more than each other. And at the moment, she was not clear-headed and inwardly strong enough to do battle. Besides that, her anger was beginning to destroy all chances for happiness.

"Okay, Dad," Mack finally said, snapping Lenny's focus back to the present. He stood up and began dragging the long tail of the phone's extension cord back to his bedroom. A bad sign his conversation wasn't going well. Lenny felt the urge to run out her front door and scream. Instead, she walked toward her room, straining to listen to what Mack was saying behind his closed door.

"Sure, Dad," she heard her son say. "I understand. Okay. Yeah, she's right here. Okay. You too. Goodbye."

Mack opened the door and without looking into his mother's eyes, handed her the phone. She took a deep breath and tried to count to three before speaking. Lenny held the phone against her chest and tried to remember what the priest had said that made her feel better about allowing herself to be angry.

"Hello," she said in her chilliest voice. Her mind exploded in cuss words she never wanted her children to say. As soon as she heard Bob's voice, she could barely listen to what he was saying.

"Look," he said, "I can tell by the tone of your voice you're mad. Lenny, something totally unexpected has come up at work. I am not lying."

"Doesn't it always?" Lenny asked sarcastically. She walked into her bedroom and closed the door. She strained to keep a scream from erupting out of her throat. She kept taking deep breaths—so many she actually felt a little dizzy. Bob continued speaking in a dead calm voice. In fact, he was talking so calmly Lenny thought he could have just as easily been reporting the weather conditions in Alabama.

"My assistant store manager has the flu or something. And you know how my work gets during the holidays. Year-end inventory, financial reports are all coming due the first of the year. Anyway, I promise, I'll try to take a week off to visit the kids in the spring. I've always thought dogwood season was the best time to visit Tennessee. I told my wife how pretty it is. She's already excited. It may sound crazy, but she's anxious to meet you. She's a pretty blonde like you. Six years younger and not as tall."

Bob always tried to work his Southern gentleman charm on her when he was up to no good. Lenny's sick stomach had turned into a headache. She remembered that the friendly priest had told her that suppressed anger could turn pretty mean. She had to speak her mind or explode.

"How great for you that you found a short wife since you always seemed to have such an obnoxious small-man syndrome," she snapped.

"You bitch! I knew you'd try to pick a fight."

"Look, you lying jerk! I'm sick of your empty promises to our children. Do you realize this is the umpteenth time this year you've made a promise to visit but haven't shown up? And it's always because of work or someone getting sick. You think if you send my child support check every month you are free and clear to live your life as you choose. I never want to speak to you again. Stop asking to speak to me. The very sound of your voice makes me furious!"

"Look here," Bob continued, "how dare you yell at me in front of Mack and Elizabeth! I love both of them as much as you do. And *you're* the one that left *me*. Remember that when you're whining about me never seeing them."

"For your information, I'm not yelling in front of our children. When are you ever going to learn the consequences of your thoughtless lying? Stop telling them you are coming to visit unless you are a mile away from our house. And as far as *me* leaving *you*—as if I didn't have just cause for that! Please, just don't go there!"

"You're just mad because I'm happy with a new wife and a new baby, and your second marriage ended poorly. But I honestly can't say I'm the slightest bit surprised."

"This discussion is not about us. This is about two little people who love both of us. Right now, Mack is trying hard not to cry. A manly thing, I guess. After getting off the phone with you, he slammed his door. He's in his room playing loud and disturbing music. And Elizabeth will soon be just as upset."

"Are you going to let me speak to my daughter?" Bob growled. "Put Elizabeth on the phone!"

"I'm walking the phone to her as we speak. She's sitting on her bed dressed in her Wonder Woman nightgown playing with Steve."

"Who the hell is Steve? One of your new boyfriends?"

"Steve isn't a man," Lenny said, clenching her teeth. "For your information, he is Elizabeth's pet mouse. Mack bought it for her after her cat died this summer. He said he was trying to save Steve from becoming snake food."

"Don't hand her the phone yet. I have one more thing to say," Bob added in his most fatherly sounding voice. "You'd better not poison the minds of my children against me! I *do* love them."

"Then live it. Try to show it, Bob. Stop just saying it," she whispered, trying to sound calm. "And *I* have one more thing to say, too. I've tried so hard for so long not to fight with you. If anyone is being poisoned it's *me*. When I hang up this phone, I'll feel sorry for you and for the joy you are missing not being with our children."

Lenny walked into Elizabeth's room, trying to appear calm. Her daughter took the phone from her mother's trembling hand.

"Hi, Dad," she exclaimed. "How's my baby brother doing?"

Lenny walked back to her bedroom. Her children so loved their baby brother. With her help, they had bought him several gifts. She would try to put them in the mail sometime next week. Lenny reached up to brush a piece of hair out of her face and suddenly remembered her unruly 'do. She walked into the hall bathroom and looked at her refection in the mirror. Her face was pale and her eyes were bloodshot. She opened a box of hair color and dotted it on her dark roots. She needed to give it at least twenty minutes, so she walked back into the living room and sat quietly in front of the Christmas tree. That's when her eyes caught sight of Mack's new favorite ornament.

When they were decorating the tree, before everything had gone sour that night, Elizabeth had discovered the German Heidi ornament had lost a leg. Mack found a large screw in the kitchen junk drawer, and now Heidi looked like a female Captain Peg-leg. They'd laughed and laughed, and Mack said he couldn't wait to show it to his father.

Heidi was damaged, Lenny thought. And the angel tree-topper was damaged. Lenny's entire household was beginning to feel beyond repair.

"Guess what?" Elizabeth suddenly asked as she skipped down the narrow hallway toward her mother.

"What?" Lenny asked, surprised at the happy look on her daughter's face.

"Dad's coming to visit for Easter. And tomorrow the mailman is bringing bunches and bunches of presents, special delivery. Dad said they cost a lot of money. But Mack and I are worth it."

"That sounds wonderful," Lenny lied. She kissed the top of her daughter's head and walked her back into her bedroom. As she tucked her into bed and turned out the light, she made sure Steve's cage was securely sealed. Then she knocked on Mack's bedroom door. She told him to turn off his music and get to sleep. Tomorrow was their last day of school before the holiday break.

As Lenny shampooed her hair, she reflected upon her perception of reality versus her daughter's. She was always striving to protect her children. She wanted their world to be perfect and happy, even though she knew her own world was far from perfect. Elizabeth may or may not be wounded by her father's long absence in her life. But Lenny hated it for both her children. It was seldom far from her mind. And Bob always had a way of tossing the guilt of their failed relationship onto her.

She turned off the water and stepped out of the cold porcelain bathtub. She stared at her refection in the mirror as she towel-dried her hair. It seemed everything she'd ever sworn she'd never do she'd gone and done. Her past did not live in the past. It walked ever present inside her head.

She opened the cabinet under the bathroom sink and pulled out a basket full of pink foam curlers. She seldom went to bed in curlers. But she wanted to look extra nice for tomorrow's office party. She used a blow dryer on her hair until it felt only slightly damp. Then she rolled up large strands of hair and fastened them to the rollers with extra bobby pins.

Once in her bedroom, Lenny opened her notebook and re-read the notes she'd taken earlier at the library. Once mature, the Desert Rose would begin to sprout several five-petal blossoms. Was Lenny mature? Could she ever blossom and grow? She searched for a pen and wrote a big number five on her notebook paper. Then she drew a circle around it. The number five might be a clue. Her Nancy Drew archetype was working again, hot on the trail of her unsolved mystery. Then it hit her. She remembered the new angel she'd just bought for the Christmas tree was missing one of its stars. Originally, there must have been six stars. But now, she only had five stars glued to her crown.

Lenny paused before closing her notebook. Was she just reaching for straws? Why didn't she just forget about trying to decode Granny's message. Then she remembered her watch had been five minutes fast this afternoon. Now the grandfather clock was five minutes slow. Were these additional clues from the spirit world? How did that realm of existence connect with those who were living? Lenny jumped down and reached under the mattress for a dream dictionary by Tom Chetwynd.

Back on the bed, she thumbed through the index. Apparently, the number five was full of symbolic meaning. Five symbolizes nature, flesh, and the body, which has five appendages—head, arms, and legs. Lenny had never thought about that before. And the hand has five fingers, too, she realized. But the meaning that leapt off the page at her was five symbolized *life*.

"Wow!" she exclaimed. That could mean that Granny's message was likely to embrace the whole of Lenny's life. She reflected back on her Jungian studies of the process of individuation. Carl Jung believed the archetype of the *Self*, was the center of the psyche and facilitator of individuation. She remembered reading that Carl Jung, when trying to seize hold of a fantasy or dream, would imagine a steep descent. And, not one to give up, he would attempt to go ever deeper in order to get to the bottom. This sounded good in theory, but until *Self* became real in her life, this knowledge did her little service. The mystery she wanted to solve was how to make this knowledge come alive in her life.

Suddenly, Lenny remembered she'd forgotten to call Dawn. She chased down the phone by following its long extension cord to just outside her daughter's room. Picking it up hastily, she dialed her friend's number.

"H-e-l-l-o," came a sleepy voice at the other end of the phone.

"Oh no," Lenny sighed. "I bet I woke you up."

"Oh, that's okay. I started to call you earlier but got distracted. What's up?"

"Bob isn't coming to visit the children after all."

"You knew it. You told Mitzi and me yesterday you knew he wasn't coming. Are you upset?" Dawn asked.

"I know I *said* it. But I didn't want to *believe* it. I kept trying to tell myself I was wrong. I kept saying positive affirmations like you said to make myself feel like he could change. You're the one who's always telling me to think positive."

"Lenny," Dawn answered sympathetically, "When you say it you really have to believe it, and see it. Besides, the only person you can change is yourself. When it comes to others, accept them as they are and see how fast they change. What do you have to lose? But don't give up. We all learn by *doing*, and not just by reading or listening to people talk. I think your positive efforts are a good start. I wish you loved yourself half as much as I love you, my dear friend. Don't get too impatient with yourself."

"Well, I've had such a cursing, hissing, and altogether weird sort of day. I even cursed an ink pen for not working. And I stole an adulteress's pencil, and yelled at my nosy neighbor who works at the university library. After that, I was almost run over by a car. Then, an angelic man told me to just let it all hang out and get mad if I wanted. And tonight, my ex-husband tells me it's not his fault our children are upset because he is not honoring his promise to visit this Christmas. He never wanted a divorce. It was my idea."

Dawn exploded in laughter. "Well, I'm sure he didn't. You are the one who objected to his secret harem. Girlfriend, you're funny when you're mad."

"Thanks, I guess. And a special thanks to you for loving me in spite of myself." Lenny felt less mad just hearing her friend laugh. When Dawn laughed her entire body shook.

"Look," Dawn said. "I know your ex-husband is acting like a jerk. I've dated lots of men like him. They say one thing, and then do another. They talk the talk but can't walk the walk. My mother always said a man is only as good as his word. But staying angry at him doesn't hurt him in the slightest. It only hurts *you*."

"I know. You're right," Lenny said. "But a really nice man told me today that it wasn't healthy to keep anger inside. I think tonight I was able to get at least some of the words I've been bottling up out of my system. From now on, I simply refuse to pretend I'm not crazy mad when I am. Trying to pretend I'm an all forgiving saint, controlled and focused, has turned me into the worst devil. I'm aware I wasn't respectful of my ex-husband's feelings. I have to admit, I still have a lot of anger lurking inside. Pretending I'm not angry has been eating a hole in me."

"Listening to the tone of your voice, I don't think you sound as depressed as you did last night. Was this nice man you keep talking about single?"

"Yes, Dawn. He *is* single, as a matter of fact. He's a *priest*, for heaven's sake. And I don't know him from Adam's house cat. I just met him on the street after I was almost hit by a car."

"Gosh, Lenny, you really have had a rough day. Maybe all you needed was to do a little ranting and raving. In *The Secret Door to*

Success, Florence said, "Change your expectations and you'll change your conditions. So maybe you should ask yourself that question. What do you expect?"

"What did I expect today? Well, certainly not everything that happened, although I *did* expect my ex to call and cancel his trip."

"Exactly!" Dawn exclaimed. "'According to your faith be it unto you.' That's in the Bible. Florence just re-worded it to make it easier to understand."

"But Dawn," Lenny argued, "so many things happened today I *didn't* expect. I'm not saying what you said is wrong. But maybe you need to loan me your book and it will help me change my life."

"Don't worry," Dawn said, laughing. "I've already got a copy wrapped up to give you tomorrow night because I know how much you loved Florence's other book."

"Dawn, I know there is deep wisdom in your words. But right now, I can barely hold a thought in my head."

"I have never met your ex-husband," Dawn replied. "But it doesn't really matter what he's like. The only person you can heal or change or do anything about is *you*. And right now, you are not happy. If you just take half the responsibility of Bob's no-show, because you always expect him to act that way, then you might just be able to let it go. You see what I mean? You'll never be able to control what he will or won't do."

"Great! Now I'm really feeling good about myself," Lenny said sarcastically.

"I'm not trying to ruffle your feathers, or put you down, girlfriend. I'm just saying we have to take responsibly for what we are sending out and helping to create."

"Do you really think because I expected the worst, I played an unconscious role in my ex's canceled visit?"

"Well, let me just say this," Dawn answered. "I once read Gandhi was known for his transformational soul power. He always imagined the man standing in front of him was trustworthy. He expected the best behavior from everybody. And they say his presence was so great even armed soldiers laid down their weapons as he passed. Now, *that's* what I'm talking about. That's spiritual alchemy! And Lenny, you need to activate that kind of soul power when dealing with your ex-husband or with anybody else, for that matter."

"Dawn, I love you! I called to blow off steam. I called to tell you about my crazy day. But you've just given me a flash of insight. Were I to think from the standpoint of my center, my God-Self, I feel I would think as Gandhi thought. I would see the best in everyone. Until this moment, I wasn't sure I even had a God-Self. But if I try to develop an expectation such as Gandhi's, I might enjoy taking root and growing in a place of peaceful expectations versus always expecting the worst."

"Well," Dawn said, laughing. "That's what friends are for. Thank goodness I finally said something that sunk into your stubborn head."

"Have you talked with Mitzi?"

"Yeah, she told me about your dream. It sounds profound. And she also told me I'm George and you're Nancy Drew. So now the truth comes out. You guys think I'm tall and manly."

"Absolutely not," Lenny laughed. "George was just athletic and liked to wear pants. But you have to admit, Mitzi makes a great Bess."

"Okay, you're right," she snickered. "I can't wait to hear more thoughts about your ghostly encounter with your grandmother. But not tonight, I'm too sleepy."

"I know how you feel. I'm exhausted, too. But thanks to you, I'm going to bed with a new attitude. I'm going to make my Granny's ghost proud. I'm going to grow some Gandhi soul power tonight. I'm going to try to believe the best about everybody. I'm sure it will feel like I'm lying to myself at first. But at least I'll give it a try. If it worked for him, it will work for me."

By the time Lenny hung up the phone, her heart felt less heavy. But she imagined the very action of persistently thinking positive thoughts would be like climbing a tall mountain. Could she do it? Or would her old mental habits of negative thinking win out, thus causing her outer world to remain unchanged?

Lenny walked over and turned off the overhead light. In bed, she grabbed an armful of pillows and nested herself between them. Suddenly, she smelled the unpleasant chemical odor of hair coloring. She tried to ignore it. It was too late to rewash her hair and try to get rid of the smell. So she got up and did the next best thing. She sprayed her rolled up hair with hairspray.

Back in bed, she allowed her paternal grandmother's quilt to cover her nose and tried not to breathe the hairspray or the terrible chemical scent of peroxide. *Maybe, room deodorizer would work better,* she thought. She walked to the bathroom, picked up a can, and sprayed her entire room. Then, she lay down in bed for the third time that night. Her head was now throbbing. Her room smelled like a stink bomb had exploded in a field of spring flowers.

Surrendering to her pain, she got up once again and walked into the kitchen for a bottle of aspirin. As she did, she noticed Lassie running toward the front door. In all the commotion, Mack had forgotten to take her out for her last walk.

Lenny walked over, patted the top of Lassie's head, and opened the front door for her. Outside, the neighborhood looked dark and quiet. She didn't bother putting the dog on a leash. She shut the door and walked back into the kitchen for a much-needed aspirin.

For safety's sake, Lenny stored all her medications on the top shelf, so she pulled up a chair to reach them and soon found the right bottle. She turned the white cap until the arrows were perfectly aligned. Then she popped off the lid. As she turned toward the sink to pour herself a glass of water, she heard a loud woman's voice. She ran to the window and saw her neighbor yelling at something on the ground beneath the neighbor's bedroom window. Lenny didn't have to guess what it was. It was Lassie.

"Here we go again," she sighed. As she set the open bottle of aspirin down, it slipped off the edge of the sink, spilling pills into the sudsy water where she was soaking the unwashed dishes from dinner.

Barefoot, adorned in only a sheer blue gown, Lenny ran out the front door. A cold drizzling rain chilled her body as she ran.

"Lassie, come home!" she yelled as cold icy chills shot up both her legs. Lassie ignored her and ran zigzag back and forth across the front lawn.

"Young lady," Ms. Tallulah yelled down from her window. "This is the last time I'm going to tell you to keep your dog, or for that matter, your children, out of my yard!"

"I'm sorry, Ms. Tallulah. I'm sorry Lassie trespassed again. But I'm kind of glad to see you. I really hate going to bed mad. I'm sorry I called you a bitch. I'm often a bitch myself. Please forgive me."

Lenny's legs were trembling. She couldn't feel her toes anymore. She stood looking up at Ms. Tallulah's window, but Ms. Tallulah didn't respond to her apology. She just closed her window and turned off the light.

As she hurried into the house, she whistled and clapped her hands. Lassie knew that meant move it *now*. The dog streaked into the house like a bolt of lightning. Lenny shut the door and stood on top of her heating vents until her feet thawed. As she stood there trembling, she vowed to think nice thoughts about Ms. Tallulah. But she couldn't think of a single one at the moment.

By the time she crawled into bed, her headache was gone. It was a good thing, because the empty aspirin bottle was now bobbing up and down next to the partially submerged greasy frying pan.

THE SNAKE

Ask and it will be given to you; seek and you will find; knock and the door will be opened to you. For everyone who asks receives; he who seeks finds; and to him who knocks, the door will be opened. Which of you, if your son asks for bread, will you give him a stone? Or if he asks for a fish, will give him a snake?

—Matthew 7:7-10

Lenny dropped into a deep sleep immediately. One minute she was noticing the rise and fall of her breath. In the next, she was watching words swirling around in her bedroom like wingless insects. As she watched them rise up and out of the ceiling she followed them.

Lenny glanced down. She was flying as free as a bird. Her house and her neighborhood grew smaller and smaller. She hardly digested this scene, when suddenly it changed. Her eyes were still cast downward and she could see her bare feet, her toenails painted with brightly glowing red nail polish. As she watched, her feet came to rest on a golden-yellow grass. She raised her head and saw she had landed near her long-ago home in Texas. She'd loved the nearby grassy fields dotted with bluebonnets. She and the father of her children had once been happy here. But it had all ended so bitterly. *Where was the wind?* She wondered. Texas always had a cold wind blowing through the grassy plains in the wintertime.

Her daughter was born in Texas—at a hospital in downtown Fort Worth. As postcard memories danced in her head, a city appeared in the distance. Instantly, she decided to walk toward it. But as soon as she started, she found she was there - downtown.

Lenny imagined herself to be in a section of Fort Worth she once adored. The streets were made of smoothly worn cobblestones. Looking from side to side, she noticed the buildings appeared different from how she remembered them. They weren't a homey western style at all. Architecturally, the buildings were ancient and gothic. In fact, it now appeared she wasn't even in the United States.

For a short period of time, during her second marriage, Lenny had worked as a part-time travel agent. She had seen these buildings once in a travel brochure. She realized she was indeed not in Texas—she was in the, City of Lights, Paris, France!

A rush of excitement traveled through her entire body, and she soaked up all the splendid surroundings, bathed by a melon-colored setting sun. She spun around and around with her arms open wide. As she did, the city's colors changed. Now, she saw more yellows and oranges. Black iron streetlamps with tiny white lightening-bug-size lights loomed overhead. She threw her head back and wondered why she suddenly felt very small in contrast.

Without thinking where she might go, Lenny started walking. As she wondered what grand sights she might see next, she saw one—the Eiffel Tower. All the lights and the colors of the sky seemed so beautiful. She remembered Vincent van Gogh writing to his brother that he tried to always look at the world with simple, childlike eyes—filled with wonder and adoration and totally devoid of judgment. Yet, as soon as he fell into "adult thinking" (judging, for example, a gray day was less beautiful to capture on canvas than a bright yellow sunflower), he wasn't able to love the world as deeply or passionately. He felt this lack of love showed in his work. If judgment was powerful enough to bring death to an artist's creative imagination, Lenny thought, it must be powerful enough to create a deep abyss, breaking her connection to God's divine light within her heart.

Viewing all the sunset's colors with the simple, childlike eyes Van Gogh so prized, Lenny wondered why she couldn't always feel this good about life, fully in the moment. As this thought entered her awareness, she suddenly smelled the foul odor of smoke. She turned around and saw a café with a red and yellow striped canopy. Sitting at one of the tables was a dark-haired man. It felt as if his gray cigarette smoke was pulling her into his field of consciousness like an unexpected calling card. He was very handsome, although not the rough and tough cowboy type who usually appealed to her. Lenny had always thought Bob, her first husband, looked like Roy Rogers. This man, however, was no cowboy. He was dressed in what appeared to be a very expensive Armani suit. He had midnight black hair and looked very European. He wore a white shirt and dark tie. On his face was a neatly trimmed mustache and beard. She couldn't see the color of his eyes, but they looked dark and mysterious. As she wondered who he was, he turned and looked at her. Then, seemingly disinterested, he coolly turned his back to her. She watched as he put what appeared to be a glass of Champagne to his lips.

Lenny suddenly felt judged, naked. She looked down to see if she really was naked. Thank God, she wasn't—she was still wearing her nightgown. She didn't even know this man, so why did his opinion of her even matter? Suddenly, Lenny remembered her hair curlers. Her arms felt as heavy as logs and she wondered why. After a bit of struggle, she felt the top of her head. To her horror, she realized they were, indeed, still in her hair. She thought about how ridiculous she must look.

Those simple, childlike eyes, adoring the beautiful sunset seconds ago, were gone in the blink of an eye. Lenny was right back in the poisonous trap of self-judgment. Thinking another person thought bad of her, so did she. Thoughts about broken dreams of yesteryear filled her head with sadness. The little girl in her wanted a happy-ever-after storybook Prince Charming. For many years she had been grieving—grieving the loss of not having a romantic storybook ending. Her second divorce was a crushing blow to her ego. She knew she couldn't rewrite her life's story. But perhaps with effort she could let go of silly fantasies about the future that caused her nothing but pain.

Lenny turned away from her handsome stranger. As she started walking, she heard a loud whizzing, rushing water sound. She turned her head toward the noise, and a beautiful, circular, stone-walled fountain rose high into the air before her.

The fountain was so beautiful it took Lenny's breath away. In the center of the fountain was a tall marble statue. The stony gray sculpture was encircled by a spray of white mist. Lenny's body began to tingle. She focused on the statue. She had been seeking center, and now she had found one.

Suddenly, the rushing water became silent. She was now somehow standing on the rim of the stone-walled fountain. Her toes were almost hanging over the edge. This change of perspective made the monument-like pedestal, upon which the statue stood, look much larger than before. Now, able to make out more details, she saw the statue was a stone carving of a man. He was muscular but pint-sized compared to the enormous world globe resting upon his back. Lenny immediately recognized it as a hideously, disproportionate Atlas.

The artist, who sculpted Atlas, had bent his back almost into the shape of a horseshoe. His head hung low, and Lenny was sure if she could have seen his face, it would be grimacing. She was just about to turn away when she heard a man's voice say in low tones, "As you think, so are you."

"I beg your pardon?" Lenny responded, not exactly sure to whom she was responding.

The statue was silent, but as Lenny stared at him, Atlas raised his head. Lenny tried to scream, but the scream was muffled as if she had a mouth full of cotton. Her statue was not wearing a man's face. It was her *own* face she was looking into! Shocked, she lost her balance and fell off the wall. But instead of hitting the water in the fountain, as she expected, she just kept falling and falling, as if she were plummeting into a well. The deeper she fell, the more frightened Lenny became. Fear gripped her heart as the walls of the well seemed to squeeze inward, like a throat trying to swallow her as she tumbled headfirst into its blackness.

Finally, her fear intensifying, she felt solid ground beneath her feet. Lenny looked up to see a pinpoint of light from a faraway source hanging over her head. The light gave her hope. Perhaps she could be rescued from wherever it was she had fallen. But the narrow, cave-like well was so deep. Lenny looked around to see if she might spot a rock, or an object to toss toward the light. Perhaps someone would see it.

That's when she noticed the writing on the wall. Moving closer, she made out three words that appeared to have been scratched into the stone with a knife. The words vibrated, as if alive, but finally she was able to read three of them; *power, will,* and *determination.*

Lenny stared at the words for what seemed like a long time. They somehow made her feel less frightened and alone. But she still had to figure a way out of the well, and at that moment, what she really desired most was a rope. Then, inside her head, she heard, *this is your rope.*

Instantly, Lenny was transported back into her bedroom, although not into her body. She stood beside herself, watching herself sleep. She had never done this before. It was as if her subconscious mind and conscious mind, possessed two different bodies. In the body she was now housed, she noticed a refreshing, calm detachment from worries of the previous day. And this body, somehow, didn't seem to be breathing. She felt as if its home existed in a world between breaths. Free from the bondage and struggles of life, she felt suspended in the air like a crystal clear veil of light. As she watched her sleeping body, she noticed something odd about her arms and hands. They appeared to be covered in words. But the words were small and impossible to read.

"This is not good," Lenny whispered. As she spoke, she was suddenly no longer looking at her body—she was back inside it. The slow, in-and-out rhythm of her breathing had returned. Then, she became aware her right arm was waving in the air. It seemed to move on its own, separate from Lenny's will. She could feel something wiggling in her tightly clasped fist. Perhaps, she still held the rope she had prayed for. She opened her eyes. They seemed glued together and opened slowly. Fear gripped her, as she immediately realized the rope in her hand was a snake—a thick-bodied, mean-looking, striped snake of the "red and yellow, kill a fellow" variety.

Then, the snake's eyes disappeared. All Lenny could see was an enormous, black, cave-like mouth with two white fangs. They were a breath away from striking her in the face. Sheer horror shot through her body, and she was about to lose her grip on the creature. Determined not to die before raising her children, Lenny flung the snake as hard as she could. As she threw it, she let out a scream that ripped her right out of her nightmarish half-sleep.

Lenny sat straight up in bed. She looked for the snake. She *knew* it was real. But how could it be? Had she suddenly lost her mind? Then out of the corner of her eye, she saw something move next to her left hand. With her right arm she whipped it sideways without a single minute of hesitation.

A small lace pillow flew through the air, knocking over her clock radio and a vase full of artificial daisies. She'd never in her life had such a real and lucid nightmare. She had felt the snake against her flesh as it had wiggled and tried to fight its way out of her hand. Worse, she still sensed its presence in the room. Her bed now appeared too lumpy for comfort. The lumps had to go. She stood up on her mattress and yanked off sheets and her Grandma's quilt. She felt better until she saw how lumpy the floor now looked.

"What was I thinking?" she whispered. Now, she'd have to clean things up, and the floor looked even more frightening. She had to get a grip on her nerves. Maybe she was having a nervous breakdown. She'd read about people having them. Perhaps this was now happening to her. But she felt as sane as ever. She was not going to act like a coward. Even brave people experience fear, she thought, but it doesn't stop them from doing whatever they need to do. She climbed off the bed and scooped the bed linens into her arms. She opened her bedroom door and tossed them into the hallway. It was still dark outside her window, and the room was a little too dark for comfort, so she switched on the overhead light.

The floor was still a total mess. Lenny began picking up daisies that were scattering all over the place. Several pink curlers had fallen out of her hair, and she picked them up and set them on her vanity. Then, she sat at the vanity, tucking her legs under her as she unwound the remaining curlers from her hair. As she did, a flash of red snakeskin caught her attention. Lenny screamed and leapt off the vanity bench and onto the top of her bare mattress.

The brass headboard groaned with disgust as it scraped against her bedroom wall. She felt foolish again, and forced herself to peep over the edge of her bed. But the red she saw didn't belong to a snake—it belonged to her snakeskin shoe. She reached down and picked it up.

Spotting its mate, she put both shoes on her feet. If something sinister was loose and roaming about, she wanted to be ready to kick it. Feeling armed and dangerous, she sat down on the bed. She needed to look up the symbolism of a snake in her dream dictionary, but this meant she would have to reach under the bed. At the moment, the last thing she wanted to do was stick her hand into a dark hiding place.

That's when the rest of her dream came flooding back to her. She had fallen into a dark well. Before the snake, she had seen her arms covered with words that were too small to read. But she had been able to read three words carved in the wall of the well: the first word was *power*, the second was *will*, and the last word was *determination*.

Right now, Lenny was determined to get the dream dictionary from under the bed. She slowly edged her way across the mattress, and then, taking a deep calming breath, she balanced her body halfway off the bed. She held onto the side of the bed with her left arm and lifted a white eyelet dust ruffle with her right hand. Then, she grabbed hold of something furry and slung it out of her way. A missing slipper was now found.

Lenny leaned further. She wiggled her fingers until they brushed against a hard surface and she felt the cloth binding of *How to Interpret Your Own Dreams*. Her orange notebook was tucked underneath the dream dictionary. She could barely touch it with the tips of her fingers. Finally, she snatched up the dictionary but dropped her notebook. As she reached back down to pick it up, loud music suddenly exploded in her right ear. She screamed, flipping off the bed head first. Her clock radio continued singing beneath her right shoulder.

Mack burst through her door and ran into her bedroom. The back of his auburn hair was sticking up like a rooster's crown.

"Mom, are you all right?" he asked, half-panicked.

"Barely," Lenny groaned. She could only imagine how bizarre she looked in her nightgown and red snakeskin high heels. Seeing his mother was having trouble getting up, Mack bent down and grabbed her right arm and hand.

"Were you jumping on your bed in high heels?" he asked with a broad grin, once he saw she was not hurt.

"I had the worst nightmare," Lenny said with a sigh. "I don't even know how to explain it because it was so odd. And it seemed so real."

"Wow, Mom. What happened?" Mack asked.

"Give me a second." Lenny bent down and placed her clock radio back on the bedside table. She sat down on the edge of the bed and told her son about her snake. Her description of the snake's colored stripes, its cave-like mouth, and its sharp teeth made Mack laugh out loud.

"Stop laughing!" Lenny teased. "I *felt* it wiggling in my hand! It felt *real!*"

Mack looked to see if she was kidding, and realizing she wasn't joking made him laugh even harder. He bent over and rolled around on the floor holding his stomach. He was laughing so hard he couldn't speak. Lassie, not wanting to miss the fun, jumped on Mack's back and began licking his neck and face. Lenny loved hearing him laugh.

"Did you say you saw a snake?" Elisabeth asked, running into the bedroom to see what all the commotion was about. "Oh boy! Where is it?" Her small, narrow feet scurried across the room as her eyes searched the floor for her mother's imaginary horror. "Mom, did you really see a snake?"

"Yes, and it's in the *closet!*" Mack screamed in mock terror. Then he jumped into the closet and dashed out waving a satin waist sash off of one of Lenny's bathrobes. He chased Elizabeth around the room with it. Lassie barked hysterically. Lenny finally calmed everyone down. She assured her daughter the snake wasn't real, and it was only part of a bad dream. But Lenny didn't really believe it.

When the children ran back to their rooms to dress for school, Lenny sat on the edge of her bed and jotted down as much of the dream as she could remember. It seemed a very odd cast of archetypal figures had paid her a visit. What they came to teach her would take some effort to figure out. She had little trouble recognizing that primarily, she had encountered poorly developed, harshly critical masculine beings. The tiny Atlas statue carrying the weight of the world on his back, Lenny could definitely relate to him. And the voice of her inner critic wore the mask of the very handsome man in the Paris café. That part of the dream was a little confusing, but it didn't seem important at the moment. Lenny immediately recognized these figures as reflections of her animus, a name Jung used for the unconscious masculine archetype within all women (as opposed to anima, the name he used for the unconscious feminine archetype that resides within all men.)

But for now, she needed to get ready for her day. She walked over and pulled her red sweater off its hanger. It smelled like the air freshener she'd sprayed in her bedroom the night before. She attached the matching faux fur collar to it and then put on a slimming pencil skirt that reached just below her knees. She looked at her reflection in the mirror. She was pleasantly surprised to see she looked more rested this morning than she usually did. She didn't know how this could be possible, having spent half the night falling down wells, and wrestling a snake.

Mack knocked on her bedroom door.

"I'm dressed, you can come in," she said reaching for a hairbrush to smooth out her curls.

"Mom, did your snake look more like a copperhead or a cottonmouth?" he asked.

"Neither," Lenny answered. "It was cherry red and lemon yellow with a really fat, worm-like body."

Mack leaned against the wall, holding his side with laughter.

"Son, just seeing you happy and laughing makes me feel happy. I'm starting to like my snake more and more. Now, go get dressed! Today is your last day of school before Christmas break."

Dressed and ready for breakfast, Lenny picked up the dirty bed linens from the hallway and headed toward the garage, where her washer and dryer were hooked up. She started a load of laundry and walked back into the kitchen.

The aspirin bottle was still bobbing in the dirty sink water. Lenny fished it out and tossed it into the nearby trashcan. All the aspirin tablets had melted into the oily water. She didn't have time to fool with washing the dishes. She pulled the stopper out of the sink and drained the dirty water. Then she replaced the stopper, ran fresh hot water into the sink and poured in more liquid soap. Satisfied for the moment, she went to check on the children.

SAND AND PEARLS

To see a World in a Grain of Sand
And a Heaven in a Wild Flower,
Hold Infinity in the palm of your hand
And Eternity in an hour!

—William Blake

Lenny and her children drove to school discussing worms, and snakes, and all creatures that crawled upon their bellies. Laughing at herself felt great medicine for her soul. By the time they pulled up in front of the school, there was no line of cars. They were running late. Some of Mack's friends were standing by the entrance waving him over. He'd already hugged his mother once this morning, so Lenny didn't ask for more. Elizabeth still allowed public hugs and kisses, so Lenny gave her both.

As Elizabeth ran toward the front door of the school, Dawn's niece, Pearl, held the door open for her. It appeared Pearl's parents were just as late as Lenny was for drop off. Lenny glanced around the parking lot. That's when she saw Dawn's brother's blue truck. But Dawn's brother was not behind the wheel; it was Dawn. And apparently, she'd been waiting for Lenny. She was waving her over.

Dawn had been hauling rock for her Grandma Mimi's Christmas present. Mimi had asked her grandchildren to build her a rock garden for Christmas. That's all she wanted. She had a low spot in her yard that wouldn't grow flowers. She decided it would make a good spot for rocks and a hardy groundcover.

Lenny looked in her rearview mirror. A car was coming, but she had time to turn her car sharply to the left and into an open spot directly behind Dawn. Lenny rolled down her window and yelled at her friend.

"Move it, you hussy!" she yelled. "You're blocking traffic!"

Dawn stepped out of the truck, laughing. She was wearing paint-splattered, bib overalls with bright red-and-white-striped socks. Her just-crawled-out-of-bed hair and overalls made Lenny laugh.

"I can't tell if you're in a good mood or a foul mood. Which is it?" Dawn teased.

"Right now, I'm wondering what Halloween witch you stole those socks from."

"Girlfriend, you don't like my socks?" Dawn said as she pulled up a pant leg, kicked off a shoe, and hiked her leg onto Lenny's open window. Her socks hugged each toe individually.

"Well, I have to admit, I sorta do! Elizabeth would *love* them. Where'd you get them?" Lenny asked.

"I can't tell you because Pearl is giving Elizabeth a pair just like them tonight at my party. She insisted on giving me my socks as an early Christmas present so I could enjoy wearing them. That girl, she can't wait to open up her presents. She's driving us all crazy."

"That is so sweet. Pearl is just a little doll inside and out," Lenny responded as Dawn lifted her foot off Lenny's car and replaced her shoe. "Well, I had an even wilder dream last night. Have you ever heard the saying, 'Red and black a friend of Jack, but red and yellow will kill a fellow?'"

"Are we talking about snakes?" Dawn asked, frowning.

"Exactly," Lenny said, nodding. "I dreamed about the 'kill a fellow' kind last night."

"Get outta here!" Dawn said with a giggle as her dark almond eyes grew large.

"I'm telling you the truth, Dawn. That snake was wiggling in my hand and it felt real. It would have killed me had I not flung it into the air. Where it went or where it came from I do not know. But I've never had such a vivid and horrifyingly *real* otherworldly type experience in my entire life!"

Lenny proceeded to describe all the details of her dream as Dawn listened with intense interest. When Lenny finished with a description of tossing the snake into the air, Dawn remained quiet for a moment before finally speaking.

"Well, I'm going to use the words your Granny always used when you wanted to Nancy-Drew something to death. Let it be."

"Carl Jung never *let it be*." He dug down until he reached into a vision of heaven. I don't want to think about this snake. But it feels too important to ignore. I know you, and everyone else, think my visions seem completely foolish and ungraspable. So do I. But don't you think I need to explore this further?" Lenny asked incredulously. "After all, look at all that has happened to me in the last two days! You have to admit this last horrifying vision is most unusual."

"And what isn't unusual about your life Lenny?"

"Nothing," Lenny answered. "Since early childhood, my lucid dreaming has shaped my relationship to the world, for better or worse. Too often, in relationships with men, I've lost my individuality. Their opinions of me mattered so much, I stopped being me, free and happy. Like last night, in the early part of my dream, before snake, I lost myself when a handsome man in a café judged me unattractive.

"Your snake was probably a symbol for your snake-in-the-grass ex-husband," Dawn said, looking serious.

"But your Gandhi story helped me so much last night. I think something was dredged out of me by your words. I went to bed trying hard to find a way to grow more open. I fell asleep forgiving everybody in the world, including myself. I want more than anything to develop more soul power by thinking the best of everyone I meet. What if this dream symbolized my getting rid of some inner judgments and unresolved anger issues with my husband. Don't you think energies like that are as deadly to one's soul growth as a snake might be to my body? I think it all fits together somehow."

"You know that does ring true to me," Dawn said. "I like that. You need to write that down. And don't drive too fast to work. But hasten on, and catch up with your visions, Lenny. They are not foolish. Your vivid dreams may feel like a curse sometimes, but they are guiding you to a greater, happier version of you. I can't wait until we have time to share the entire dream together."

"I'll try to write it down later," Lenny said. "Thanks for your kind words. I needed to hear them. But right now, I've got to get to work."

The friends hugged and Dawn hurried back to her brother's truck. Once again, Lenny decided to drive to work without playing the radio. She needed silence. She wanted to mentally map out her busy day. She and the other secretaries would exchange gifts during their fifteen minute break. Then at one o'clock, they would have lunch with all of the coaching staff in the athletic cafeteria. She'd heard the food was fabulous, which she figured it probably had to be in order to pull in good recruits. After work, it was Dawn's church choir program, followed by an after-party at Dawn's house.

As Lenny turned onto the Alcoa Highway, she thought about how quickly she and Dawn had bonded. They had actually only met three years ago. But it felt as if their sisterhood stretched back much further. Elizabeth was actually responsible for bringing the two together. Dawn often helped her brother drive his only child, Pearl, to school. Pearl and Elizabeth met in kindergarten and became fast friends.

One morning, not long after kindergarten had started, Elizabeth had insisted on wearing multiple barrettes. Lenny figured it was because her hair was so baby-fine it wouldn't stay in place. But when Elizabeth begged for additional pigtails beyond her customary two, Lenny had thought it a bit odd. It had taken a lot to talk the child out of it.

Later in the week, Dawn picked up Pearl, at the same time Lenny arrived to pick up Elizabeth. The two girls ran out of the school building holding hands and giggling. Seeing Pearl's braided, multiple pigtails on each side of her little head, Lenny immediately understood Elizabeth's envy. She'd forgotten how little girls love to look just like each other. Coordinating fashions with a best friend was something she herself fondly recalled, although now, she tried hard not to dress like anybody else. She figured the suppressed artist in her was trying to express her uniqueness.

Lenny remembered the first day she met Dawn. She was wearing a dark blue wool business suit, with a large rhinestone angel pin perched on her shoulder. Her neck was graced with a lovely strand of pearls.

"Hello," Dawn said in a friendly voice, beaming a wide and incredibly beautiful smile as she extended her right hand. "My name is Dawn. You must be Elizabeth's mother."

"Yes, I am," Lenny answered. "And I think our daughters are best friends."

"Oh, she's not *my* child, just my heart in pigtails!" Dawn had said, her grin getting even bigger. "I'm her Aunty Dawn. Pearl has been talking about Elizabeth every day since school started. She cried the whole week before school began and even insisted she was too sick to go when the day arrived. My brother and I were betting on how soon her teacher would call asking us to pick up our crying child. But she met Elizabeth, and that cured her."

"My Elizabeth couldn't wait to go to school," Lenny shared. "And she talks about Pearl all the time, too. Let me tell you, convincing her that her wispy blonde hair can't make a head full of pigtails like Pearl has not been easy."

Both women laughed. Then, Dawn mentioned that with Pearl being an only child, she might overcome some of her shyness if Elizabeth visited her after school for a play date.

"That sounds great," Lenny responded. "Elizabeth would love it!"

On the spot, they picked a day that was good for both of them. Lenny would drop off her daughter on the way to take her son to football practice. Then she would pick her up on the way home when practice was over.

Soon, the two women started scheduling their *own* play dates. Dawn was an avid hiker, and Lenny loved hiking but hadn't gone since her Granny's death. Spending long hours on the trails in the Great Smoky

Mountains National Park, had given them lots of time to get better acquainted.

On a short hike to Abrams Falls one day, Lenny had remarked how much she liked Pearl's name. Dawn explained Pearl's name came from her Grandma Mimi.

"So your Mimi's name is really Pearl?" Lenny had asked.

"No," Dawn answered, laughing. "Here's the story. My brother's wife got pregnant before they got married. They were young and had a lot of student loans. They were torn apart as to what to do. Neither one was ready for marriage. And they were both afraid to tell their parents. My brother finally broke down one night and told Mimi. They've always been as thick as thieves."

"What did Mimi say when she heard the news?" Lenny asked.

"Best advice I've ever heard her speak. She said, "when life kicks sand in your shell, make a pearl.""

"So they did!" Lenny exclaimed, laughing.

"Yes. And that's how Pearl got her name."

"That's a beautiful story," Lenny said. "Is that why you like wearing pearls?"

"Well, I guess you can say that. When my brother's wife graduated from college, Mimi gave her a string of pearls. So when I got my bachelor's degree, she gifted me, too."

"On her teacher's salary, I'm sure that wasn't easy," Lenny said, shaking her head.

"Her? She's as tight as they come. But generous when the occasion feels big."

After hearing Dawn's story, Lenny shared with Dawn how Elizabeth got her name. Lenny's ancestors, on both sides of her family tree, were from the Blue Ridge Mountain region of Georgia. After Lenny's parents divorced, her mother's mother had moved in to help raise Lenny and her two siblings. Granny arrived with a big metal trunk full of family keepsakes. Granny shared several items from the trunk, including her mother's infant moth-eaten bathing suit, with an appliqué of a pumpkin on the belly. There was also her grandfather's handcrafted, leather baby shoes, awards he won at work, and his wedding shirt. Granny's modest

1920 wedding dress had been carefully folded up in tissue paper in the trunk, as well. But it was the love letters from Granny's mother to her father Lenny loved best.

The letters were inked in fancy Victorian-style penmanship, and they smelled like faded violets. The letters had all been signed, "Your loving wife, Elizabeth," and Lenny quickly fell in love with the name. Elizabeth's husband was part Cherokee, but when Lenny begged to hear Granny's stories about this branch of the family tree, Granny's lips got tighter than a new girdle.

Before long, Lenny's reflections and memories of when she and Dawn met had driven her straight into the employee parking lot. She hardly remembered the ride to work. Lenny stepped from her car. The air was as cold as the steel gray sky looked. Today was the day she should have worn her stovetop boots. Instead, she opted for her red snakeskin heels. She sprinted as fast as she could toward the athletic building, slowing down only slightly as she made her way up the steep flight of concrete steps.

A PAPER ROSE

The mythological figure of the Universal Mother imputes to the cosmos the feminine attributes of the first, nourishing and protecting presence. The fantasy is primarily spontaneous; for there exists a close and obvious correspondence between the attitude of the young child toward its mother and that of the adult toward the surrounding material world.

—Joseph Campbell

Those who enter through the side door of University of Tennessee's Stokley Athletic Center, immediately walk upon an indoor track arena. If you're wearing tennis shoes, no one in front of you can hear you coming. But that's not the case if you're wearing high heels. When Lenny entered the building, the sound of her steps echoed down the long hallway.

A couple of basketball players were running laps, and Lenny envied their energy and physical fitness routine. If she wasn't walking in the woods, among evergreens and hardwoods, Lenny didn't like exercising. After two years of fulltime work, while raising kids, and going to school three nights a week, Lenny thought it aerobic just to get out of bed.

Mindlessly, she watched the athletes run past her. Then someone in tennis shoes, suddenly, appeared behind her, inches away from her right shoulder. Lenny turned toward the figure, and saw it was a man she didn't recognize. His smile looked almost *too* friendly. She half-smiled back, turned away, quickened her pace, and held tight to her purse.

He looked safe, she thought, but she didn't want to take any chances. He appeared to be somewhere in his fifties. For a brief moment, Lenny wondered if he was the secret lover of Ms. Red from the library. His salt-and-pepper hair matched his tweed sports jacket, which screamed "teacher!" with its tan leather elbow patches.

"I know something about you," the man said, chuckling.

Lenny stopped in her tracks. She'd heard those lines before. Was it some kind of cosmic pickup line?

"What do you know?" Lenny asked carefully, not certain she wanted to hear the answer.

"I can tell you're a happy person. I saw it in your eyes when you smiled. A lot can be read by looking into someone's eyes," he said grinning ear to ear.

Lenny hated to tell the man his intuition was way off the mark. As they continued to walk down the hallway, silence filled the narrow space between his broad shoulders and her red sweater.

"Tell me something," he said with a suspicious wink. "What would you like to be when you grow up?"

Lenny looked him in the eyes to see if he was serious. This man was definitely a charmer like her first husband, who would have easily said something like that. It raised Lenny's suspicions immediately. But remembering her previous conversation with Dawn, how Gandhi believed the best about everyone, Lenny switched off her judge, and began to think kind thoughts about this man. She decided to play his game until her hand was safely attached to the outer door of her office.

"A child," she said looking up at him without a trace of a smile. A smile, after all, might give the man the wrong signal.

"Why, young lady! That's the best answer I've heard all day."

"Well, it's still early," Lenny reminded him.

"No," he said shaking his head. "You win the prize!"

He reached across his chest and removed a red crêpe-paper rose from his lapel pocket. She hadn't even noticed it before he took it off.

"Oh no, really," Lenny said, blushing as she shook her head. "That was a silly answer. I doubt it's worthy of a prize. And besides, I'm sure you'll hear a better answer before the day is over."

"I'm absolutely confident I'll not hear such a wise answer again. Not today or any other day. The prize belongs to you," the man insisted.

"You're making me blush," Lenny said, feeling her cheeks grow rosy.

The man stopped walking and stood holding out his hand, offering her the paper rose.

"You must accept your prize, little girl. Now, go and have yourself a very merry Christmas," he laughed.

Lenny looked down at the paper rose in his hand. As she took it from him, she checked to see if he was wearing a wedding ring. And he was. If this was Ms. Red's professor, she understood her attraction to him. The man nodded goodbye, turned, and left without a word.

Lenny stood in the hall for a moment, astonished. After all, strangers didn't give her paper roses every day. Smiling, she walked a little further and was soon unlocking the inner door to the football office. For the first time in a long time, she was the first to arrive. For some unknown reason, traffic or faulty alarm clocks must have slowed her other coworkers from getting to work on time. She checked the clock above the doorway. She was only running five minutes late, which seemed almost impossible. She quickly dismissed this oddity, turned on the lights and hung her blue cape in the closet. She hadn't bothered to put it on in the car, but she might need it later on today. A cold front was moving into East Tennessee.

She sat her purse on top of her desk and searched for her desk keys. Almost immediately, after transferring the phones from the night service, her desk phone rang. It was her coworker Katy. When she got to her car this morning, she discovered one of her tires had a slow leak. She had to take it in for repair or replacement. She told Lenny she'd be running late. Lenny promised to give the bad news to their managing coach. But Katy assured Lenny not to worry—she'd definitely make it to work by lunchtime.

Lenny hung up the phone. Then she opened her pencil drawer and retrieved a long hatpin leftover from a homecoming game corsage. She pinned the red rose to her sweater. Then she took out her compact mirror and admired her paper prize. The kindness of this stranger had oddly enlivened her. She put away her mirror and walked into the break room to make coffee. One of her coaches always complained her coffee was too weak for his taste. She filled the metal container to the highest mark. If this didn't wake him up, she thought, nothing would.

Yesterday, her thoughts primarily focused on her unfriendly neighbor, Ms. Tallulah, and then Bob. She lacked the will or the power to change how she felt about either one. But she wanted to try. It felt good last night to at least try to apologize to her grumpy old neighbor. You can take a girl out of the South, but you can't take good old-fashioned Southern manners out of a girl.

Back at her desk, Lenny tore December 22 off of her desk calendar. The newly exposed photograph depicted a snow-capped mountain with its mirror image reflected upon the still waters of an enormous lake. The scripture was taken from the 23rd Psalm of David. It read, *He leads me beside quiet waters, he restores my soul.*

As Lenny thought about the mountain's reflection, an idea started forming in her mind. She opened her purse and once more took out her cracked compact mirror. Opening the compact, she gazed at the unevenness of her reflection in the shattered glass. As a human being, she realized, she was a living expression of millions of cracked thoughts and emotions, just like her reflection in the compact mirror.

Then, she looked back at the photograph. *A mountain stays where it is,* she thought to herself, *just like Granny said a center does—it stays put.* But the mountain's reflection was altogether different—that was a moving thing. From one day to the next, the reflection probably changed. When the sun is shining, the reflection looks just the way it does in the picture, Lenny thought. But if it's cloudy and gray the next day, the reflection would look very different—even though the mountain itself doesn't change.

By 9:45 a.m., Katy had arrived, wearing a trench coat and carrying a wet umbrella. Katy talked about how lucky she was that her slow-leaking tire didn't become a blowout on the interstate. By noon, all the secretaries were buzzing around their bright orange Christmas tree. The head football coach, Coach Masters, arrived with four of the most beautifully wrapped gifts Lenny had ever seen. He beamed when he explained his wife was great at gift-wrapping. It charmed Lenny to hear him speak so proudly of his wife's creative talents.

While all the secretaries were excitedly sharing, or good-naturedly complaining about their holiday plans, the main line rang. Lenny hurried to pick up the receiver. The man on the other end insisted on talking to the defensive coordinator. Lenny tried to explain he'd just gone into a staff meeting, and was not talking calls, but the man on the phone was not getting the message. He was angry, and felt he had valuable advice that would improve the team's chances for a bowl win. He refused to leave his name and instead launched into his planned speech.

Lenny often took calls like this after a losing game, and she hated it when the callers were rude. But today, she actually enjoyed it and doodled on her steno pad as the caller replayed the entire football season over the phone, not realizing Lenny wasn't really listening. First, she drew a rose with a black ballpoint pen. She loved to sketch with pens instead of pencils. They translated her feelings onto paper in simple black and white, no muddy grays to fuss with. Her rose grew larger as she drew. She'd left the center open. After all, she wasn't sure where center was. Then, still drawing, she tucked a tiny newborn baby into the center of her rose. Like this morning's stranger who suddenly appeared out of nowhere, this tiny baby popped into Lenny's head and spilled out of the end of her pen.

"Have you heard a word I've said?" the caller suddenly asked angrily. Lenny snapped her attention back to the phone, realizing the man had paused in his discourse, expecting a response from her that never came.

"Oh, I know how you feel," she told him with as much sympathy as she could muster. "I get emotional about our losses too. But I'm simply not allowed to interrupt a staff meeting with your suggestions."

"I hear voices in the background. Sounds to me like you're not telling me the truth."

"Oh, that's the secretarial staff. We aren't included in staff meetings. Actually, we're in the middle of our office Christmas party. But like

I said, I'll be more than happy to take a message. I didn't catch your name."

"I said it three times. I don't think you've heard a word I've said, young lady!" He sounded exasperated.

The caller was right, but Lenny didn't know how to respond. "Well, I'm all ears now," she said cheerfully.

The phone line went dead and Lenny shrugged as she replaced the receiver in its cradle. She smiled down at her drawing and tucked it into her top drawer just as the phone rang again. This time it was Mitzi, and Lenny filled her in on the highlights of the snake dream, promising to give her more details at the after-concert party at Dawn's house that night.

Mitzi told Lenny she had found the dream workshop handouts she had promised to share with her, thinking they might help Lenny decode her Granny's message.

"Bess, darling, you're so sweet and perky," Lenny teased.

"Bess was perky?"

"No, *you* are," Lenny said, laughing.

"Hey, Dawn told me about your ex not being able to keep the kids so you can go to the bowl game. I know you have family in town, but I'd love to stay with Elizabeth and Mack for the three nights you'll be gone."

"Mitzi, I can't ask you to do that," Lenny said.

"You didn't ask me," Mitzi responded. "And besides, I owe you for taking care of Gray while I was on vacation."

"One cat doesn't equal two wildcat children."

"It's final!" Mitzi declared. "After all, you can't say no because that's my Christmas gift to you. Otherwise, I'll have to go out at the last minute and get you some store-bought stuff you probably don't need or want. Come on, Lenny. I really want to do this for you."

Lenny took a deep breath. It was just like Mitzi to do something wonderfully unselfish as a gift. As stunned as Lenny was at the generous offer, she also knew there was no saying no.

"I'm trying to think of a bigger word than 'thank you.' But I can't think of one."

"It's perfect," Mitzi whispered. "Because I know you mean it! See ya tonight!"

At 12:15 p.m., the phone lines were transferred to another office. The entire football staff, along with the other athletic office personnel, left the building and paraded merrily toward the athletic cafeteria. The food all looked extraordinarily lush and rich. It was served buffet style. By dessert time, Lenny knew she couldn't eat another bite. But then, someone walked by her carrying a bowl of ice cream, dripping with rich, dark brown, hot syrup. She not only got the ice cream, she also got a dark chocolate brownie, and smothered it with both hot fudge and whipped topping. She might get sick, she thought. But it would be worth it.

While no one was looking, Lenny unfastened the side button of her pencil skirt. It felt good to be able to breathe on her way back to the office.

9
SHARED REALITIES

Time, space, and knowledge localize experience, focusing our interests upon a fleeting point of view. No permanence is found. No permanence seems necessary. The movement of being moved appears to be life's quest. A reality shared, none more exclusive than another. Wholeness seeking wholeness as structures come and go.

—Carl Garant

After the staff had returned from lunch, they eagerly gathered around the office's bright orange Christmas tree. Coach Masters handed each secretary her gift and then said since the gifts were all alike, everyone could dive in and open them at the same time.

The women excitedly peeled off the beautiful wrappings, and each delighted wholeheartedly at what she found—a Fitz and Floyd ceramic rabbit. The rabbits had white bodies with gray fur markings as an overall pattern. On top of each one's back was a removable lid, and a pale-pink ceramic Christmas bow sprinkled with holly served as the lid's handle. Lenny's bunny reminded her of Elizabeth's book, *The Velveteen Rabbit*. Lenny had promised to read it to her daughter on Christmas Eve, and now the universe had gifted Lenny with her own beautiful rabbit.

Lenny gently held the bunny up into the light. His eyes caught her attention. When she looked into them, she thought her new bunny gave her a very knowing look. His sweet mouth, indented beneath his nose, was turned up. He seemed to approve of her as much as she delighted in him.

To everyone's surprise, the gift giving wasn't quite over yet. The equipment manager, who enjoyed complaining the head coach gave away too many jerseys to fans, gave each of the secretaries bright orange sweat shirts and pants. Then, around three o'clock, Coach Masters told the secretaries to take the rest of the day off. They all flew toward him with hugs of thanks.

After he left, the secretaries exchanged their ornaments. Lenny was the new girl in the office, so she opened her gift first. When she did, her eyes filled with tears. In her hands rested a round ornament with a floating universe of dancing stars. It was the same ornament she'd bought for Katy, and wanted to keep.

"Don't you like it?" Katy asked her nervously.

"No, Katy—I *love* it!" Lenny exclaimed. "Now open your gift and you'll see what I mean!"

Katy did as instructed. "Well, this is a strange coincidence," she said looking puzzled. "Where did you buy my ornament? I drove all the way to Maryville to buy your gift!"

"Well, I live in Maryville, so I didn't have to drive as far as you," Lenny said, laughing.

Soon, the secretaries went back to their desks to get ready to leave, and Lenny decided to call Dawn. She was so excited about Mitzi's offer to keep her children she couldn't wait to share the good news.

"Mitzi already told me," Dawn said, chuckling. "No more castor-oil face for you!"

"You know, I had a really scary morning, but it has ended up being the best day I've had in a long time. I feel…well I'm having trouble explaining how I feel because it feels so new. I feel like a weight has somehow been lifted off my shoulders. But I'm not sure exactly sure what has changed about my life. Maybe, I'm growing a little soul power."

"That's big in itself, Lenny," Dawn said in a serious tone of voice.

"I know," Lenny agreed. "And right now, I'm having trouble chasing back crazy happy tears."

"Those aren't crazy happy tears. They're cleansing tears, Lenny."

"Well, I guess you're right. If working on my bad habit thoughts and words have anything to do with my current happiness, I'm glad I shook myself loose from that snake. He was mean."

"How do you know your snake was a 'he?" Dawn asked.

"I don't. But just now, when you asked me that question, that's what came to me. Wasn't Eve's devil snake in the Garden of Eden a male?"

"Yeah, good point. I always thought the devil snake was as male," Dawn giggled. "We were both spoon fed Bible stories as little children, Lenny. Too often, I don't pay attention to what I might be creating in my life from those early years. I often feel the more positive my daily affirmations become the more unwanted thought patterns and negative beliefs resurface. Like telling myself over and over I am beautiful, until I pass by a mirror and see every flaw known to mankind. My inner critic is a mean creature, like your snake. I pretend she doesn't exist, but she does. That's what I admire about you Lenny. I thought about it all day today. You aren't afraid to examine everything in your life. It challenges you, excites you, frustrates you, sometimes it makes you feel lonely and afraid, but you never run away from what you discover about yourself."

"No, I just fling it across the room, then worry about where it landed," Lenny laughed. "Do you ever wish what you hoped for, dreamed about, and believed as a child had come true?" Lenny asked.

"You mean, learn A-B-C and your life will be A-B-C simple?" Dawn asked.

"Yes," Lenny answered. "That's exactly what I mean."

"Well, that would be nice. But that's just not the world we live in, Lenny. What is good for some is not necessarily good for all. But every planet has its place in the sky. And every life has its own purpose, its own special place and time in which to grow and evolve. Granny saw you wandering in a desert and reminded you that you are a beautiful soul in spite of what you think about your past history. Remember my Mimi's sand story? When life kicks sand in your shell, make a pearl. Well, you are a Desert Rose. Maybe that means life has kicked a lot of sand in your shell. And whether you can see it or not, you are growing. Your Granny didn't ask you to change your past, which you keep trying to wish away. She asked you to grow—right now, today, where your two feet are planted."

"Dawn, you're so wise. You always say what I need to hear," Lenny responded. "Oh, and speaking of roses, a complete stranger handed me a paper rose this morning. At first I thought he was hitting on me. But he didn't ask for my phone number. He just asked me what I wanted to be when I grew up."

"Did you tell him a fashion designer?" Dawn asked. "You're always whining about that."

"No," she said reflectively. "Actually, I let that dream fly away years ago. I told him I wanted to grow up and be a child."

"Honey, you don't have to grow into one. You're already there," Dawn said, giggling.

"Dawn, do you think my inner child is center?" Lenny asked. "Today, I was doodling on a piece of paper while I was talking to a caller on the phone, and I ended up drawing a rose and putting a baby in the center of it."

"Jesus said you must enter the kingdom of heaven like a child," Dawn answered. "That makes as much sense as anything else I could come up with. I like it."

"We've been talking too much about me lately," Lenny said, changing the subject. "Tell me how your day's been going."

"You know," Dawn said in a quiet tone of voice. "I had an odd experience myself today. Actually, I'd almost forgotten about it. I'm glad you're asking me to share it, because I want your opinion. This afternoon, when I was working on Mimi's rock garden, I had the radio tuned to an oldies station. Suddenly, a really, really old song came up. The lyrics went, 'I'm in the mood for love.'"

"Wow, that is old," Lenny said.

"Yeah, I know," Dawn agreed. "Usually, this station plays the same standards over and over again. Anyway, I was humming, and I stopped to rest while the song was playing. I looked over at a really smooth round rock—and this is the really weird part of my story—I saw Grandma Tiny's face!"

"I can't wait to see that rock!" Lenny exclaimed.

"No, silly! The rock is just an ordinary river rock with a few shadowy patterns to it. I only saw my Grandma Tiny's face in my mind's eye. Anyway, when I heard 'I'm in the mood for love' on the radio, Grandma Tiny was the farthest thought from my mind. I don't think I've talked very much about her. She was from a small coastal village in Japan. My grandpa was in the army when they met."

"Was your Grandma Tiny fond of the song you heard playing?"

"I don't know. She died suddenly, in her sleep, while I was in elementary school. The story I'm about to share is a silly memory, but one I treasure. I remember clearly a visit with Tiny the summer I discovered mood lipstick. She never wore any makeup, but I tried to put some of my lipstick on her for fun. She just giggled and kept hiding from me. We turned it into a game."

"How funny," Lenny said, laughing.

"On my lips, the lipstick looked hot pink. And she'd shake her head saying, 'No, no, no.'"

"So did you ever convince her to try it?" Lenny asked.

"I begged her until she finally gave in. And on *her* lips, the lipstick turned a bright red. When she saw herself in the mirror she wiped it off saying, 'Hooker, hooker, hooker.'" Both Dawn and Lenny broke out laughing.

"What a cute story Dawn. Thank you for sharing it with me," Lenny said when she could catch her breath. "It also makes me realize those we have lost to death are only a thought away. I don't think heaven is very far. Do you?"

"It's as close as our own heart," Dawn responded.

"Truer words have never been spoken."

"I guess one must be childlike to believe in experiences that can't be measured or tested by the rational mind. Maybe that's why only a child can enter the kingdom of heaven." Then, abruptly changing the subject, she added with a giggle, "By the way, I've told Joseph all about you. He can't wait to meet you." Joseph was Dawn's new boyfriend, and she was eager for him to meet her best friends.

"I can only imagine what you've told him," Lenny said, sighing.

"Well, all I can say is do your best not to act too normal. I've told him you're my crazy artist friend. Don't let me down. He loves eccentric people like you."

"Me? Act normal? I wouldn't know how. And I'm a terrible actress. So I can assure you, I won't disappoint him."

"Hey girl," Dawn said with mischief in her voice. "After 'hello, nice to meet you,' tell him your snake story."

"That would do it, Dawn," Lenny said, laughing at the thought.

By the time Lenny hung up the phone, the office was empty. She had brought her orange notebook to work so if the day got slow or boring, she could write down her thoughts about her snake dream. She hadn't gotten a chance to do that earlier, so she decided to do it now, before she left. Opening up the notebook, Lenny wrote down as much of the dream as she could remember. When she was done, she unpinned her paper rose and taped it onto a blank page, pressing it down with the weight of her palm.

As she turned off the office lights, she looked out the window. A slow misty rain had shifted into a downpour. All the other offices were locked and her umbrella was in the car. All she had was a small, plastic fold-up rain poncho she kept in her desk drawer. It wasn't much, but at least it was something. Thus armed for the bad weather, Lenny hurried down the hall and through the door, her red shoes clicking all the way to the employee parking lot.

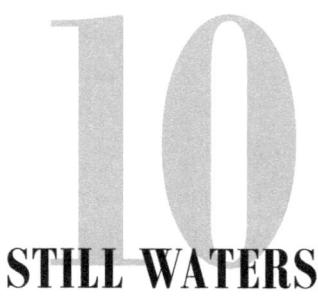

STILL WATERS

When people say I am wise, or a sage, I cannot accept it. A man once dipped a hatful of water from a stream. What did that amount to? I am not that stream. I am at the stream, but I do nothing. Other people are at the same stream, but most of them find they have to do something with it... I stand and behold, admiring what nature can do.

—Carl Jung

With her first step into the street, Lenny lost her one-handed grip on her plastic poncho. It bellowed and flopped to the ground like a deflated balloon. She couldn't run in high-heeled shoes, so she hugged her gift bag and purse tight to her chest beneath her blue cape. If the bag got too wet, it would break. She had to protect her treasured bunny.

The rain was coming down so heavy she could hardly see. As Lenny looked upward trying to wish herself into her car, she stepped into an enormous puddle of water. With nothing to do but surrender, she didn't even try to miss the rushing waters that cascaded across the uneven parking lot. Soon her heel dug deep into an unseen hole. She barely prevented herself from having a bad fall. It was an awkward movement and just enough to unlatch the single button holding her cape around her neck. The cape sailed away, but Lenny couldn't stop to catch it.

Once at her car, Lenny placed her wet gift bag on top of the hood. She fumbled for her keys and unlocked the passenger-side door. Once her package was safe, she took off her shoes and threw them onto the floor of the front seat. Then she ran across the slippery blacktop and rescued both her cape and plastic poncho. The warmth and beauty of her dry-clean-only Christmas sweater was now a thing of the past.

Sitting back in her car, she surveyed the damage and slapped her hand against the steering wheel in disgust. If she had only left work when the other secretaries had left, her sweater wouldn't have been spoiled beyond repair. *They* had listened to the weather. *They* had been prepared in their sensible shoes and tote bag umbrellas.

Life was a spinning wheel of absurdity, Lenny thought. This morning, she was thankful for being late. A memory ago, the universe had gifted her with a paper rose from a stranger, and a beautiful ceramic bunny from the coach. But right now, she just felt walloped.

Lenny stuck the key in the ignition and turned the heater dial to high. Cold air blasted her in the face, chilling her to the bone. She turned it off quickly. When she turned on the windshield wipers, a screeching sound sent more shivers down her spine. The rubber on one of the wiper blades had apparently rotted so badly it crumbled off in the heavy rain, allowing the bare metal blade to scrape across the glass.

Lenny looked out at the halo-like arch that formed across her windshield with every pass of the wiper blades. The rain was too heavy for driving, so she sat and waited for it to slow down. She was glad the temperature outside wasn't freezing, or all the rain would have turned into a snowy blizzard. Tomorrow was Christmas Eve, Lenny remembered, and it would be hard to find an open garage to fix the wiper blade. The place Katy had gone to was right off Kingston Pike, she remembered, which wasn't far away at all. And Coach Masters had sent the secretaries home two hours early, so if she left now, she would probably get there before the garage closed. Suddenly, the universe was her friend again.

To buffer the irritating scrapping, Lenny turned on her radio. It didn't really help. But the heat did—after the engine warmed up. Her teeth chattered as the radio crooned, "Chestnuts roasting on an open fire…" As Lenny's car moved forward, her mind moved in reverse. Why had she left her umbrella in the car this morning? Why had she bought an expensive dry-clean-only sweater on her meager budget? Why had she married the first two men who asked her?

Then, at the first red light, she caught herself thinking of her children and praying their bus had left on time so they wouldn't end up like their drowned-rat mother. The light turned green, and as Lenny struggled to see out her foggy windshield, her mental talk shifted gears again. If she'd never married, she wouldn't have her two wonderful children. And if she'd stayed miserable in her second marriage, her jealous husband would never have allowed her to work full time or to even think about going back to school. Lenny's life could have turned out a lot worse.

She also remembered she'd removed her paper rose before leaving work. Had she forgotten to take it off, it would now be nothing more than a spitball. Even though the rose's value was pennies, compared to her ruined dry-clean-only sweater, the thought warmed her heart.

A block away, she spotted the all-service gas station Katy had spoken of. She clicked on her turn signal and patted her brake. The driver behind her was driving too fast. He blew his horn and almost crashed into the back of her car. As he missed Lenny's car by inches, she gasped. Quickly recovering, she couldn't help but feel lucky all that was wrong with her car was a rotted wiper blade.

The station had a nice long overhang at the front door. Lenny was already soaking wet, but she didn't want to get any wetter. A tall man wearing grease-stained overalls came out to greet her and she explained her problem. He pulled off her blades and told her to wait in her car until he could check to see if he had a replacement. The man went back inside, and Lenny watched him through the big glass window as he studied a long row of narrow boxes. Then he waved for her to come on in, so Lenny left the car in park and hurried into the waiting area.

The man told her to have a seat and he'd be with her shortly. There was only one chair available. It was avocado green vinyl and smelled of cigarettes and motor oil. Her wet clothing and hair hugged her with icy fingers. She couldn't even imagine how she looked. As she scooted her legs up under her body for warmth, she snagged her stockings on a split seam of the chair upholstery, ripping an enormous hole in the back of her pantyhose. She sighed as the last ounce of vanity slowly dripped away into the puddle of rainwater she was leaving on the floor.

Lenny had not planned on changing her clothes before attending Dawn's church program. She was all girly-girl. She loved to dress up for any occasion. But tonight, the football trainer's gift of bright orange sweats was calling her name.

The tall mechanic returned, his fingernails black with layers of old grease, and mumbled about having trouble finding the size of blades for her car. He smelled like a gasoline-soaked rag. He handed her a slip of paper with the cost of the new wiper blades.

"It only took a minute. I don't charge labor for small jobs like this," he said in a friendly tone. Then noting her bedraggled appearance, the man added, "It looks like you just went for a little swim in the lake!"

"Yes!" Lenny exclaimed. "And I feel just like I look!"

She paid the cashier with cash. The unplanned cost of new blades was not as bad as she expected. But often, she was down to the bare minimum in her checking account by payday. She'd never budgeted on a monthly basis before this year. It was still hard for her to pay unexpected expenses.

The cashier, noticing her wet clothing, offered her a free cup of coffee. Lenny accepted with gratitude. She decided to sit back down and wait for the rain to slow some before driving home.

The sound of water as it cascaded off the canvas overhang and metal guttering was so mesmerizing to Lenny her mind began to wander. When she was inside and warm, nothing was more calming for her than the sound of a heavy rain. But outside, the storm was a monstrous force to be reckoned with. Lenny realized she could choose to respond with acceptance, although she admitted to herself more often than not, she reacted to life like the mindless driver who had almost plowed into the back end of her car. Had that driver felt mentally tossed and battered all day long? Had he ever been given a paper rose for a silly answer? She felt certain he'd not. She was glad she no longer felt angry with him.

Lenny hadn't had a chance to reflect on the day's Bible verse from her desk calendar. It was one she knew by heart. She'd memorized it long ago in Sunday school. She leaned back in the foul-smelling chair and sipped her coffee. She closed her eyes and thought about King David's still waters. She imagined he liked to lay down in grassy meadows staring up at the heavens. No doubt, he was much more capable of finding center, staying put, than Lenny. One minute she was on an emotional rollercoaster. The next, she was caught in mindless motion like a hamster on a treadmill. Could life be lived any other way?

She threw her empty white Styrofoam cup in the nearby wastebasket, and waved a thank-you to the clerk, hurried back to her car in her squeaky high-heeled shoes. For the rest of the drive home, Lenny wondered just how wild her life must look from the clarity and height of her Granny's point of view. In one way, she envied those who had passed on. She'd only feared death because it meant separation from her children. Death might bring long, drawn out pain like her Granny experienced. But it could also be quite sudden, like Dawn's Grandma Tiny. If Gandhi were a mountain lake, Lenny mused, he would definitely mirror heaven's stillness.

As she drove into her driveway, her children were standing in front of their frost-covered storm door, drawing snowmen and writing words she could not read. They were both grinning from ear to ear, seemingly recovered from yesterday's broken promises. The hearts of children mend quickly, Lenny thought. Why her own heart did not, she did not know. She longed for a hot shower, dry slippers, and a cozy robe. But that wasn't going to happen tonight. Her hair tightly plastered to her face and neck, she unloaded the car and hurried into the house.

"Gosh, Mom, your sweater looks like road-kill," Mack joked.

Elizabeth reached for Lenny's bags. She opened the damp gift bag, searching for additional presents.

"Nothing for you," Lenny said with a smile. "No presents until Christmas. Except for Nikki, and I'm giving her a card with shopping money," she said, handing the babysitter a card with her name on it. "Hope you like it, Nikki."

The babysitter opened her card and thanked Lenny for the ten-dollar bill.

"By the way, did you hear it might snow tonight?" Nikki asked as she put on her coat.

"I heard there was only a small chance," Lenny answered, "but like the children, I hope this time the weather man gets it right."

Nikki seemed more talkative than usual tonight. Lenny was glad the shy girl had finally warmed up to her. They said their goodbyes and Nikki slipped out the door.

"Mom," Elizabeth said, "you promised we could open Dad's presents on Christmas Eve. Remember?"

"Did they even come?" Lenny asked. As she said this, she knew she'd broken Gandhi's number-one rule. She wasn't thinking the best of Bob. Lenny looked under the tree and noticed several new packages. She smiled and hugged her daughter, who was obviously overjoyed.

"Well," Lenny said. "I don't remember saying you could open your father's gifts early. But that sounds like a great idea. And afterward, you can call him and let him know how much you liked his presents."

Elizabeth squealed with delight as Lenny walked into her bedroom to peel off her wet clothes. She took a quick hot shower and returned to the living room wearing her bathrobe, minus its sash.

"Mack, where is my robe sash?" she asked her son.

"Your what?" Mack asked. "Oh, you mean the yellow terry snake. I think it's still in Elizabeth's room. I'll get it for you."

She looked down at the new stack of presents and dismissed the negative thoughts she had about Bob. After Mack returned with her sash, she told the children about how her cape blew off in the employee parking lot. Their laughter seemed to make ruining her sweater almost acceptable.

Attaching her sash to her robe, Lenny walked to the garage and put the damp sheets from the washing machine into the dryer. Then she walked back into the kitchen and attacked the sink full of headache-free pots and pans.

WALKING TREES

He took the blind man by the hand and led him outside the village. When he had spit on the man's eyes and put his hands on him, Jesus asked, "Do you see anything?" He looked up and said," I see people; they look like trees walking around."

—Mark 8:23-24

Elizabeth seemed lost in her own little world. She was shaking the Christmas packages, and then listening to each one, hoping it would speak its contents to her. The gift piles had grown considerably. Lenny bent down and examined them closer. She counted at least ten new boxes. Their father's sudden generosity helped to soothe some of the sting of his no-show. She walked to the kitchen repeating her new mantra, "I'll think the best...I'll think the best."

"You think what's best?" Mack asked.

"Ms. Tallulah," she said trying not to mention his father. "I'm doing my best to think the best of her."

Lenny needed to fix a quick meal for supper. She decided on a good old-fashioned breakfast, Mack's favorite. She made canned biscuits, eggs, bacon, and buttered grits. After supper, she didn't feel like dressing up. Instead, she felt the need to slip into her new bright orange sweat pants and sweat shirt. Dawn had warned her due to all the lights on the living Christmas tree, the heat in the church would be turned off. Lenny decided to also wear her long coat and leather tennis shoes.

She told the children to dress in their warmest clothing. While waiting on the children to change, she made herself some hot tea. At the kitchen table, she picked up one of her favorite books, Kahlil Gibran's *The Prophet*.

On Joy and Sorrow was her favorite chapter. Lenny felt the need to read it again, because it seemed as though the last two days overflowed with both. A verse jumped out at her:

> *And is not the lute that soothes your spirit*
> *the very wood that was hollowed with knives?*

Last night, Bob's actions had cut a deep wound in her heart. She mentally prepared for the worst, and it had happened. What role had she played in distancing him from her children? If any, it was certainly unintentional. If the symbolic wood of Lenny needed to be sliced and diced, she hoped to become a soothing instrument, and not a pair of angry drumsticks beating on everybody's last nerve.

Mack walked out of his room wearing a sloppy football jersey and baggy pants. She almost sent him back into the bedroom to put on more presentable attire but changed her mind. Elizabeth wore a rainbow-colored wool sweater and checkered slacks. Nothing matched. In an odd way, it looked cute.

As Lenny brushed her daughter's hair, she thought about how often she worried too much about outer appearances. A healing story from the Bible immediately popped into her head. It was about the first time Jesus used his own spit to heal someone. The attempt gave the man only half-sight. And with half-sight, he saw people as walking trees. Then Jesus performed the healing all over again, and the second time, the man saw clearly. Lenny wondered if perhaps his first sight, following the initial healing, was more about seeing the energy of people—maybe they looked taller with long tentacles of light, like an aura. And just maybe, Lenny thought, that's how spirits see human beings, like the blind man with half-sight. Lenny made a mental note she wanted to paint what that might look like. She found it much more fun to express herself with visuals than trying to rationalize life with plant-like terminology.

Before they went out the door, Lenny took her new ornament from Katy out of its gift bag. She held it in her hand and shook it up. The stars danced in swirls. She hung it high on the tree beneath the watchful eye of their new tree angel. Then, they piled in the car and were on their way.

They arrived at the church fifteen minutes before eight o'clock. Lenny was astonished at the enormous turnout. The church was a large red brick building with steep concrete steps and large white columns holding up the overhang of the roof. Although, this was one of the largest churches in the area, it appeared to be overflowing with a sea of people. Several friendly volunteers were busy accommodating late arrivals in metal chairs three rows deep behind the last pew.

The church windows were all open, as Dawn had warned. Lenny and the children kept their coats buttoned up. Chatter and movement filled the air with excited anticipation.

As soon as the lights were turned off, Lenny's eyes started tearing up. A sudden and unexpected cold wave of regret and self-criticism seemed to come out of nowhere. It felt heavy, like a hope against hope of having a different past. She kept thinking about the half-healed blind man. Squeezing her eyes shut, she silently prayed for the power, determination, and will she would need to finish the inner healing she knew had just begun. Trying to bulldoze these stubborn thoughts out of her head wasn't working. She silently prayed for clear eyes and a second round of healing.

The deeply fragrant greenery of the living Christmas tree gave her the sensation of being in a pine forest. There were so many evergreen branches the choir was almost completely hidden. She could hear them climbing what must have been a wooden structure. Everyone grew silent as they marched onto the stage one by one.

The music told the story of the birth of Jesus. Each song was orchestrated with brilliant flashes of white lights, as well as every color in the rainbow. Elizabeth had trouble seeing some of the scenes, so Lenny lifted her up on her lap. The evergreen scent, the music, the chilly air, and the wonderful orchestra were pure holiday magic.

Lenny felt she must have been hiding behind heaven's door when the gift of song was handed out. Although she loved music, she couldn't sing a note. In junior high, she had tried to join the school choir. Her best friend at the time had talked her into going with her to tryouts. Lenny figured she could slide in unnoticed because, after all, a choir was just people singing in a large group. But that didn't happen. One by one, each of the students were ask to stand up and sing a song of his or her own choosing.

"You rat!" Lenny had exclaimed to her friend. "What the heck have you gotten me into?"

Before her friend could answer, the choir teacher heard them talking.

"Okay," the teacher said sternly. "Since you two can't remain quiet, you're next." The teacher pointed her finger at Lenny. Lenny wanted to run out the door—but she was sitting by a really cute boy.

"Who me?" Lenny asked.

"Yes, you," the teacher scolded.

Lenny hadn't known what to do. The only songs she knew the words to were Beatles songs. Lenny gave her friend a mean look. Then she walked to the front of the class. She sang the first thing that came to mind:

Wellll..shake it up baby now, shake it up baby.
Twist and shout, twist and shout.
C'mon c'mon, c'mon, c'mon baby now, come on baby.
Come on and work it on out, work it on out.

The students exploded in laugher. Lenny's friend was bent over like a pretzel. But rather than feeling embarrassed, as she had feared, Lenny actually felt a little empowered. The cute boy in the back of the room began clapping his hands to the beat of Lenny's song. It had made her feel more cool than foolish. Unfortunately, the teacher wasn't the least bit impressed.

"Young lady," the teacher said sternly. "We'll have no horseplay in my classroom. Do you understand me?"

Lenny had no recollection of what happened next. But that was definitely the last time she tried to sing in front of an audience. Since choir was an elective class, she elected to never to return.

In the closing moments of the living tree program, the rainbow-colored Christmas tree lights turned into a blazing white cross, a wonderful reminder of God's forgiveness. God knew His children. He knew the paper-flower love they often loved each other with. And He also knew deep down, Lenny was a Desert Rose capable of finding her season in which to blossom. This thought made her smile.

Soon, the program ended and everyone's cars seemed to be pulling out of the church parking lot at the same time. The air was bitingly cold. Dawn's house was within walking distance from the church, but it was definitely too cold to walk. Walking trees and singing trees filled Lenny thoughts as she drove the few blocks to Dawn's house. Within minutes, she and the children were busy unloading the car and carrying in an armload of gifts.

LOVELY FRIENDS

Love is the only freedom in the world because it so elevates the spirit that the laws of humanity and the phenomena of nature do not alter its course.

—Kahlil Gibran

Dawn's neighborhood was built in the late 1950s and early '60s. The houses were narrow and long, without a central hallway dividing the rooms. Her home was perfect for a single woman or someone with a small family. She had turned the second bedroom into an office, and its most spectacular feature was its highly polished hardwood floors. Lenny's children loved to take their socks off and slide all over the house. So did Dawn and Lenny.

Dawn's decor had a strong oriental flavor. Pictures of both Buddha and Jesus hung on the living room walls. Because Dawn didn't have much of a green thumb, her houseplants were mostly plastic with one exception: she grew violets in her kitchen window. It must have been the perfect spot for them, because they thrived there even though she ignored them. Even so, Lenny never entered Dawn's house without being greeted at the front door by the fragrance of fresh cut flowers—not to mention the appearance of Dawn's cat, Ms. Kitty.

Ms. Kitty looked like a tiger, and she often acted like one. She loved to unravel small area rugs, so Dawn had stopped buying them. Her hardwood floors were old and heavily varnished and they made for a great dance floor in her large living room.

Lenny and her children were the first guests to arrive after the concert. She knew where Dawn hid her house key—under a plastic angel wearing a grapevine halo. As she opened the door, Ms. Kitty greeted them with a meow but then ran when she saw the children. She was expecting to see her mistress. Elizabeth chased after the cat while Lenny hung up coats. As instructed, she handed Mack a box of matches to light all the house candles. It looked as if Dawn had at least forty of them scattered about.

The house smelled of hot cinnamon, orange juice, and heavenly lemonade. Lenny walked into Dawn's kitchen. Her friend had already started a slow simmering pot of Swedish glogg. Lenny poured the reddish brown brew into a cup. It was a sweet, warm, and welcoming hello.

The front doorbell rang, but before Lenny could answer it, Pearl dashed into the house. Her parents followed close behind. Pearl joined Elizabeth, and they both scurrying about looking for Dawn's petrified cat.

Trays of Christmas cookies, ham and cheese snacks, and garlic-smothered pretzels and peanuts were offered in generous white bubble glass containers. Lenny took out a couple of vegetable and fruit trays from the refrigerator. Dawn had added fresh flowers to the platters, and they looked wonderfully festive. Next, several plates of homemade cookies were unwrapped. Each Christmas, Dawn made several different types, including clever angel-shaped cookies with chocolate faces. Lenny's favorite was Dawn's peanut butter buckeyes, and she was glad to see Dawn had made plenty of them.

The hostess arrived soon after, still singing a carol. Her new boyfriend was holding her arm. He matched Dawn's height and had a slightly darker complexion and a heavy shadow of a beard three days in the making. Dawn's last boyfriend had been a longhaired hippy-type who talked endlessly about going to Nashville and landing a big-label recording contract. Lenny couldn't help thinking Joseph was a nice change of pace for her friend.

"Please, don't wait on me. I hope you all have helped yourselves to some refreshments," Dawn said as she took off her coat.

Dawn's brother Mike and his wife headed toward the kitchen. Mike was shorter than Dawn, but otherwise they looked almost exactly alike. Dawn had gotten her father's height, while Mike had gotten their mother's. Dawn often wished it had been the other way around, but even so, Mike was strikingly handsome. His shorter stature didn't seem to matter to his wife, who was several inches taller than him.

Dawn put on some jazzy music. After so many long nights of rehearsals, she'd had her fill of Christmas carols for the year. Several choir members dropped by, and soon the small house was filled with warm bodies. Mitzi arrived late and unescorted. She and her new boyfriend, Steve, had not gone to Dawn's church program because he had wanted her to meet his parents, who were hosting a small gathering of relatives. Steve had stayed at his parents' house to visit with his out-of-town cousins. Mitzi, wanting to make a good impression on Steve's parents, was dressed to kill in gold high-heeled shoes and a forest green, velvet dress.

"I bet you thought I'd forget these, didn't you?" Mitzi said as she handed Lenny a stack of the promised, dream workshop handouts.

"No, I did not," Lenny responded, giggling. "I'd actually forgotten you were bringing them. But I *did* remember the Christmas presents."

Walking into the room and hearing their conversation, Dawn declared, "I vote we open gifts as soon as possible!" She was carrying two cups of hot glogg and handed one to Mitzi as she complimented her friend on how fabulous she looked. Dawn was dressed casually, in her favorite blue jeans and an oversized white blouse that was heavily starched. Lenny thought it looked very sophisticated with her pearl necklace. For the first time in her life, she was under dressed. But it felt deliciously warm and cozy.

"I'm sure the children will like that just fine," Lenny said as she walked over to a paper bag full of wrapped packages. She handed Elizabeth a gift to give to Pearl and the children all ran into another room to find Pearl's gift for Elizabeth.

"Here's your gift, Mitzi," Lenny said, handing her friend a wrapped package.

"First, open mine," Mitzi said, laughing. "You already know what it is, but I can't wait to see your face when you open it."

Lenny smiled and opened a white envelope tied up with a red ribbon. It was a small piece of poster board with stick figures and headshots of Mitzi and Lenny's two children baking cookies. A dog and cat were playing together beside a table and two chairs. Above this scene, she had drawn a large picture window with a black magic marker. Framed inside the window, she had and pasted a picture of an airplane cut from a magazine advertisement. Lenny's photo was glued to the side. On the bottom of the poster board, Mitzi had written the following message: *This ticket good for three days of spoiling your children rotten while babysitting. Merry Christmas! Love, Mitzi (Bess)*

"Well, thanks a lot, Mitzi," Dawn teased, looking over Lenny's shoulder. "How will I be able to top your fabulous gift to Lenny?"

"Don't worry about that, Dawn," Lenny said, laughing. "My greatest treasure on earth is having two of the loveliest friends a girl could ever have. And I mean that with all of my heart."

Lenny put her arms around Mitzi first, and then Dawn. They hugged her back and chatted about how good it felt to see her in such a light and happy mood.

Mitzi handed Dawn her gift next. It was a black and white paisley print journal that looked quite handsome. Mitzi, who perpetually struggled with money, had been thrilled to discover it during a particularly good clearance sale at the Big K. And because Mitzi's gifts always came from the heart, she'd thought of a way to make it extra special.

"Oohh, I *love* it, Mitzi!" Dawn cooed.

"Open it up!" Mitzi said, excitedly. "There's something inside." When Dawn opened the journal, she saw Mitzi's handwriting on the first page.

"Dear Dawn,'" she read aloud. "'Our friendship is such a treasure to me, so I hope you will use this journal to write down many of your treasured thoughts (as well as memories of some of our crazy times together) and then give it back to me next Christmas! I'll even start you off with a great quote! Love, Mitzi.'" Below her note, Mitzi had copied down a Haiku from a monk named, Nanpaku, and Dawn read that, too:

> *Quite apart from our religion,*
> *There are plum blossoms,*
> *There are cherry blossoms.*

"Wow, Mitzi," Dawn said, clearly touched. "What a great idea for a gift! I can't wait to fill it up and give it back to you. But that quote—it's so deep! It reminds me of Lenny's rose dream. I hope you won't expect any of *my* musings to be quite *that* profound!" she continued with a chuckle.

"Don't worry," Mitzi reassured her. "I'm sure whatever you decide to write will be absolutely perfect!"

"Okay, my turn," Dawn said, giving Mitzi her gift. Unwrapping the present, hidden under several layers of bubble wrap, she found a ceramic pixie sitting on a sprig of mistletoe. It looked exactly like Mitzi, and Mitzi was delighted.

"Wow!" Lenny exclaimed. "I guess Dawn and I were thinking along the same lines! Now, you *have* to open my gift. Dawn, you, too!" Dawn and Mitzi opened their gifts from Lenny, who had painted them watercolor fairies, hoping to capture their natural spirits in an unusual and unexpected way. Mitzi's painting was a pixie with short hair sitting atop a pink Lady Slipper. Lenny had chosen a Lady Slipper because they'd seen one growing beside a trail on a springtime hike. The dress of her fairy was made of woven strands of leaves and grass. Her shoes looked like wild orchids. Lenny had titled this watercolor "Snappy Slipper." Mitzi squealed with delight.

Dawn's painting depicted a nature sprite dancing beside a Jack-in-the-pulpit. Dawn was easily the best dancer of their group of friends. She could move her whole body to any song, and watching her was like watching moving poetry. The title of her watercolor was "Dancing with Jack, Dreaming of Joseph."

Dawn hugged the watercolor to her chest and laughed until tears rolled across her cheeks. She hesitated for a few minutes before showing it to Joseph, who had been chatting with one of Dawn's fellow choir members. When he saw the painting, he just shook his head and smiled at Lenny.

"Lenny," Mitzi said, giggling, "You once told me you wanted to be a fashion designer when you were younger. Well, silly, you certainly became one. Just look at how sweet my pixie looks in her strappy ivy clothes and her cute little pink shoes."

"Well, I just have one question for you Lenny," Dawn said, looking from her painting to Mitzi's. "Why is my dancing diva wearing only her birthday suit?"

"You know artists never like to explain their work," Lenny giggled. I honestly just paint what comes to me," Lenny said, shaking her head and laughing.

Within a short time, many guests began to make their exits. A small cluster of people were gathered in the kitchen, saying their goodbyes. The three friends and Joseph sat cross-legged on floor cushions in front of Dawn's fireplace, which was filled with large, glowing white candles.

Dawn insisted Lenny share with Joseph her ghostly visit and snake dream. They all gave their take on what a snake meant to them. Mitzi shared she had read once that a snake is often depicted as the counterpart to the hero. For after all, how could a hero be a hero without an enemy?

They all agreed having an enemy made good daytime drama, yet having one creep up in the night was very unpleasant.

Joseph said he believed animal dreams often represented spirit guides. Dawn laughed. "If that's true Lenny, where do you want your snake to take you?"

"Stop!" Lenny screamed. "I don't want a snake taking me anywhere. Surly, that can't be what my snake was all about. But I have to tell you something, I have noticed that *is* a little odd. From the moment I flung the snake away from my body, I have felt better—both inside and out. I can't explain it. But it's true."

"That makes sense," Joseph said intently. "Think about the medical insignia of the staff with two snakes coiled around it—it's called a caduceus. The staff of Moses, which symbolizes the healing power of God, is often drawn with one snake. And the Hopi tribe uses snakes in their Snake Dance at the end of summer to bring in rain, which (metaphorically speaking) cleanses the earth. By what you just said about feeling so much better, I think your snake was all about healing—regardless of your obvious fear of them. But tell me your first impressions. What do *you* associate with your particular serpent?"

"Death," Lenny sighed. "By its fangs and coloring, I knew immediately it was poisonous. And the second thought I had was that it was a devil—probably stemming from the Bible story about the serpent coiled around the Tree of Knowledge in the Garden of Eden."

"That's got a lot of meaning as well," Dawn said. "Let's think about what knowledge you might have received from this boy snake."

"Boy snake?" Joseph asked.

"Yeah, Lenny and I think her snake was definitely a boy," Dawn said, laughing. "Lenny's had a lot of trouble lately with some of the men in her life. And other parts of her dream before seeing the snake were pointing toward the masculine."

"I just thought of something else," Mitzi said. "In my psychology class, we once had a discussion about how unmasked demons are always the most dangerous. Maybe you unknowingly uncovered something dangerously destructive within yourself that was poisoning your life. And once you saw it on some level of consciousness, it had to go. You held it in your hand and flung it away from you. So you felt better all day—even though you weren't aware of the reason why."

"That fits nicely into other parts of my dream prior to seeing my snake," Lenny responded. "I love you guys. I love that you don't think I've lost my mind. I'm not always sure. I often feel when dream-walking I'm more consciously aware than in my wakeful body."

"Lenny," laughed Mitzi, "I don't think you are even going to need my dream workshop notes. I think we've just solved a truly awesome mystery. Here I am, thinking I'm Bess, your partner in solving great mysteries. And all we needed was a man to help solve this case. Welcome to our little band of detectives, Joseph."

"Uh, I beg your pardon," Dawn said, chuckling as she gave Joseph a tight squeeze around the neck. "I love you guys. But I'm not sharing my man!"

"A big thanks to all of you," Lenny said. She reached out and shook Joseph's hand. Then Lenny watched as Joseph's face turned toward Dawn's in complete adoration. He was so perfect for Dawn, and as Mitzi said, a welcome addition to their small circle of friends.

After concluding her snake was all about healing, Lenny shared the rest of her dream. She talked about the puny little Atlas and her critical and unfriendly stranger as well as the three words scratched on the walls of her stone-like tomb. Suddenly, as she was speaking she recalled another almost forgotten symbol that felt burned into her forehead two weeks earlier. She wasn't sure if it was connected to her inner-male being puny and frail. But it felt important to share it with a man. Dawn had already spoken of Joseph's interest in esoteric subjects like numerology and sacred geometry. She tried her best to describe what she'd seen flash before her eyes just before falling asleep. Mitzi insisted she draw it on a napkin.

Lenny got up and walked over to a nearby basket where Pearl's crayons were stored. She chose a dark red color and everyone watched as she drew a large red valentine. Then she sliced the heart down the middle with a straight line. On the left side she drew a circle with a dot in the center. On the right side she drew an equal-armed cross. As she held up her drawing she noticed everyone looked as puzzled as she felt. Dawn was the first to speak.

"Well Joseph, let's hear what you have to say," she giggled. "I'm just seeing a broken heart with crazy symbols."

"I'm happy to help you out, Lenny," he answered. "But please keep in mind, all that I tell you is based on my own personal experiences. But I would like to say I strongly believe that for each of us, our greatest power rests not in our physical strength, but in our inner core, where the eternal source of our energy resides. This is what came to mind when I looked at the circle with a dot. Call it the hub, the Self, or whatever you wish to call it. Lenny's grandmother told her a center stays where it is. And it does. Also, the center point where the two arms of the cross meet is fixed, an unmovable point. Also, if you look at the shape of the heart, it has two points. One that rests at the point where the two curved lines flow downward. The second point occurs where they meet at the bottom of the heart. If you use your imagination, it could definitely reflect two equally matched individuals or mirrored images united and coming together as a whole."

"Valentine's day comes to mind when I look at it," Mitzi smiled.

"If you are right and I need to see with my own eyes what this symbol means, I see a broken heart. I see a longing and loneliness for a perfect mate. But something also tells me this can't possibly happen on the outside of my life, until my inner male starts lifting his own weight in my life. An inner male, female kind of balance is what I'm trying to say."

Dawn giggled. "You're definitely the most un-masculine woman I've ever met, Lenny. I can't see you coming into a strong masculine anything!"

Joseph patted Dawn's hand and looked deeply into Lenny eyes.

"I don't think Lenny's divided heart is about anything that's happened or symbolic of anything she needs outside her own heart. I do think real love involves giving not taking, not possessing, not needing to seek approval from a beloved. That isn't love. That's just manipulation. Destructive love is indeed blind, because it doesn't see what it can give, only want it lusts, desires, needs, and even demands from another. Perhaps for reasons unknown, this is the kind of love Lenny has attracted in the past. But in my opinion, something deep within her is coming out. Her healing snake is definitely a positive symbol of this. Now, she's preparing her heart for greater things. And I think the other two symbols represent great things to come."

"Wow," Lenny sighed. "I love Dawn too much to be jealous. But I can't help but envy her right now. You are a wonderfully wise man Joseph. My past love affairs were like emotional storms. There were no survivors in the end. Yet, seeing the two of you together makes even me feel calm and happy. It gives me hope real love does exist."

Dawn reached over and hugged Lenny. She looked back at Joseph and whispered something in his ear. He smiled and nodded his head.

"Dawn knows I hesitate to give you my opinions about your visions Lenny. But since it seems to help, I'll continue. The circle with the dot often means curriculum, the beginning of everything, the point of beginning, the starting point. This is the first state before out of it the flower of life gets created. You can say it is one second before day one."

Joseph stared into Lenny eyes, and stopped talking. Lenny jumped up and started dancing around in circles. "I love it, I love it, I love it! And flowering, I love you used that word!"

Dawn had just sipped from her cup and spit it out all over her white shirt. Mitzi looked puzzled and wasn't sure if she'd missed something. As Lenny plopped back on the floor, Dawn hurried to the kitchen for a damp cloth. They had all stopped laughing by the time she returned.

"Okay, you two, what happened while I was gone," Dawn said with a large wet circle on her chest.

"Nothing beautiful," Joseph smiled pulling her down beside him.

"Joseph mentioned flowering and that's exactly what I felt my Granny wants me to do," Lenny whispered wiping tears from her eyes. "I honestly had no idea my Granny's message held within its simplicity, so much wisdom. But just sharing it with my lovely friends makes me feel so genuinely happy. I haven't felt this way in a long time."

"You can't stop now, Joseph. You haven't told Lenny what the equal-armed cross symbolizes."

Joseph shook his head in agreement. His dark brown eyes grew narrow and far away. He hesitated briefly before speaking.

"In my opinion, the greatest battles in life are always within our own self. I speak from personal experience. It is often when I'm in denial about certain negative thoughts or influences that things get worse. I think your divided valentine heart is definitely a powerful yin/yang symbol. The hidden power of sacred geometry is uniquely personal. But I don't mind sharing my take on what it says to me. I wear a similar cross for protection. It can also mean you are at a crossroads. The four arms point in four directions. And like the circle with a center, as I said earlier, this symbol also has a center point from which the straight lines branch out."

"Your grandmother told you a center says put. So Lenny, how have you not stayed at your center?" Dawn asked.

"Dawn," Lenny said shaking her head. "I am so off center I can hardly count the ways. My energies are scattered. I forget where I'm going, what I've just said. I'm always in my mind. And my mind is like a monkey jumping from this thought to the next. And my monkey mind is mean. It insults me, criticizes me and reminds me of everything I should have done, could have done or didn't do."

"Well said," Mitzi laughed. "But we love you anyway!"

"Souls can easily be seen as seeds," Joseph continued. They germinate and eventually flower in their own season. I think you are in a germinating stage of growth. Instead of spending so much time in your mind, spend more time examining your heart. I think this symbol is pointing you in that direction. Perhaps it's as simple as finding out at what point you stopped loving yourself. This original center, once fully embraced, can become a major starting point in your quest for a happier, more balanced life."

All three of the friends looked at each other and then clapped their hands.

"Thank you for your beautiful words of wisdom," Lenny said. "Dawn and I have been reading a book about the power of one's thoughts and words. Your words are helping me even more to make sense of my life in ways I have never imagined. It now makes sense that in a recent dream, words appeared on both my body and in my deepest, darkest, innermost depths. Words can heal, or they can destroy. "

"That reminds me, Lenny," Dawn said suddenly, jumping up to retrieve something from across the room. "I completely forgot to give you your Christmas gift. You know it's the book I promised by our favorite metaphysician."

"I already love it," Lenny said, hugging her friend as Dawn handed her the gift. Along with the book, were a pair of read and white, candy cane socks. She laughed and told Dawn she'd enjoy wearing them with her new bright orange football sweats.

Soon after, the party broke up. Lenny's children fell asleep on the way back home. As she tucked her sleepy children into their beds,

Lenny thought about how important her friends had become in her life. During her second marriage, she seldom saw them because it had made her husband jealous. His possessive nature, and the lost freedom to be with her friends, was the root cause of most of their quarrels and unsolvable tensions. Their last argument almost caused her to lose sight in her right eye. She turned her head to dodge his angry arm, but didn't quite make it in time. That was the last straw. She talked about the incident once to her girlfriends during happy hour. But after that, she asked them to not bring it up. It was too full of painful memories. During this heart breaking reflection, she valued her friends even more. She silently said a prayer of thanks for having such lovely friends who truly cared about her—who, like Gandhi, never seemed to notice her shortcomings.

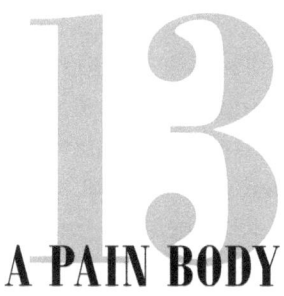

A PAIN BODY

The field of time is the field of sorrow. All life is sorrowful. And it is. If you try to correct the sorrows, all you do is shift them somewhere else. Life is sorrowful. How do you live with that? You realize the eternal within yourself. You disengage, and yet, re-engage. You—and here's the beautiful formula—participate with joy in the sorrows of the world. You play the game. It hurts, but you know that you have found the place that is transcendent of injury and fulfillments. You are there, and that's it.

—Joseph Campbell

Soon after arriving home, Lenny curled up in her nest of pillows, and feel sound asleep. As she drifted away in peaceful slumber, she felt herself being carried into a lush, green forest. She became keenly aware of birds twittering back and forth and the sound of rustling leaves—or was it footsteps?

Feeling slightly alarmed, she began to walk away from this unknown rustling. And she thought about fleeing, she was suddenly out of the forest and standing on the edge of a rocky cliff. The next sound she heard was a groaning sigh. It echoed across the high mountain where she stood. Lenny thought there might be a lake in the valley below, but she didn't want to look down. The sound kept growing louder, and as it did, she thought she heard a human-like moan. Someone might need her help!

Lenny stepped toward the edge of the cliff in case she suddenly needed to jump. Looking down, she found she had been right—a beautiful lake lay in the valley, its still water mirroring both the mountain and her image. Thinking it odd she was wearing a gray wool scarf wrapped tightly around her neck, Lenny stepped back away from her rocky ledge. She was having difficulty breathing from the pressure on her throat. She reached up and tried to loosen her scarf, but when she did, she immediately felt claw-like fingers clutching her throat.

Lenny screamed and began to run. But her vocal cords no longer worked, making her feel helpless and weak, fear zapping all of her strength as monstrous claws continued to strangle her. Fighting to break free, she wanted to see her attacker's face, so she turned her head sharply to the right. Suddenly, she was unfastened. She no longer wanted to run away. Fueled by sheer will and determination, Lenny became the aggressor, grabbing her foe's arm as she twirled around to look into the eyes of a grotesque being. Whatever it was, its features reminded her of Gollum from the J. R. R. Tolkien novel, *Lord of the Rings*. Her son had insisted she read it only a few months back. And she was glad she listened to him. Otherwise, she would now be feeling a lot more fear.

The creature's wrinkled skin looked like brain matter. His limbs were long and bony, his hands and fingers were knotted, ending in tapered hook-like fingernails. He had long, stringy horse-like hair, and he hopped on his two legs like a frog. Lenny squeezed down on his arm as he tried to wrench it free. Looking at him sent cold shivers up her spine.

"I'm not taking you home with me," Lenny scolded, thankful her voice had returned. "Who are you? And why are you trying to kill me?"

"Paaaain," the horrid creature gurgled.

"Yes, I'm probably giving you a lot of pain. But you started this. I want to know why you tried to kill me!"

"Lovely," he said spitting the word out as if it tasted foul in his mouth.

"What do you mean by 'lovely?'" Lenny asked. "You're not making any sense."

"Deep joy pushed me out," he answered. "Your lovely friends are taking my space," he moaned.

"Thank God for that," Lenny said. "I still don't know who or what you are."

"I am as you have made me," he growled between clutched teeth.

"I do not believe you," Lenny insisted. "You make me feel sick to my stomach just looking at you."

"Goooood," he purred.

"Stop this insane game you're playing!" Lenny commanded. "Anything lovely or good has nothing to do with you trying to strangle me."

"Good is what I am," the creature replied. "Read your little *Prophet* book: 'For what is evil but good tortured by its own hunger and thirst.'"

"Are you saying you are good tormented into being evil?" Lenny asked, staring into the creature's repulsive eyes.

"Stop looking at me!" he hissed, turning away from her.

"I've learned recently that evil doesn't like to be found out or stared at. Angry snakes have gotten the best of me lately. I don't know where mine went, but I don't doubt the two of you are friends. I'm not letting you go until you explain yourself to me."

"You made me as I am. Ask yourself," the creature said, spitting yellow liquid from his clenched teeth.

"Well, you remind me a bit of Gollum, and I both loved and hated him," Lenny said, more to herself than to the creature. "Maybe you represent good *and* evil to me. Are you a thought form I created because of these strong contradicting feelings?"

"Maybe," he hissed.

She wasn't completely satisfied with this answer. While she pondered what to ask next, he began to circle around, twisting the arm she held into a tight ropelike tentacle. She feared he was getting ready to attack her.

"Stop circling!" she barked in her most threatening tone.

The creature started jumping up and down. His legs twitched as if they were in a hot pan of grease. Thread-like veins bulged out of his forehead. His hair whipped about on his head as if swatting an unseen fly. It reminded her of a pony swishing its tail. He threw back his head, and a hollow mean laugher erupted from his hideous open mouth.

"Now you know why I look as I do," he said rather disgustedly. "I'm your pain body."

"You're my *what*?" Lenny asked, totally confused.

"I'm your pain body!" the ugly creature snapped back.

"Okay, I heard you," Lenny said. "But I don't know what you mean by that. And you have yet to explain why you jumped on my back and tried to strangle me."

"I thought you were going to jump," he answered. "I tried to stop you."

"You mean you thought I was going to jump off that cliff?" she asked, incredulously. "That's absurd! I would only have done that if I needed a way to escape."

"No, I knew you would not jump," the creature said, sounding insulted. "But unseen hands could have pushed you."

"Well, if anyone wanted to push me off a cliff it would be you," Lenny responded. "And why would unseen hands push me?"

"To see if you would fly," he said, with a sinister laugh.

"*Fly*?" Lenny asked, surprised at this positive turn of his story.

"Where would that have left *me*?" the creature asked in a devilish whisper. "You know so little. For instance, why do you think you hate my hair so much?"

"I don't hate your hair," Lenny said, suddenly trying to be polite. "But if I did make you up in my mind, I'm not sure why I made you so grotesque looking. That's all."

"I'm created by thought and I can read your thoughts, Lenny," he scolded. "Let go of my arm and I will tell you about my hair."

"Okay, I get it!" Lenny exclaimed. "You read thoughts because you are some kind of hideous thought form I've dreamed up. I'll let go, but no more attacking me from behind and strangling me."

He nodded, and she let go of his arm.

"I don't like my hair, but you gave it to me," he said with a sigh, sitting down on the ground and unraveling his long, tangled arm.

"Stop saying I made you anything," Lenny pleaded. "If I did create you, it was on a very bad day. I must have been really angry or something. I'm certainly not aware I did such a thing. So tell me why I created you with long white horsehair."

"No birthday pony!" the creature screamed, writhing in great emotional distress. The sound of his voice echoed down the valleys below them.

"Wait a minute," Lenny said. "What are you saying? Because I didn't get a birthday pony as a child, you grew horse hair?"

"Unrequited longings are pain. I'm your pain body!" he screeched. "How hard is it to understand good and loving wishes unfulfilled are the most powerful creators of pain?"

The Gollum-like creature's face began to fade as Lenny mentally traveled back in time. She watched herself at six years old, swinging on a rusty blue metal swing set that sat in her yard growing up. As she kicked her legs high into the air, a large dark-colored pickup truck loaded with hay drove into their long winding driveway. A man got out and unloaded several bales of hay.

"Tell your father he doesn't owe me a thing," the man said. "He fixed my television with a new tube and didn't charge me a penny." Then he waved goodbye to her and climbed back in his truck.

"Okay," Lenny smiled and waved goodbye as he drove off.

Lenny had been begging her parents for a pony. Suddenly, joy flooded her soul. She was getting a pony for her birthday, but the pony was to be a surprise. She decided not to say a word to her parents.

The next day, her mother decorated the house with pink and yellow balloons and blue paper streamers. She dressed Lenny in her new yellow Easter dress for photographs. Lenny remembered thinking she would have to take the pretty dress off before she rode her pony. It had surely been delivered during the night. She raced outdoors. The hay was still stacked up, but the vacant grassy lot beside her house was empty. No pony! Frantic, she dashed into the house, wailing that her pony had run away.

"Lenny, that hay isn't for a pony," her mother said, laughing. "Where in the world do you get such a crazy idea? You know we can't afford to buy you a pony. That hay is for planting grass seed."

In a flash of light, the replay of a childhood memory was gone. Lenny was back with the horrid creature, staring at his horse hair.

"That happened so long ago," she whispered, feeling more like a kid than a grown up. "I was just a child, a dreamer who believed her dreams would come true. All little girls think thoughts like that."

"I only go where thoughts take me," the creature said with a know-it-all smirk.

"Well, I no longer want a pony. So, maybe if we're both lucky, your ugly hair will fall out," she said, feeling put out by his cocky attitude.

"You've got everything backwards," he responded. "You are only good when you are one with *all* of yourself. If you seek wholeness, you must look where you least want to look. My hair is formed from broken dreams, wishes that died before they were tasted; critical remarks of others you believed fully formed my body. If you hate what you have made me, uncover your deepest wounds. I knew you could not fly. The hands you do not see - saw it."

He suddenly shrieked loudly and vaporized into a misty gray cloud of smoke right before Lenny's startled eyes. Then, becoming aware of her breath, she drifted into a deep trance-like world where thoughts and words were not allowed.

TWO WORLDS

Who looks outside, dreams; who looks inside, awakens.

—Carl Jung

Morning arrived without the sound of loud music from an alarm clock. Both Lenny and her children slept until almost 10:00 am. It felt good not to rush out of bed. Lenny lay under the covers and enjoyed not moving her body. After a delicious moment of not feeling disturbed, she yawned and stretched. Carefully crawling out of bed, she slowly walked to her bedroom window and looked out at the world. The rain had stopped, but there was no snow in sight. The children would be disappointed. Thinking of that, she vaguely recalled having had a dream about childhood disappointment. But the memory flew out of her head as quickly as it had flown in.

She went to the kitchen and made coffee as she thumbed through her recipe box for her sugar cookie recipe. She marveled at how wonderfully late she had slept. She felt not the slightest bit of anxiety. Although, this relaxed and peaceful feeling was refreshingly new, Lenny didn't want to question it.

First on her to-do list for the day was baking cookies. After she mixed up a large mound of buttery batter, she placed it in the refrigerator to chill for about an hour. She sat down and started reading the paper as she drank a creamy cup of brewed coffee. When the dough was cold enough, Lenny got out two metal cookie pans and greased the bottoms with a stick of butter. Then she formed tiny balls of dough, plopping them on the first cookie sheet. She opened the oven door and scooted the metal sheet inside. Then she went back to reading the local news. Before long, Mack walked into the kitchen, looking like he'd lost his best friend.

"Mom, did you look outside?" asked the boy, who was wearing the same clothes he'd worn the day before.

"Yes, I know, it didn't snow last night," Lenny answered.

"I wish they'd quit saying it will, when it never does," he huffed.

"Weather is unpredictable, like women," Lenny teased. "And please tell me you're not wearing those same clothes again today…"

"Gosh, Mom," Mack interrupted before Lenny finished her sentence. Why are you in such a bad mood? Last night you said I could wear what I wanted."

"Put on clean clothes, Mack. And pick out something less holey and raggedy. You're not wearing the same clothes over and over every single day. And I'm *not* in a bad mood!" she replied, raising her voice.

The foul aroma of burnt sugar drifted out of the closed oven door.

"Mack, now look what you made me do! If you hadn't distracted me, I wouldn't have burnt these cookies!"

"Mom, why are you so mad?" Mack asked. "Remember what you told me when I missed that long pass at my last football game?"

"What?" Lenny said pulling a tray of way-too-crispy cookies with thick black edges out of the oven.

"Everybody burns the cookies sometimes."

"I said 'biscuits,' but thanks for the reminder."

Lenny scraped the ruined cookies into the trashcan and plopped the second batch into the oven. Mack stomped out of the kitchen to change his clothes. Lenny picked up her 1982 dishtowel. It smelled foul, so she threw it into the trashcan atop the charred cookies. Pushing out the old year felt as good as pushing out stale pain and hurtful sorrows.

She awoke this morning feeling more rested than she'd felt in a long time. She'd had no disturbing dreams. At least, she didn't remember having one. In fact, she remembered something about a birthday pony.

Mack was wrong. She had not been in a bad mood at all, but a rested, happy mood. However, it deed feel as if it was about to fly away. That reminded her—in her pony dream there was something about thinking she could fly. But she didn't remember where she went or what she saw.

Her day, still new, was not going as she had expected it to go. Did it ever? But Lenny also realized living without hope makes the heart sick. She remembered so many mornings she got out of bed with a song in her heart. And before nightfall, her simple, child-like wonder of being alive, drifted away like a cotton ball cloud. A sick heart was not good fertilizer for growing soul power. But a thought is just a thought, until it is seized. She decided she would scrap the bad ones out of her head, much like the scarred metal cookie sheet in her hands. Maybe, Mack saw something lingering in her disposition she couldn't see. Being a single parent wasn't easy. It would make her life easier if her husband lived close enough for weekend visits. But, regardless of mood of the moment, without doubt, a certain kind of heaviness around her heart was definitely gone.

"Mom, why are you staring into space looking weird? Are you still mad?" a small voice asked.

"Elizabeth! For the last time, *I'm not mad!*" Lenny exclaimed, raising her voice. "You two need to stop making crazy assumptions. How many times do I have to tell you guys? I'm not mad."

"Okay!" Elizabeth yelled back at her mother. "Then why are you yelling?" The girl stomped back into the living room without waiting for a response.

"I don't know," Lenny said as she opened the oven door. Her second tray of cookies needed a few more minutes. She followed Elizabeth's trail into the living room, where she and Mack were watching cartoons.

"Look guys, I'm sorry I was yelling. It wasn't your fault I burned the biscuits," she said to them.

"I thought you were making cookies," Mack said without looking up at her.

"I *am* making cookies. I meant to say 'cookies.' I don't know where my brain is these days," Lenny said. "Anyway, I wanted it to snow as badly as both of you. It's never snowed enough in Tennessee to suit me. But that's almost like asking for a miracle. We often have snow in January, so I guess we'll just have to wait until then. Now let's forget about the snow and try and have fun today! Okay?"

"Sure," said Elizabeth.

"Mom," Mack said, "I was in a good mood until you ragged on me about my clothes. You've been in a bad mood all week."

"You are, Mom. I saw you throw our dishrag into the trash. You had a mad look on your face," Elizabeth chimed in, mimicking her mother's frown.

"See, Mom, I told you so," Mack said, delighted to have his sister's support. He walked over to the window and opened the drapes to check on the weather. As he did, he picked up a handful of buckeye chocolates from a star-shaped candy dish.

"Mack," Lenny said with an exasperated sigh, "Please stop eating chocolate balls for breakfast. You need something with vitamins. And I will also need something to offer guests, if we have any."

"I smell something burning," Elizabeth said, sniffing the air.

"Oh, shit!" Lenny yelled, running toward the kitchen.

Her children giggled. Lenny didn't swear in front of them often, and they seemed delighted this slip confirmed their mother was indeed in a bad mood. Lenny threw the second batch of cookies into the trash. She plopped the last batch of batter into the oven. This time, she was going to sit glued in front of the stove. Their nagging her about being mad almost pushed her into a foul mood. Was that the same as her always expecting Bob to lie to her and the children? It seemed likely, she concluded, especially if everyone had enough soul power to influence small matters with the power of his or her intention, like Gandhi.

Lenny's new intention was to think the best of every face that stood before her. She hadn't managed that perfectly so far, but after all, even Gandhi had to start at some point. She was determined to, at least, make an effort. She'd be more careful with her thoughts. She'd write the one she wanted to keep in her journal. For it was beginning to feel obvious, if a strong thought married a feeling, a new archetypal character popped into her dreamscapes.

Lenny slipped her hand into a Santa Claus oven mitten, and checked her cookies. The last batch of cookies came out fine. Lenny wasn't a Betty Crocker. She preferred digging in the dirt, and planting flowers, to baking. But good mothers baked cookies for their children, and too often, Lenny felt like a bad mother—especially when her children wanted her to act happy even though her heart was breaking. That, in a nutshell, was what her entire second marriage had been about. She constantly struggled with feelings of guilt over putting her children through an unhappy second marriage. She feared they all three had unhealed scars from that union. Guilt was a terrible robber of present moment joys. Someone once told her guilt was lack of faith in a loving God. But if Jesus was right, and the kingdom of heaven was within, she needed to find a way to forgive herself.

"Elizabeth!" she called out. "Come and help me decorate these pitiful sugar cookies."

Elizabeth ran in and gleefully sprinkled the cookies with a small shaker of colorful confetti. Mack came in, too, and together, they all ate several warm and perfectly baked cookies.

As she washed the dishes afterward, Lenny spied Ms. Tallulah filling up her bird feeders. At least she loved something, Lenny thought sipping the last drops of her cream filled coffee. She wanted, intended with all of her heart, to think positive thoughts about her neighbor. Maybe this was a good way to start.

Suddenly, she heard Elizabeth's voice as if from a faraway place.

"Mom, did you hear me?"

"No. Sorry, honey," she said, her attention returning to the kitchen. "I was watching Ms. Tallulah feeding birds. What did you say?"

Elizabeth turned toward the window. "I don't see any birds," she said.

"They flew away when she walked outside," Lenny answered.

"I don't blame them," Elizabeth said, giggling. "She's a mean witch!"

"Honey, I don't like you talking like that," Lenny said. "I know I've called her that and worse, but now I'm trying to think the best of her. Maybe she's just lonely. We don't really know what has caused her to act the way she does toward her neighbors."

"Fine, I won't call her a witch," Elizabeth said. "But what I asked you was if you wanted to hear a poem I wrote about Santa."

"Of course I want to hear your poem!" Lenny answered, delighted. "But give me a hug first."

Elizabeth walked over to Lenny, who hugged her daughter and kissed the top of her head. Lenny thought she smelled like honeysuckle shampoo and soup. Elizabeth began reciting:

> *I hear some hoofs upon my roof.*
> *Might it be Christmas Eve?*
> *And Santa comes down my chimney.*
> *I love him and he loves me!*
> *That's why I'm happy.*
> *But only once a year he comes.*
> *But I am lucky that he does come.*
> *For I love him so.*

"Oh my goodness," Lenny said with a smile. "I love it, Elizabeth! That's the sweetest poem about Santa I've ever heard!"

"Good grief, Elizabeth!" Mack yelled from the living room. "Haven't you ever heard you're supposed to love baby Jesus more than Santa Claus?"

"Shut up!" Elizabeth yelled back.

Her brother walked into the kitchen wearing a pair of jeans with a long diagonal slice across the left knee.

"All you ever think about is Barbie this and Barbie that!" he griped. "How do you think poor Jesus feels? Aren't you forgetting it's *His* birthday?"

"Mack," Lenny said, pointing at the rip in his pants. "Please don't tell me these are the only clean pair of jeans in your closet. We're going to visit relatives today. I don't want them thinking we are poverty stricken."

"Gosh! Are you going to be like this *all day*?" he asked.

"He cut them with his Boy Scout knife," Elizabeth tattled. Lenny suddenly realized the girl had chocolate smeared on her upper lip.

"Elizabeth, stay out of the chocolate balls!" Lenny said, raising her voice.

"It's not cool to wear new jeans, Mom," Mack protested. "Only nerds wear new jeans." He left the room in a huff.

"Well, God forbid you should look like a nerd," Lenny called after him. "Fine! Be cool! Wear whatever you want. I surrender. We are going to be happy today if I have to smack you guys around this house to get us there."

Lenny chased after Mack, who ran from her as she circled around the coffee table with her fingers wiggling in tickle mode. Barking, Lassie ran back and forth between Lenny and Mack, as if trying to herd them. Elizabeth ran into the room, wanting in on the chase. Soon the house released the heavy lingering odor of burnt cookies and foul moods.

After the tickling game had been exhausted, Lenny returned to the kitchen. "Do you think Santa will get me everything on my list?" Elizabeth asked as her mother finished washing the dishes.

"I hope so," her mother answered. "Go get me your list. I'll check it twice to see if you've been naughty or nice!"

"Mom, that's Santa's job, silly," Elizabeth said, giggling.

"Oh gosh, you're right," Lenny said with a smile, hugging her daughter. "But I'm his helper, so get me your list and I'll check it for Santa."

Elizabeth ran out of the kitchen and soon returned clutching her list. She chattered on and on about how Magic Curl Barbie's hair could really be curled, how Disco Barbie really danced, and how one doll wore Jordache jeans just like hers. She sounded like a toy commercial.

"Hey Mom," Mack said entering the room with a sly grin on his face. He'd overheard his sister's list. "I hope Santa brings me a G.I. Joe doll wearing Red Bull jeans. I can't wait to put a chew of tobacco in his pocket."

"Mack!" Elizabeth screamed. "Mom, make him stop! He's making fun of me!"

Elizabeth leapt across the room and tried to punch her brother in the stomach. He hopped just out of her reach, and Elizabeth missed and fell on her knees, bursting into tears.

"Mom!" Elizabeth screamed. "Make him stop teasing me," she begged as she tried to buzz saw her brother with both fists flying.

"Stop teasing your sister, Mack!" Lenny yelled. "I'm not going to play referee all day today. And Elizabeth, silly words said by your brother shouldn't upset you so easily. And stop hitting him! You know he'll win if you two wrestle."

Silly words, Lenny thought to herself. Silly words, cruel words, spiteful words, gossipy words, mean words—they all had the power to hurt a person. It wasn't only sticks and stones that could cause pain after all. We're all so different. What hurts one person might not hurt someone else. She needed to remember that herself. For if a person constantly lived off center, Lenny imagined, his or her life would be swirling sideways—up one minute, down the next—in constant day-to-day drama. This was exactly the life she had been living, but desperately wanted to change. Could anybody other than a lonely yogi on a mountaintop stay God centered for good?

Still smiling about his clever joke, Mack poured himself a glass of milk and returned to his cartoons. Lenny knew he loved his sister, but that didn't stop him from delighting in stirring up her temper. Lenny remembered treating her younger brother the same way when they were growing up. She remembered teasing him, and like Elizabeth, he got mad easily. She now wondered why this behavior had ever given her so much pleasure. She remembered how Lassie's puppies loved to chew and sharpen their teeth on each other. Perhaps, this behavior was a wild, free-spirited, untamed part of every human psyche. Some people tamed it, but others never even tried. She prayed Mack would try to tame his inner wild before she had a nervous breakdown.

"Is Santa invisible like God and the Tooth Fairy?" Elizabeth asked, following her mother into her bedroom.

"Well," Lenny said, "Santa is more like the Tooth Fairy. And God can only be seen as a reflection in the life of someone like Jesus. God spoke one word, the world exploded into creation, and here we are.

So no word can really describe what form He might take. He's like a Father to me. And I like to think He and Mother Earth are somehow married. But we can imagine Him in lots of ways. I'm sure He doesn't mind a bit. Jesus said to look inside to find Him."

"Are people bad when they don't believe in Santa?" Elizabeth asked next. "I know a boy at school who doesn't believe in Santa or God. But I forgot to ask him if he believes in the Tooth Fairy."

"No, people aren't bad because they don't believe the way you believe," Lenny said gently. "After all, which would you rather do? Argue with someone or play and have fun?"

"Play and have fun," Elizabeth answered, smiling. She seemed very sure of her answer.

Thankfully, she ran out of questions, which was good, because Lenny was running out of answers.

Mack, suddenly, walked into the bedroom, a big grin plastered across his young face. "Hey Mom," he said, "I need to read you my poem. I just wrote it."

"I'd love to hear it," Lenny said, smiling.

"I like January because it is the best time to build snowmen," he said. "I like to throw snowballs at my sister and make her cry. And I like to throw her in the snow and that makes her cry."

Mack had barely finished uttering the last word when he got the reaction he'd hoped to get from his sister. Elizabeth chased him down the hall, and Lenny soon heard them tumbling and wrestling. Mack was laughing hysterically and Elizabeth was screaming furiously at him. But this time, Lenny decided to just let them fight it out. Maybe all sisters and brothers act this way. As she made her bed, she thought about how vividly clear her dreams had been of late. And she was glad she had simply rested in dreamless sleep the night before.

15

AN ALCHEMY MOMENT

The job of the soul, of course, is to cause us to choose the grandeur—to select the best of Who You Are—without condemning that which you do not select.

—Neale Donald Walsch

Christmas Eve turned out to be a marathon. By late afternoon, the weather conditions grew worse and the local news reported the strong possibility of an ice storm. Conditions in Nashville were already getting bad and it was moving east toward Knoxville. This bumped up visits to each of Lenny's parent's homes. To please Mack, she did two quick loads of laundry. He wanted to wear his white football jersey, and Lenny wanted to wear her new orange sweats again. In case of ice, they needed to dress warmly.

Laundry done and everyone dressed, Lenny packed both gifts and children into her car. They soon arrived at Lenny's father's house. He lived in a beautiful valley at the foothills of the Smoky Mountains. His wife, Lenny's stepmother, was a fabulous cook, and the kitchen table had so much food, it was hard to find room to set down a dinner plate. After an early supper, everyone sat in the family room while Lenny's stepbrother, who had driven up from New Orleans, played his guitar. He always had everyone in tears with funny stories and jokes. Today was no different. He and Lenny's younger brother were much alike. They were always considered the life of any party. When the two of them were together, they competed, telling one outrageous story after another.

Unfortunately, due to the weather, everyone cut the evening short. A few hours after their arrival, the family exchanged gifts and Lenny and her children were soon off to the next stop. The long stretch of road, winding its way up to a hilltop cabin, where her other set of parents lived, was gravel. The sky looked dark and foreboding as her car bounced atop the rough and bumpy road. Still feeling inspired by the fun music at her father's house, Lenny turned the volume of her radio up high. Driving in the loud, noisy car made the slow drive a lot more fun.

As her car wound up the steep hill to her mother's cabin, Lenny spotted a lot of new decorations. Her mother was a member of the local garden club. In fact, she had actually helped organize the new club after she had moved from town into this more rural community. Along with a large display of lights, her stepfather had built a wooden tree-shaped structure on which sat a dozen white poinsettia plants. Lenny couldn't remember seeing anything as lovely as this flower tree.

After exchanging gifts and catching up on the latest news with her stepsisters and their families, they sat in front of a roaring fire while eating chocolate cake and drinking cocoa and coffee. Lenny's children told their grandparents how much they loved their gifts and what they hoped to receive from Santa. When Lenny's stepfather came in carrying a load of wood, he told her that sleet was now falling. Lenny quickly packed up their gifts and headed home with her children.

The visibility was terrible on their drive back. Lenny suddenly thought about how horrible it would have been had she not been able to get new windshield wiper blades yesterday. At the moment, she couldn't think of anything as wonderful as those new blades. She dared not to imagine what might have happened on this winding road had her wipers fallen apart tonight, instead of yesterday afternoon. Maybe, like the young priest said, she did have an angel in her pocket. She didn't hear a peep from the back seat. Mack was reading instructions for a game with a new camouflage flashlight. Elizabeth was dressing and undressing a Barbie doll.

"Hey guys," Lenny said, looking at them in her rearview mirror. "As soon as we get out of these mountains, let's go visit our favorite Christmas lights–that crazy house just a few blocks away from our neighborhood."

"Oh boy!" Elizabeth said, with an enthusiastic giggle.

"Great!" Mack agreed. "Maybe they've added some new displays this year," he speculated, smiling broadly.

"Only if they planted new shrubbery," Lenny responded, laughing. "They strung lights on every single thing in the yard last year."

Lenny didn't take her usual route home. Instead, she took a back way so they could see the overly-decorated house ablaze with holiday yard art. The street usually had little traffic, except at Christmas. The third house at the end of the lane was so gaudy it just had to be seen to be believed. And the children loved it.

Her mother's garden club awarded ribbons to the best decorated homes in their community. Lenny laughed at the thought of this house winning a blue ribbon. But for the joy it gave everyone, it should. After a day of burnt cookies, arguing over clothes, the kids' constant bickering, and the bad weather, laugher was good medicine.

Even before their car drove close to the small brick rancher, they could see it blazing against the foggy mist of falling sleet. The oversized plastic cartoon characters were the most delicious of all the displays. And Jesus wasn't left out, either. A pint-size manger scene rested atop a bale of hay in the center of the yard. As soon as Lenny saw the bale, she vaguely remembered dreaming about hay. She'd have to look it up in her dream dictionary, she thought, if she remembered it by the time she got home.

"Oh, look, Mom!" Elizabeth exclaimed. "They have a new Tweety Bird!"

Tweety sat in a dogwood tree right next to the manger scene. Pooh Bear hung in another dogwood tree several yards away. Spotlights shone on each of their faces as well as on a large snowman at the base of one of the trees. The rest of the yard was filled with Disney characters, ironically dressed in summer attire. A wooden painted Daisy wore a polka-dot bikini, and Donald held a rope, about to lasso a snowman wearing a Santa hat.

As they slowed their car to take a long look at the yard, Lenny saw two shadowy figures peeking out from closed draperies in a darkened room. The lights from the shrubbery glowed brightly across faces of an elderly man and woman. Lenny suddenly had the urge to cry. She choked it back, and rolled down her window to wave at them.

"Mom, those people just waved back at us!" Elizabeth cried out.

"I know," she answered. "Haven't they given us a fun gift this year? Do you have any idea how much effort must have gone into putting all this stuff up?"

As she drove onto her street, Lenny couldn't stop wishing those two fun-loving strangers were her neighbors, instead of Ms. Tallulah. As she unloaded the car, Mack took Lassie for her evening walk. Elizabeth ran into the house to sort her father's gifts under the tree into two piles for unwrapping. As Lenny unloaded the last bag from the car, she glanced toward Ms. Tallulah's house. Just as she suspected, her neighbor was looking out her bedroom window. Lenny thought about pretending she didn't notice. But continuing to wish away her mean neighbor wasn't going to change anything. And besides, she realized, that would be wasting an opportunity to practice her newly acquired wisdom of soul power, which, as Dawn had said, was nothing short of spiritual alchemy. Lenny decided the practice of seeing God in everyone, watered your own God seed. Feeling empowered and even a little hopeful, Lenny waved up at the woman peering out the window. But instead of waving back, Ms. Tallulah quickly disappeared into her dark house. *Well, at least I tried*, Lenny thought to herself.

Once inside, she placed newly unwrapped gifts under her tree, took off her shoes, and watched her children unwrap gifts from their father. Most of the presents were clothes. He'd also included checks for them to go out and buy something they hadn't received. One of the gifts he sent Elizabeth was a beautiful music box with a dancing ballerina. She was dressed in a pink satin tutu with rolls of ruffles gathered around her waist. Elizabeth played the music box over and over again. It was a hauntingly sweet melody that Lenny had never heard before. She felt relieved that she'd somehow been able to release some of the lingering anger she'd felt toward Bob.

After the gifts were all unwrapped, Mack called his father. When both children finished talking with him, he asked to speak with Lenny. She dreaded talking to Bob, but she wanted to try hard not to repeat their earlier quarrel. Taking the phone and placing the receiver to her heart, she silently prayed, *Lord, help me see him with new simple, child-like eyes. Eyes without judgment or anger.* Then she put the phone up to her ear.

"Merry Christmas!" she said in her cheeriest voice.

The phone went silent. Lenny wondered if Bob had fainted from shock.

"Merry Christmas to you," he said in a dry voice. "I want you to know I'm still really mad at you."

"Well, I'm absolutely not mad at you," Lenny said, and she almost believed that she meant it. In her head, she started repeating over and over: *Love, love, love, not hate.*

"Well, I'm glad to hear that bit of good news," he said. "Lenny, you'll never change. When we were married, I never knew if you were going to greet me at the door with kisses or whack me over the head with a frying pan."

"I never hit you with a frying pan," Lenny said with a laugh. "But now that I think about it, I sure wanted to a few times."

"Well, I have no idea what's come over you, but I'm glad you've stopped hurting our children by hating me."

Lenny hesitated before speaking. If she denied hating him, that might not be the entire truth. Did she really hate him or did she hate his constant lying? Either way, she was supposed to think the best of him, so she pretended that he wasn't a liar but was instead a man of his word. That felt like a lie. But, if it worked for Gandhi, it was worth giving it a try.

"I'm sorry if you think I hate you," she responded. "I don't like how you break promises. I hate it when you say you will do something, and you don't. But I have not always been fair with you. And it does affect the children. Please forgive me," she said. "And I really appreciate your sending the gifts special delivery. It was very considerate of you. The children are fine—they understand why you had to cancel your visit. And they absolutely love their gifts. All the clothes you sent to Elizabeth, didn't exactly fit. But she will grow into them. Thank you. It helps me out a lot when you buy them school clothes. And Elizabeth's dancing ballerina has been playing nonstop since she opened the box. By the way, what song does the music box play?"

"I don't know," Bob said quietly, no longer sounding angry. "The box it came in originally arrived at my store damaged, so I put it in a different box. I might have another one in one of my other stores. I'll check. You know, when I saw one of my sales clerks unpacking it, I knew it was perfect for Elizabeth."

"Yes, it was," Lenny agreed wearing a warm, and sincere smile. She could tell that he was caught off guard by her compliments. He enjoyed bragging on himself. And hearing Lenny praise his choices for gifts eased some of their tensions. By the time Lenny hung up the phone, she felt both at peace with him and proud of herself. Quick thinking helped her side-step her way out of another angry confrontation. It was a *huge* improvement over their last phone call.

She walked into the bathroom and brushed her teeth. After getting ready for bed, she looked at her herself in the mirror.

"I think I'm actually starting to like you," she whispered to her reflection.

TEAR SEEDS

And then a strange thing happened. For where the tear had fallen a flower grew out of the ground, a mysterious flower, not at all like any that grew in the garden.
——Margery Williams *(from The Velveteen Rabbit)*

Before the children went to bed, Lenny heated a saucepan of milk for cocoa at story time. Elizabeth handed Lenny her copy of *The Velveteen Rabbit*. The classic tale was also one of Lenny's favorite books. Mack wasn't interested in the story, so he stayed in the kitchen, working out the rules of his new board game. Before she started the story, Lenny flipped Elizabeth's book over and read the back cover to set the mood: *There was once a velveteen rabbit that lived with a stuffed horse and many other toys. 'What is real?' asked the Rabbit one day. 'When a child REALLY loves you, then you become real,' said the horse. The rabbit hoped that wonderful thing would happen to him someday.*

By the time she'd gotten to the end of the book, Lenny was wiping tears away from the corner of her eyes. She felt a strong kinship with the tattered and worn-out rabbit. And when he magically became real, it was almost too much to bear. To Lenny, being real meant always being comfortable about *who* you are. And she didn't know if she had ever really felt real. And most importantly, had she ever felt really loved? This morning, she had awoken more in the present moment than she'd felt in years. A heavy tightness around her chest was gone, as if a trauma that had once strangled her had broken loose. Her lucid dream of shaking off a snake had seemingly shaken off years of suppressed anger toward her first husband. Right now, she wasn't ready to even think about her second husband. She would save that hard work for after Christmas. She wondered if the process of individuation, true self-discovery, was simply uncovering what she had created, *unreal*, verses what God created _*real*? Perhaps unlike the velveteen bunny, she was created real, but by her *own* creating, she had become unreal. If so, spiritual awakening wasn't about becoming real or about transforming like a caterpillar into a butterfly. It was beginning to feel more like setting a golden winged Self free from a prison of poisonous thinking and false identification. If God is love, as the poets and sages wrote, then so was her center. Yet, most of the time she didn't loved or lovable. And psychologically, this was not where she wanted to spend the rest of her life. Alive, breathing, but constantly feeling disconnected from her others as well as herself. A God-Self —a center stays where it is, was beyond her reach.

"Mom, I asked you a question. Are you listening?" she suddenly heard Elizabeth ask.

"Sorry sweetie. I'm so happy we read your bunny story tonight. I was just lost in all the magic. What did you say?"

"I asked you if you thought the Nursery Magic Fairy was prettier than the Tooth Fairy," Elizabeth said, referring to one of the characters in the story.

"Well," Lenny said, hesitating only slightly. "She certainly dresses better. And the book did say the Nursery Magic Fairy was the loveliest fairy in the whole world. Her face was like the most perfect flower ever seen. And don't you love the artist's drawing of her dress?"

"Yes! It looks *adorable*," Elizabeth giggled, her eyes sparkling. "I love dewdrop pearls. But do you think she felt wet all the time?"

"Maybe she felt a little damp in the mornings," Lenny answered. "The grass feels wet to my feet even in the summer sun. But at the same time, it feels nice. I don't think she minds. At the library, I read about a gypsum stone in the desert that sometimes blossoms into the shape of rose petals. It only needs a little moisture to blossom."

"Are you kidding, Mom?" Mack asked, walking back into the living room with a cup of hot cocoa, spilling a long drizzle of brown down the front of his t-shirt.

"No, Mack. It's called a Desert Rose. Next week, while I'm off work, we'll plan a trip to the public library and I'll show you a picture of it. It's technically called a *gypsum rosette*. Arid, sandy conditions mixed with just a little moisture help Mother Nature create magic in the desert."

Elizabeth jumped off the couch and ran into the kitchen for more cocoa, oblivious to the fact that in voicing her explanation to Mack, Lenny had experienced what could only be called an "aha" moment. Her Granny's message, what she'd been trying to say in the simplest of terms, was suddenly coming alive inside of her. For the last two days, she'd been totally and insanely obsessed with chasing down the meaning of Granny's visit. And now, just sitting with her children, with her mind completely off of the message, its meaning had gently landed like an ever elusive butterfly.

"That sounds pretty cool," Mack said, smiling. "I can't even imagine a rock looking like a flower."

"I didn't know such a thing existed, either," Lenny said. "Nature is such a marvelous teacher, if we take the time to see and experience her. By the way, I promised to read two books tonight. What book have you chosen to read, Mack?"

Mack jumped up and ran back down the hallway. He returned carrying an oversized family Bible. The only time it was opened was during the holiday season. Lenny often placed a miniature nativity scene atop the Gospel of Matthew. But this year, she'd not been able to locate it.

"By the way, have either of you seen our little manger and figurine set?" she asked.

"You know where it is, Mom," Elizabeth said with a surprised look on her face. "Remember? I asked you if I could put it in Steve's cage and you said *sure*."

"I did?" Lenny asked with a surprised look on her face, not at all remembering she had given her daughter permission to put the manger in the mouse's cage. "Well, I can't even imagine where my mind was when I said Steve could have it."

She had to admit her mind constantly swirled in and out of daydreaming. She couldn't help but feel more than a little disturbed by how often she found herself saying and doing things unaware. Could old mental habits be broken? More and more, Lenny wanted to live in a place of constant awareness. Never feeling disturbed by little annoyances, like burning sugar cookies. To be at peace with herself, her enemies, the entire world, no matter what kind of wildness was standing in front of her – this was her dream center. A place she would never want to leave.

"Mom, don't take it away from him. He really likes it," Elizabeth pleaded dragging her mother out of her thoughts.

"Well, that's nice to hear. But next year we'll buy him a rat toy or draw him a paper Christmas tree."

That seemed to delight Elizabeth. Mack just rolled his eyes.

"Now, let's read about the first *real* Christmas," Mack said, plopping the heavy book into his mother's lap. "I'm too old for kid stuff."

"But my toy bunny became real," Elizabeth reminded her mother.

"Yes, he did become real," Lenny said, patting her daughter's leg. "And sometimes, just like with the velveteen bunny, our life gets really hard and we cry and cry. And like magic, things change for the better."

"Like tonight when you were nice to Dad?" Mack asked.

"Mack, do you think I'm not nice to your father?" Lenny asked, feeling more than a little hurt. She thought she had covered up her true feelings about Bob pretty well in front of the children.

"No, Mom," Mack said. "I'm not a kid anymore. I can tell when you get upset and mad. And every time Dad asks to speak to you, you get that mad look on your face."

"I guess I'm not a good actress," Lenny said. "But I'm going to let you in on a secret. I'm trying not to dislike him so much. And tonight was my first attempt. So things went pretty well tonight, don't you think?"

"Yeah," Mack said nodding his head in agreement. "I guess they did."

Lenny took a deep breath. A part of her wanted to scream out just exactly why she looked so mad when Bob asked to speak to her. But it would only hurt her children. Perhaps she had been swallowing those poisonous feelings for too long, she thought. Perhaps the poison had finally come up and out of her system for good. She hoped so. As she'd seen so clearly looking down the mouth of her snake, poisonous, angry and bitter thoughts were deadly. They were thought forms, Lenny-made archetypes, anxious to rob her and her children of their peace and happiness. They were not real. They were not God created. But if she continued to manifest and feed them with her negative thought patterns, she would indeed remain lost to her true Self. A lovelier, more stable, and grounded self. And with it, she would loose a happier, healthier way of spending the rest of her life.

Hurriedly, she began reading aloud the passage in the Bible where Joseph meets an angel: "But while he thought on these things, behold, the angel of the Lord appeared unto him in a dream, saying, 'Joseph, thou son of David, fear not to take unto thee Mary thy wife: for that which is conceived in her is of the Holy Ghost.'"

"Do all angels wear pearl and dewdrop dresses like the Nursery Magic Fairy?" Elizabeth asked, interrupting her mother's reading.

"That's dumb, Elizabeth," Mack scolded. "The archangel Michael doesn't wear sissy-looking nightgowns. He wears armor and a man-skirt!"

"It's not dumb, Mack," Lenny scolded back. "I'll bet Elizabeth's angels wear dresses of pearl and dewdrops just to please her."

"Women!" Mack exclaimed with a sigh. "They're always thinking about clothes."

"Well, I want an angel *and* a Nursery Magic Fairy to watch over me!" Elizabeth exclaimed.

"That'll probably happen, Elizabeth," Mack said, sounding frustrated with his sister. "But only because you're full of stuffing like your old bunny."

Elizabeth screamed and hit her brother over the head with her pink Easter rabbit. Mack responded in kind, and soon they were wrestling on the floor.

Lenny closed the family Bible and started counting out loud. If she got to three, the children knew, she'd give them her meanest look and send them to their rooms. Mack and Elizabeth jumped back onto the sofa by the time Lenny had gotten to two.

Lenny continued reading, *"Then Joseph, being raised from sleep, did as the angel of the Lord had bidden him, and took unto him a wife."*

"Mom," Elizabeth interrupted again, "does God get angels to do His work because He doesn't have wings?"

Lenny quickly shot Mack a warning look that made it clear he was not to slam his sister with his words.

"Elizabeth," Lenny said, "I think God created angels as messengers. He needs to stay in heaven. He's like our center. Everything we see in the world burst forth from Him. And so, like little sheep who often get lost, we need all the help we can get. That's why He created angels."

"Yeah, you're right!" Mack exclaimed. "If God went off on some adventure, all the planets would go rolling around like bowling balls slamming into each other!"

"Mom," Elizabeth said. "Mack's scaring me!"

"Both of you need to stop talking," Lenny warned. "Santa is on his way. And it will be morning by the time I finish reading this one chapter. No more questions! It's past your bedtime and Santa will be here soon!"

"Sure, Mom!" Mack said, winking.

Elizabeth was asleep by the time Lenny reached the end of the page.

"Mom, what's a Nazarene?" she asked sleepily, waking up on Lenny's last word.

"Not tonight, Elizabeth," Lenny answered. "It's way past your bedtime."

After the children were in bed, Lenny switched on the television and watched "A Christmas Carol." Unlike Scrooge, she was never frightened when a deceased spirit made a call during her sleep time. However, in broad daylight, she reasoned, it might be another story.

Once, while working at the hospital with Mitzi, Lenny had dreamed of Mitzi's deceased mother, who had died of heart disease. At the time, Lenny didn't know Mitzi very well. Lenny had brushed away the dream at first because she felt too embarrassed to tell Mitzi about it. Then, before the week was over, she had another dream about the woman. This time, Mitzi's mother insisted Lenny give her daughter a message.

She had said, "Tell Mitzi I love her. And I'm proud of her."

The second time she visited, Lenny awoke and scribbled down the message as she remembered it spoken. She described what Mitzi's mother was wearing. It was a beautiful sparkling black pantsuit, fitted at the waist with bellbottom sleeves. It looked whisper-thin and dusted with silver moonlight glitter. Lenny, surprised by the encounter, instantly fell back to sleep.

The next morning, she had given Mitzi her mother's message—the whole thing, including the notes she'd written about her attire. And much to Lenny's surprise, Mitzi believed her. Although Lenny hadn't known it at the time, Mitzi's inner battles had gotten her down. Her mother's simple message of continued loving concern was thankfully, very appropriate. As Lenny shared with Mitzi what her mother was wearing in the dream, Mitzi laughed out loud. Then, with tears welling up in her eyes, she whispered, "Mother always wore black. She thought it made her look thin." As it turned out, this was the one clue that had made Mitzi believe she had encountered the spirit of her mother.

That experience also brought the two women closer together. Lenny thought about how the clothes of spirits and angels really were what dreams were made of. Stardust sprinkles and morning dewdrop pearls. Like Mack had said, women are always thinking about clothes—both in this world and in the afterlife, as well.

Lassie trotted out of Mack's room. She must have been wondering why Lenny wasn't in bed. The dog stared up at her with sad eyes. "Up," Lenny whispered. The dog jumped on the sofa. "You can't sleep either?" she asked into Lassie's curious brown eyes. Lassie wagged her tail, happy for Lenny's attention. Cozy in Lenny's lap, Lassie licked Lenny's hand as Lenny rubbed Lassie's white fluffy chest.

"My life is weird, Lassie," Lenny whispered. "But it's never boring. And I'm sort of glad in an odd kind of way. Do you think I'm weird, Lassie?"

Lassie looked deep into Lenny's eyes and wagged a happy *Yes, but in a good way.* Dogs seemed to know so much more than their masters gave them credit for knowing.

As the Christmas television show ended, Lenny tiptoed into the garage. She carefully opened the trunk of her car and removed hidden presents. Back in the living room, she silently scattered them under the tree.

She posed Elizabeth's new Barbie doll inside her pink convertible. She arranged Mack's new football atop his shiny new skateboard. Then Lenny walked back into the kitchen. As she did, her body suddenly shivered, covered in goose bumps. She checked the thermostat. It registered normal. She checked to see if the windows were closed and made sure the door was locked. Everything was tightly sealed.

Still feeling cold as she walked back into the living room, Lenny pulled a tattered quilt from the hall closet. It was a family treasure made from scraps of clothing worn by her father and his eight siblings. As she lay back down on the couch and covered herself up with the quilt, she noticed the colored lights of the Christmas tree dancing upon the squares of the quilt, as if calling them back to life. Lenny looked up at the ceiling and watched rainbow dots flashing on and off.

Elizabeth had left Santa a snowman cookie and a small glass of milk. Lenny reached down to pick up the cookie and bit the head off the snowman. It was store-bought and tasted stale. Lenny put it back down on its plate and drank the pasty taste out of her mouth with the last drop of leftover cocoa. Then she polished off the glass of milk. Lassie, who had jumped off the couch when Lenny got up to get the presents, was now curled up close to the heater vent by the front door. It was her favorite spot, besides someone's lap.

Lenny leaned back on the coach and caught sight of her new tree-topper angel. She studied her crown of stars. Five was a symbol of life, a symbol of nature, she recalled. It seemed to suit her just fine. Lenny wondered if the white angel missed her sixth star. The one she lost before Lenny bought her. What star had Lenny lost?

As a child, she used to wish upon stars every night before going to bed. She was slightly younger than Mack was now, when her parents divorced. She remembered the pain. And she also remembered vowing this would never happen to her. What a laugh. She had dragged herself, and her two children, through not just one but two divorces. She definitely had two star-wishes ripped off of her crown. And like the gooey spot left on the angel's head, a broken childhood dream is the stickiest grief to let go.

Tears rolled down her cheeks and she let them come. *A mother can cry on Christmas Eve as long as her children are safe in their beds sound asleep,* she thought. As she patted her eyes with a nearby pillow she let her thoughts fly by without caring where they went. She wasn't going to follow them tonight. She was way too tired for that. She just wanted to rest in the fragrant arms of her Christmas tree.

A wet tear tickled her right ear. And as it did she heard a soft whispering voice say, *"Arise."*

BLACK PONY

There are times when fear is good. It must keep its watchful place at the heart's controls. There is advantage in the wisdom won from pain.

—Aeschylus (525 - 456 BC)

As if on command, Lenny's heavy earthly body felt amazingly light as she rose off the couch and out of the house. Her living room vanished before she could even open her eyes. Her new world was void of color and form. This made her feel slightly tense and disoriented. She couldn't tell what was up or down. It almost appeared as if she'd been swallowed by a brown paper bag.

Feeling heavy once again, Lenny felt her eyeballs fluttering rapidly behind her closed eyes. As she continued to concentrate on this bodily sensation, a black image appeared. Startled, she almost turned and ran. But as the image came into focus, Lenny realized the form standing before her was a black pony. He was a raven beauty. But he was prancing about as erratically as her eyeballs had been fluttering only moments ago.

"Please stop," she begged. "Whatever you're doing, you are making me feel sick at my stomach."

"I'm simply exaggerating your feelings," he snorted. "You're constantly exaggerating meaningless moments and taking things personally. It would be best to remain silent and think before taking something to heart."

"Well, *you* need to stop stomping about, and I'm sure you're right. What is your name and why are you here?" she asked.

"I am Fear," he said matter-of-factly.

"I've never feared horses," Lenny said. "But years ago, I wished for a pony just like you. Of course, I didn't get it."

"I know your past well," the black pony said. "One seldom grows up and leaves it behind. The little self of your creation holds many secrets. Tonight, you have reached the level of awareness, vital to your well-being, to learn about natural fear. I am one of many inner teachers. I'm from the Animal Kingdom. Not a single animal, including the human kind, could survive without natural fear."

"But I've always believed one *should* be afraid of fear," Lenny said, remembering the famous quote from Franklin D. Roosevelt, who told the nation's citizens, when inaugurated in 1933, *the only thing to fear was fear itself.*

"Wrong," the pony snorted indignantly. "All creatures of Creator need to know when to be afraid. The fears of mankind have grown outrageously dense and very real. But Creator didn't create those fears, humans did. You created you own fears, Lenny. And your children will do as they see you doing. You need to teach them the difference between what is a watchful intuitive eye and what is nonsense. I am that watchful eye."

"Do you have a name?" Lenny asked.

"Just call me Fear. You already make your life more complicated than necessary. I want you to awaken with awareness of our visit. I want you to stop allowing fears of future failure to set in motion the certainty you will fail in what your heart and soul longs to accomplish in this lifetime."

For a few minutes, Lenny just watched the pony with the velvety smooth coat circle around and around her. His long tail and mane glistened against the dull color of their empty, brown world.

"Have we met before?" Lenny asked. "When I was a child, before I feared I would fail at everything I tried to accomplish, I think I saw a picture of a horse called Black Beauty. And it stirred a deep longing in my heart for a pony just like you. How in the world did this longing turn into fear?"

Fear, the pony, walked over to Lenny and looked deep into her eyes as if he was trying to see his own reflection. "I think," he said, "if you wrote down all the things you've feared since childhood, you would discover a lot of nonsense fears wrecking your chance for a happy life."

"To write about all I've feared, I might have to go back to when I was a newborn child," Lenny said, laughing. "I'm not sure I would know exactly where or how to begin. I've never thought of myself as being a particularly fearful type. But now that I think about it, I think I fear a lot more than I have ever felt comfortable admitting."

"A dreamy artist like you shouldn't lack the inspiration to get started," the pony responded. "Just draw what comes, and let it tell you your story. Then decide if you believe it or not. That way, you will make room for Creator's watchful eye."

"And you are that eye," Lenny said, smiling and beginning to understand.

"Indeed, my eyes are without judgment," Fear said, nodding in agreement. "It's really quite simple and uncomplicated. If you live in the moment, you need only feel fear when I am present. I am not a way of life. I shall always come when I am needed. I give you natural instincts of when, what, where and whom you should beware. I was created for this purpose. A seed of fear is planted in everyone. Water me with loving acceptance, and I will not grow into a problem. The higher the vibration of love, the freer you are from the wrong kind of fears. It is that simple."

"Nothing in my life is simple or uncomplicated," Lenny said with a heavy sigh. "Absolutely nothing!"

"If you say so, you'll create it. No doubt about that."

"But Fear, I don't *want* to create a life full of devouring fears. I hate even admitting I'm constantly afraid of being judged for all of my past failures, two of which ended in divorce. And I'm miserable about not being able to even date, fearing I will make the same mistake over and over again."

"I can't help you Lenny," Fear responded. "What you give your power over to becomes what you create. You are the creator of your life. I am not. I am natural fear. I was created to help your species survive. Nothing more, nothing less. When you let things come and go without attaching a story to them, you will find your center. It is a worthy quest for the spiritual warrior. And let me assure you, it will feel wonderful once you arrive. At the root of your worst fear is deep loneliness. You feel different, separate from others. You long for companionship with a like-minded other. But your fear of being hurt by love, is growing thicker by the day. Seek ye first your Center, then you will become like a strong magnet, attracting all the good things your heart desires."

"I don't like to think I fear falling in love, or the judgment of others, but I do," Lenny admitted. "You are right, Fear. And this feels very wrong to me. Jesus said one should never judge, but I think I'm much harder on myself than I am on others."

"And so are most, when it comes down to it. When you speak falsehood, believing you are your past, losing touch with your true Self, and believe it, your God-self, a mini-creator, brings it to pass. For as the great Greek philosopher Aeschylus once said, *God's mouth knows not how to speak falsehood, but he brings to pass every word.*'"

"So you're telling me my Higher Self will let the false thoughts I think and talk about come to life?" Lenny asked. "I cannot help but be reminded of books that have come to me saying this very same thing. But I am not God. And I certainly do not wish falsehood to come to pass by my every word!"

"God is in an earthworm, but the earthworm isn't God," Fear answered, looking a little frustrated. "When you didn't get a birthday pony as a small child, you feared none of your wishes, hopes, and dreams would ever come true. I am a wish turned upside down. A fallen star from the crown of your possible good. You keep replaying the same old records Lenny. I dwell at the bottom of your unconscious mind. But tonight, you uncovered me with willful determination. In my purest manifestation, I am natural gut-instinct. If you constantly ride the wild horse of fear, it will run away with your life. As you draw closer to

Center, your seeing eye will open. Not just in a dream, but you will take these clear eyes into your day-to-day living.."

Now, Lenny was the one pacing back and forth around her Fear pony.

"This is how I felt when I first saw you tonight. It is movements an animal makes when it becomes afraid. Now, tell me how you're feeling," he said.

"Slightly agitated by the idea of making something out of nothing, angry that I've let fear rob me of freely loving, and feeling like a victim, not in control my life," Lenny said. "I'm feeling regret and wishing I'd not lost a star from my crown. I'm sad that not only did my life not work out as planned, but worse, I've lost so much precious time in grief. No wonder I'm having so much trouble trying to appear happy in front of my children. They see the truth. I used to have their clear eyes, *your* eyes. All day today, they saw the real me and I was so full of fear I was unconsciously very angry about it. I was mad. My children saw this in me, but I was blinded by my closed adult eyes. Maybe that's why I was so mean-spirited to my ex-husband. Not that I don't think he deserved my anger at times. But I could have been more skillful in expressing my suffering to him. I know he has his own steep mountains to climb. I can't honestly say, if measured and weighted, his bad habit energy would weigh more than my own. At first, I felt great relief expressing my angry feelings to him. But now, I ask myself, can I truly be happy knowing another person is suffering from my critical words. I judged him all cloudy and gray, and saw myself all sunflower yellow and right. This isolating judgment is enough to make me truly want to change."

"Goodbye, Lenny," Fear said suddenly.

"*No, Fear!*" Lenny cried out in a sudden panic. "Please don't leave me! I feel safe with you. Safer than I've ever felt in my entire life."

"I can never leave you, Lenny. I'm a part of your very essence. Remember: '*The reward of suffering is experience.*'"

"Aeschylus said that," Lenny responded. You've quoted him often tonight. But I never really understood the true meaning of those words before now."

"What you read has been imprinted in your mind," the pony continued. "Spiritual truths have a way of finding expression in the material world. You are well on your way to finding what you seek, Lenny. *'When a man is willing and eager, the gods join in.'*"

"That's another quote from Aeschylus," Lenny said, smiling. "I'm beginning to think he had a Fear Pony just like you."

"He had a horse, Lenny. But that's a tale of a different color."

Lenny smiled, and as quickly as Fear had appeared he was gone. Lenny soon realized she was no longer inside the paper-bag brown world. She was calmly adrift in an inky night sky. Lenny wasn't sure why, but Fear's visit had given her renewed courage.   "Thank you, Fear," she whispered into air that seemed thick and full of life. The black night had never felt or looked so beautiful. For what seemed a long time, she drifted within the endless void of empty space, unafraid. Surely it was true, she thought, when one was ready, their teacher would appear, even one named Fear.

She drifted along in blissful silence, until suddenly, she felt slightly disoriented, a little dizzy. A flash of light appeared. It shot forth from the heavens like a falling star. The sky was suddenly ablaze with a million stars.

A WHITE UNICORN

We might naturally think of white as the simplest and purest of colors, and until the time of Sir Isaac Newton this was the general opinion. We know now, however, that the white light of the sun is not simple, but is made up of rays of all the colors which our eyes can perceive.

—Walter Sargent

The starlight danced around Lenny like a summer field full of fireflies. The flashes of light buzzed as they flew by her, and she was feeling hypnotized by their movements when suddenly, she detected the pleasant aroma of baby powder. She turned around to find its source. Expecting to see a newborn infant, she found instead a sparkling white unicorn covered in diamond-like glitter.

"Oh, my goodness!" Lenny said with a gasp. "Are you a fallen star?"

"No," said the unicorn in a female voice. "Unlike your black pony, I represent your heart's desire."

"Did I create you, or are you a creation of God?" Lenny asked.

"Creation is not a lesson I teach," she answered. "I teach desire, the fuel that will take you where you want to go. Where do you want to go Lenny?"

"I don't want to go anywhere right now," Lenny said, feeling mesmerized by the unicorn's beauty. Is your name Desire?"

"No, my name is Color," said the unicorn, walking toward Lenny. She was much larger than Lenny first thought. As the unicorn bent low, Lenny looked into her eyes and saw they were crystals. They reflected Lenny's face much like her broken compact mirror—dividing it into many smaller reflections. Lenny quickly looked away, feeling confused. She suddenly felt as if she were several places at the same time. She flashed back to seeing herself asleep on the couch, and then just as quickly, Lenny was back inside her dream body with the unicorn named Color. After a long pause, Lenny asked about her name.

"Is Color a name I gave you?" Lenny asked.

"That's an odd way to speak of someone's name," answered Color. "I have come to offer you the gift of simplicity. I think you desire this but have not witnessed its value until now."

"Then you have come to teach me simple desires?" Lenny asked. "I just had this conversation with a black pony named Fear. And as I said to him, nothing in my life is simple."

The white unicorn stared at Lenny with her crystal eyes for what seemed like a long time. Color was much more still and tranquil than her black pony. As Lenny thought about the difference between them, Color finally spoke.

"Lest you become even more confused, Lenny, let me explain something. I am not here to teach you about polarity. Everything is dual on the physical plane. Are you not already familiar with the principle of polarity, which states everything in creation has an opposite?"

"Yes, I am," Lenny answered.

"Good. I am not the opposite of your black fear pony. I am here to bring into your awareness how the center which you seek is much like the color white. Your heart's greatest longing is to return to this center. It cannot be easily found, for it is not what it seems to be in your logical way of thinking. Center is not a place—it is beyond thought. But when you find it, you will wonder why it took you so long to realize it is not something you can find."

"Then are you saying I should *not* seek center?" Lenny asked. "I'm feeling even more confused, and this lesson doesn't seem very simple."

"Your ego is always identifying with form, endlessly seeking and losing itself in form and things, be they thoughts or emotional attachments. Desiring to satisfy the soul with such unsatisfying forms of energy makes you feel lost and afraid. But when you live life from center, these types of empty desires vanish. Like the color white, the concept of center only appears to be simple. White is not blankness, or the absence of color, but actually holds *many* colors—all of them, in fact. And when you go to your center, you integrate all the parts of yourself and bring them together. Do you understand?"

"I think I do," Lenny said, feeling the wisdom of what Color had just said settling into her being. "In the last two days, I've heard and read much about finding center. But it still seems illusive and difficult to incorporate in my day-to-day living. Granny said center always stays where it is. So how did I lose mine?"

"Only the child you once were can help you see how center was lost to your thinking," Color replied. "In reality, it has gone nowhere, because center indeed stays where it is, as your Granny said. But that is not for me to teach you. This is your inner child's gift to you. If you are sincere, and open to going ever deeper, and deeper within yourself, she will go with you."

"Then please tell me, how do I find this child I once was, my inner child?" Lenny asked.

"You can't find her," Color answered. "But when she no longer feels afraid, *she* will find *you*, and then you will find what you are seeking."

Lenny wondered how her inner child—even if she did eventually manage to feel safe—would ever find her, especially since Lenny felt unfocused, too scattered, like the reflection of her face in Color's crystal eyes. A couplet written by William Blake, one of Lenny's favorite poets, suddenly popped into her head:

> *The wild deer wand'ring here and there*
> *Keeps the human soul from care.*

"Does my soul, my Self, my center, watch me wildly wandering here and there?" she asked Color.

"Yes," Color said, nodding. "And to witness this and to see it clearly will be enough to keep you at center in the midst of many of life's storms. I cannot say this is easy. But I can say it is a simple concept when you learn to apply it *before* you react to whatever comes your way—or more accurately, before you react to whatever you attract to yourself. I shall leave you now, Lenny, but know you are on the path toward all you seek."

Color vanished, and once again, Lenny felt so disoriented she could not tell up from down. For a long time, she felt as if she were wrapped in a protective, warm blanket void of color and form. Suddenly, she heard her grandfather clock chime five times. She awoke, slightly startled to find she had slept most of the night on her living room couch.

19

A CLOSED DOOR

Let the little children come to me, and do not hinder them, for the kingdom of God belongs to such as these. I tell you the truth, anyone who will not receive the kingdom of God like a little child will never enter it.

—Mark 10:14-15

Finding herself on the couch at five o'clock in the morning surprised Lenny. But more surprising was her total recall of her dream. She got up from the couch and walked into her bedroom to retrieve her orange notebook. Then she took down shorthand notes of everything she could remember about her dreamtime encounters with a beautiful black pony named Fear and a magical white unicorn named Color. By the time she was done, Lenny felt wide awake, but it was too early to get up. She pulled back the covers on her bed and lay her head down on the freshly washed sheets. As she thought about how wonderful they smelled, she was soon fast asleep once more.

Again, Lenny was surrounded by the color brown. But this brown felt alive and even lush, and she seemed to be deep in the belly of some sort of wooden structure. She stretched out her hands to discover the space that surrounded her was relatively small. It almost felt like the interior of a coffin. A rush of panic shot thought her, but her fear gave way to a feeling of surprise as she realized she could make out certain forms and shapes outside of the wooden structure she occupied— including branches and, when she looked up, the cracked foot of her white angel tree-topper. It dawned on her she was somehow inside the trunk of her Christmas tree.

"Can you hear me?" she called up to the angel. A strong remembrance of speaking to two horses was still on her mind. And she couldn't help wondering if dolls or toys became real in ethereal planes of existence. "How did I shrink? And however did I get inside my Christmas tree?" She waited, but the angel did not respond. Apparently toys and dolls become real only in storybooks.

"Please," she pleaded with the silent angel, as if she were Lenny's only hope. "Send down a popcorn strand so I can climb out of here. But no more snakes!"

Both in dreams and in waking life, Lenny often felt the need to be rescued by a prince, a rope, or even just a helping hand. This was not good, she sensed. She wanted to be able to rescue herself, but so far she had not been successful.. The two men whom she had married were both controlling and enjoyed her need to be loved. But soon after each marriage, Lenny realized what they offered her was not the love she craved. There seemed to be something lonely in her nature that craved companionship, but at the same time needed to feel independent and free. Neither of her husbands were big on giving her freedom—at least not Lenny's idea of freedom. The love they offered Lenny felt possessive, more about what they wanted or needed, less about giving her their truth.

As Lenny sat thinking about her inner conflicts with men, a beautiful door appeared. It looked medieval or Spanish in design, with ornate carvings cut deep into thick burgundy wood. She reached out to grasp a knob in the center of the door, but it wouldn't turn. So she knocked. Nothing happened. She knocked several more times, but still nothing happened. A thought crossed her mind. Maybe she needed permission from the other side before it would open. If so, whom, she wondered, should she ask?

As a wave of frustration hit her, she had an impulse to kick the door like a spoiled child. But that idea seemed a bit rash. Once, years ago, when she was in her teens, she kicked a door when she was mad at her Granny. She was being scolded for breaking a forgotten household rule.

She'd really wanted to cuss, but she knew better. Instead, she kicked at her closed bedroom door—and had ended up breaking her toe. Sometimes, she thought as she pondered the mystery door, it might be better to just leave closed doors alone. After all, did she really *need* to see what was behind this one?

Most definitely, she heard herself thinking almost before she was finished asking herself the question. Lenny remembered having dreams of walking through doors before. According to her dream dictionary, doors were a symbol of transition from one realm to a new realm, from the uninitiated to the holy. Clearly then, this closed door held secrets Lenny was not yet ready to receive or was simply not prepared to accept. Perhaps her inner Nancy Drew was too tired to look for clues. Deflated, she sat for what seemed like a long time, and her frustration eventually gave way to a quiet acceptance. And as it did, Lenny felt a certain inner tightness begin to loosen.

She had barely recognized this sensation, when her surroundings began to expand and grow outward forming a large circle. She was now in the center of a large stadium. *I'm in a Spanish bull-fighting arena!* She thought to herself. *How did I get here?* She recognized her new surroundings from travel brochures she'd seen for Spain. As the arena's tall walls rose up around her, she felt prepared to handle whatever bulls lurked behind them—as well as whatever might be lurking behind that stubborn wooden door she'd not been able to open. She saw it in the distance, still closed.

Then she remembered Color's words about her inner child. She was the one who would show Lenny how she had lost her center. When the child felt safe, Color had told her, her inner child would find Lenny. But how was her inner child ever going to feel safe when Lenny was so used to being afraid? Lenny thought of Fear and the lessons her black pony had taught her. If danger did approach, Fear would let her know if it was time to fight or flee—she was sure of that.

With Fear's lesson still fresh in her mind, Lenny realized she'd never felt as safe as she did at that very moment. And then she thought about Color, and what the beautiful white unicorn had taught her about the power of desire. A childlike longing bubbled up in Lenny's heart, and she remembered how wonderful it felt to be full of joyful anticipation and belief in impossible dreams.

Lenny closed her eyes and drifted back in time. She imagined herself the child she was before too many broken dreams and wishes took her away from her belief that even the most seemingly impossible dream could come true. As she pictured herself as a child, her body became lighter. She felt like a leaf detaching from its tree branch and ready to fall to the ground. With great strength of will, Lenny let go. She was no longer afraid to drop into the unknown, hanging in uncertainty for as long as she needed. Almost at the point of her surrender, she was drifting, content to feel powerless. And as she concentrated on her newfound willingness, a loud screech filled the air.

Lenny opened her eyes with a start. Her mystery door was now open wide.

TWO CHAIRS

Life without Rebellion is like seasons without Spring. And Rebellion without Right is like Spring in an arid desert.... Life, Rebellion, and Right are three-in-one who cannot be changed or separated.

—Kahlil Gibran

Lenny rose to her feet, delighted the heavy, once-unmoving door had opened. She had not kicked the door as she'd done as a rebellious teen. Back then, she had wanted to kick at rules she did not wish to follow. She'd felt the same way about the rules religion imposed, too. She loved the teachings of Jesus. They embodied all that she knew to be true. But, at the same time, she found a lot to rebel against in her traditional and strict Christian upbringing, where everything was a sin. After meeting Dawn, she was now filled with a passion for studying mystery schools, mythology, and the ancient philosophies of Ancient Egypt and Greece. Questioning ideas and exploring the truth of all others, she realized, were assets of a rebellious nature, while impulsive emotional outbursts, like kicking at doors, were definitely among its drawbacks. And this time, because Lenny had managed to keep her rebellious temper in check, she'd been able to open the mystery door. Now, she was most anxious to see what was on the other side.

There were only two beings Lenny hoped to meet behind this door. One was her soul mate, if such a man truly existed. The other was her inner child, whom Color had told her would help her discover how

Lenny had left center. At this moment, Lenny knew no other desire but these two.

She walked toward the open door. Then, just as she was within a few feet of entering, she heard Elizabeth's voice—although she couldn't figure out exactly what she was saying, or to whom she was speaking. Lenny had not expected to meet Elizabeth. On several occasions, she dreamed of visiting her children. Right now, she was more than a little curious about why her daughter might be a part of this most unusual dream.

She crossed the threshold. After walking a few steps further, Lenny noticed long, dark purple shadows stretching before her and simultaneously sensed a presence behind her. Whatever was behind her was making the shadows grow longer and longer. With a strong desire to face her fears, Lenny walked straight into the shadows and turned around. Puzzled, she found herself staring at two huge chairs made for giants. One was a child's highchair, the other was a wheelchair.

Lenny had hoped for a spiritual treasure of profound delight. But the ridiculous sight of not one, but two giant chairs made her laugh out loud. Like Alice in Wonderland, she had somehow shrunk—first to land inside her Christmas tree and now to enter the domain of an unseen giant. This didn't seem like a step forward in finding center!

Both chairs disturbed Lenny. Like the mystery door she'd just walked through, they were ornately carved like something belonging in a Spanish cathedral. Being a lucid dreamer all of her life, Lenny was well aware of the significance of certain symbols. But, before she could think of anything significant, she began to have an uneasy feeling the chairs were judging her. They did not look at her with simple, child-like eyes. Or, perhaps this wasn't true. Perhaps the highchair represented nothing more than her need for nourishment of a spiritual nature. She could deal with that. But the wheelchair—this she flat-out disliked. Perhaps its presence indicated that whatever was crippling her was still tight around her legs, hindering her walk through life. Or worse, would she be unable to move under the weight of this lesson? She wondered if the wheelchair would scold her, as so often Granny had done when Lenny was in the prime of her rebellion years.

Then, the idea of mind pictures came to her. She played this game as a child and later learned it was a great way to meditate. One meditation she experimented with was picturing a stage with a black curtain. On this curtain, you tried to visualize golden letters, which would eventually spell out words or phrases—messages from your spirit guides or at the very least, your unconscious mind. The goal was to make what you were imagining so real you clearly saw the curtain and the letters. Lenny tried this now, although she could only get the letter "L" to appear. Nothing more would come, and she got so frustrated she had to stop.

She glanced from one chair to the other, hoping they would somehow reveal their story to her. But after several minutes, nothing happened. Lenny wondered if perhaps the oversized chairs were nothing more than reminders to enjoy simple pleasures like taking walks and giving thanks for daily nourishment. But if this was all they meant, she couldn't help but feel a little let down. She had expected so much more behind the door.

Feeling mentally scattered, she decided to focus first on the chair she liked the least. She stared intensely at the wheelchair. But still, nothing happened. And just as she was about to switch her attention to the highchair, Lenny noticed a large man appeared to be sitting in the wheelchair.

She looked into his eyes. He looked much like the handsome man at a Paris café she'd seen in her earlier dream. This same man was back, testing her, she decided. She did not look away nor did he. They stared into each other's eyes for what seemed like a long time. Lenny didn't move a muscle. But then without warning, as quickly as he had appeared, the man vanished, leaving the wheelchair empty once more.

The man of her dreams was never the man she thought he was, Lenny thought, feeling a pain in the pit of her stomach. In fact, was *she* even the person she thought herself to be? Was all her uncertainty about never getting what she really wanted crippling her spiritual growth? With humility, Lenny bowed her head and relived, in her mind's eye, many failures and broken dreams of the past. Her hope deferred had made her heart too sick to continue trying to solve the unsolvable mysteries of life.

Lenny turned away from the chairs without knowing why. As she pivoted, she was surprised to find she was looking straight into the face of the child she had been at age five.

"Do not be frightened," whispered the child. "Fear will break our ray."

"We have a ray?" Lenny asked, wide-eyed.

"Oh, yes," Child responded, smiling. "In your understanding, that means if you get frightened, you won't be able to see me anymore."

Lenny nodded she understood, remembering what Color had told her. "You are right to warn me about being afraid, because I have been afraid to beckon you," she said. "I'm not sure I ever want to relive being five years old again. But I've been told it is very important to meet my inner child, if that is who you are."

"I am this in you," Child said with a warm smile. Lenny recognized Child's voice as her own by its vibration, and she immediately understood why she thought she had heard Elizabeth before she walked through the doorway. Elizabeth, at seven, sounded much the same as Lenny did at Child's age.

"Have you come to show me how to stay put and how to find center?" Lenny asked, hopefully.

"All you need to do to find center is to find joy in just doing," Child explained. "When you learn to vibrate with joy, you will find vibration alignment with All. Joy is a magnetic power that reaches out into the universe attracting everything like itself. Find joy Lenny. Then you will be like an arrow moving toward a target. I cannot say more than this. This is all I know."

She looked up at Lenny and then lowered her head as if suddenly sad. Then she looked up and smiled. Lenny suddenly noticed they were wearing identical pale blue cotton nightgowns. As if reading her mind, Child picked up the edges of her nightgown hem and began rocking back and forth as she stared up at Lenny.

Lenny touched her abdomen with her hands and looked into Child's eyes. She felt a strong connection to Child, as if they were attached by an invisible umbilical cord. The longer Child rocked, the more attached Lenny felt to her. Then suddenly, Child walked over and took Lenny's hand before leading her to stand in front of the oversized wheelchair.

"Granny sat in a wheelchair in the hospital," said Child.

"I know," whispered Lenny. "It hurt me to see her too weak to walk."

"It hurts Creator and our angels when you cannot walk," Child whispered shyly, as if she were disclosing a secret.

"But I *can* walk," Lenny said, squatting down until she was eye level with Child.

"As you see, I do not see," said Child. "Inner kingdoms are full of bridges, and these are connected to both your heart and your voice. You must be centered and balanced to cross inner bridges. You have many thoughts and say many things to yourself in your head that make you stumble and fall. But with my simple eyes, you can witness where both the good and bad seeds you've scattered have fallen. Your voice is a bridge for angels and animals on the other side to walk across. As you expand your inner space with less noise and mental chatter, we can walk over those bridges. But we do not come uninvited. Nor can you enter our realms without passing each challenge set before you.

"So I passed a challenge, and that is why the door opened. Is this correct?" Lenny asked, feeling proud, but at the same time confused.

Child nodded, smiling. "I walked to you on the bridge of your voice," she answered.

"What word did I say you walked on?" Lenny asked, still puzzled.

"I walk on *all* of your words, but mainly the words with the strongest emotions. I wrote these words on the walls of your deep void. This is a place inside you were you first began to feel alone."

"Are you talking about *determination*, *will*, and *power*?" Lenny asked, remembering the three words she saw written on the walls of a well. "I remember these words very well, Child.

"Those were messenger words sent to help rescue you. While you live inside a physical body, you are a bridge between *I Am* and *I am not*. *I am not* is only conscious of a physical body and its appetites. And *I am not* feels lonely all the time. *I Am* lives as One with the Universal Mind."

"So if I am a bridge between *I Am* and *I am not*," Lenny asked, "and *I Am* is God, then is *I am not* the absence of God? Is that why it lives in a deep void?"

"No," said Child patiently. "Like the rhyme says, *'There is no spot where God is not.'* There can never be an absence of God, who exists in everything and everyone all the time. *I am not* is merely the absence of the *awareness* of God's presence. That's why it occupies a deep void." Lenny nodded. What Child had been saying felt true to her heart, although confusing to her intelligence.

"This place of Love, where *I Am* dwells, is a place I wish to go. This sounds like my true center. Can you take me there?" Lenny asked. "Your heart will take you there when it is no longer crippled with self-criticism, judgment, guilt, regret, fear, and pain," Child explained.

"I suppose then," Lenny said, "the wheelchair is my symbol of all that you just said. And maybe the highchair represents how I have not nourished myself with acceptance and love. Chairs are typically considered a symbol of our attitudes—the places where we choose to sit. Both of these chairs speak loudly to me now, however, it does not feel pleasant to see them. I wish they would disappear."

"But that is only one way to see them," Child responded. "Remember *I Am* is in everything and everyone. My voice cries to you to be angry no more. Be happy instead. I am part of you, I am your innocence, and I connect you to your childhood. You cannot uncreate me, Lenny, but you can hide me."

Lenny watched as Child continued to rock back and forth holding up the ends of her gown. The more she rocked, the more her mind began to get clearer and clearer.

"It matters nothing to me what others are choosing, or not choosing. I am always pleased with myself. I certainly am. But you worry these chairs are judging you, tearing down your ego structure—your conscious mind, who you think you are," Child continued. "You like your attitudes and beliefs. You are offended when another person thinks you are wrong and you feel you are right. This way of thinking feeds your ego, Lenny, but it starves your soul. *I Am* wishes that all of his children walk in soul's power. Those who always see the best in everyone, always first see the best in themselves. "

"I believe you, Child" Lenny said. "Many saints and sages have written similar advice. I see why Jesus said, one must become as a child to enter the kingdom of heaven. The bridge to heaven must only be walked with a loving and trusting heart—the heart of a child. Even though my rational mind does not yet understand all of this, something deep inside me *does* understand—because what you say fills me with great peace."

Child stopped rocking and looked up at Lenny with knowing eyes.

Lenny took a deep breath, and then she added, "Child, I've spent days longing to know the true significance of my Granny's message. Do you know fully why she called me a Desert Rose?"

"Yes. But first I wish to show you something," Child said, taking Lenny's right hand. "You will like this lesson, Lenny. Do not be afraid, or your fear will break our ray."

"I can't imagine being afraid of you—you are so loving," Lenny said, looking down at Child. As they walked, Lenny noticed the ground was strewn with beautiful grains of soft and glistening sand. "You know," she whispered down to Child," I have lived in fear a long time. My black pony helped me realize this about myself. It wasn't really all that hard to admit, I was simply shocked to see it. And seeing it so clearly through Fear's eyes has changed me, Child. I am not the person I used to be."

"I know," Child said, smiling up at Lenny. They drew close to the highchair. Child climbed up on the bottom rung, and Lenny sat down beside her.

"Where do you get your nourishment?" Child asked.

"You mean my spiritual food?" Lenny asked. Child nodded.

"Well, I love my Bible, but I don't always feel fed at church. I'm not Granny," Lenny answered. "I don't read my Bible and memorize verses anymore, but the words still live in me and have much meaning. I follow my heart and constantly strive to explore whatever new ideas and philosophies come to me, seeking truth wherever it can be found. I enjoy studying different faiths, and I respect all their ways. But I also know I must choose my own path. Because I believe no two souls are alike, it would be foolish for me to think what feeds my soul would feed another's soul."

"Yes," Child said. "This is true. But remember, what goes into your mind, wanted or unwanted, invites an experience. Too much study of fear-laced reading grows unwanted fears."

"Yes, very wise words, Child. As I nourish myself with what resonates to my inner being, I hope to reach a level of understanding that will make me more loving and more tolerant with everyone else in my life. Jesus taught this when He said to love others as you love yourself. But since I obviously have not been able to truly love myself for a long time, I have indeed loved others as myself—which is to say, very little indeed."

"Joy is the nourishment your heart needs," Child said in a comforting voice. "The well in which you fell also provided nourishment. Much nourishment takes place when your physical body sleeps and your dream body walks. Remember your snake left you with an image of an open mouth, Lenny. You must pay attention to what words you fill your own mouth with. Someday, I see your heart will bud in self-love. And as this bud unfolds, it will naturally blossom into loving others because you will truly love yourself. As in nature, love's petals are delicate and cannot be forced to open."

"My heart shall always treasure these words, Child," Lenny said with a faraway look in her eyes. Currently, I have an enemy neighbor I'm trying to love. But I guess I need to first love myself, then loving her will be a piece of cake."

"You cannot love something you do not understand," Child said. "To understand all is to forgive all. But to forgive anyone else, you first have to forgive *yourself.* Loving others comes after this, but never before."

"Then take me into forgiveness ," Lenny said impatiently. "I want to go where Love is not, in order to put love where it longs to be."

Child jumped off her perch, and Lenny followed. She scooted sand back and forth with her toes, looking down intently, as if she was listening to a voice Lenny couldn't hear.

"Okay. I will do this," Child whispered, although Lenny had no idea to whom Child was speaking.

"Forgiveness is fun to unravel," giggled Child. "Now I wish to show you our tapestry. It is our next lesson." As soon as Child said these words, a bright light flashed across Lenny's eyes, and for several seconds, she could see nothing but white.

21

THE TAPESTRY

Thread is an ancient symbol. It can be a sign of the umbilicus, which in turn is connected to the thread of karma, or fate, which weaves its way through your life. Look for the thread of truth throughout the circumstances of your life.

—Denise Linn

As the brilliant white light began to fade, Lenny saw the tapestry. Hanging suspended in midair, about eight feet high and ten feet wide, it looked absolutely stunning. But looking was not enough. Instinctively, Lenny walked over and touched it. As she did, she noticed each thread felt as if it were alive with many memories—much like Granny's quilt.

Some threads were knotted and knurly while others were tightly woven and smooth. Patch-like patterns of every color (including some Lenny was sure she'd never seen before) were scattered about in a totally random fashion. But this seeming chaos actually enhanced the tapestry's breathtaking beauty.

As Lenny studied the tapestry, an odd thought crossed her mind. She'd long ago envisioned becoming a fashion designer when she grew up, but a teen marriage and early pregnancy had ended that dream. Even so, she still passionately considered herself cut from artisan cloth. She'd never tried to imagine what that artisan cloth might look like, but now, gazing at her tapestry, she realized it must look exactly like this.

Lenny looked down at Child. She wasn't looking at their tapestry. She was looking at Lenny.

"See?" Child said, smiling. "Now tell me what you see to hate or do not forgive about yourself!"

"If my life is found in this work of art, absolutely nothing," Lenny answered. Suddenly, Child was covered in what looked like rainbow fireflies. She reached out to touch Child, and when she did, these same colored lights covered Lenny's hands and arms. As she looked back at the tapestry, she saw it was glowing—as if its strands of thread had been transformed into brilliant rays of light, borrowed from the nearest rainbow.

"Look at us!" Lenny said, laughing with delight.

"The breath of God is Light. Light and Love are One. And they make everything beautiful," Child said, giggling so hard she almost fell to the ground.

"Do all souls have a tapestry?" Lenny asked.

"Yes," Child answered. "But no two are alike."

"Where did the light from my tapestry come from?" Lenny asked.

"God and Light are One," Child said, still smiling. "When you turned away from this Light, you walked forth, feeling unnourished for a long time. You moved away from your true source of sustenance. Trying to find it in a human relationship was disastrous. Was it not?"

"Yes," Lenny said, feeling regret for seeking in others the love she did not feel she possessed in herself.

"But now," Child continued in a whisper, "seeing what love is *not* helps you to see clearly what love *is*."

"Well, I definitely learned the 'what is not love' lesson over and over again," Lenny said, shaking her head. For a long time Lenny just stood, staring at her tapestry. She'd often remembered wondrous and vividly colorful dreams. But tonight was the most splendid rainbow dream of them all. It nourished her soul, and she never wanted to forget it. She intuitively knew every thread and all it represented.

"When you were small," Child said smiling up at Lenny, you drew black lines around all your colors. Do you know why you did this?" Child asked.

"I had almost forgotten about that," Lenny answered, looking down at Child. "I didn't want my colors to run into each other. I liked to keep them separate. Nothing in my life felt like it was under my control, so I must have thought I could control my colors by holding them in with dark lines."

"When one lacks the nourishment of Light, one cannot move. One gets stuck inside a shape, a prison of his or her own creation," Child explained. "Look Lenny. Do you see this knotted patch of color on your tapestry?"

Child pointed to several long red and yellow stripes. Lenny nodded, trying to follow the stripes as they wound through several of the tapestry's bright patches of color.

"This is your snake before you thought him into form," Child said.

"Oh my!" Lenny said as she studied the ribbons of color. She immediately recognized the energy attached to these threads of light. But she did not hate the threads of the tapestry as she had hated holding the neck of her angry snake.

"Try to manifest this circle over here," Child said, pointing to a beautiful white splash of glittery thread.

"That one looks like the sun," Lenny said, admiring it.

"What you have not lost, but only forgotten, resides here," Child said, smiling. "When you ponder the great, the great will come. These threads hold knowledge that will cut though your black threads of separation and illusion. See? There are no black threads surrounding the circle."

"I had not noticed that before you pointed it out to me," Lenny said carefully, leaning in closer for a better look. For a long time she looked from the red and yellow threads to the brilliant splash of white. Slowly, she began to imagine she could tell each patch of color apart, as if she were looking at pictures in a photo album. She wondered about the colors of the men loved and lost in her life, including her inner masculine.

"Yes, they are here," Child said, reading her mind. She pointed knowingly at several dark and light shades of blues with black and brown boarders.

Lenny nodded, not at all surprised Child had known her thoughts and certain she was right, even before Child confirmed it. After a long quiet stretch of contemplation, Lenny spoke.

"I think fencing in my relationship colors, with demands and expectations, has caused me to miss the spontaneity only true love can give," she said, looking down at Child as Child looked up at Lenny. "I drew the black lines because I wanted to feel safe. I didn't want to live in an atmosphere of suspicion and jealousy which I did most of the time. But at one time, all of my relationships were beautiful. I have no regrets. Not any more.."

Child beamed. "And now do you see how silly you've been, trying to wish away your past?" Child asked. "Would you tear apart this tapestry to remove the colors you do not like?" A mischievous smile spread across Child's face as she watched the truth dawn on Lenny.

"I think you know the answer to that question!" Lenny said, laughing. "Yesterday, I wanted to erase my life story. But right now, I wouldn't change a thing about my life. I'm certainly aware I've burned the biscuits more than once. And I've often gotten stuck and depressed and angry when things did not go as planned. My threads have gotten knotted and tangled in places. But I am not ashamed of my tapestry. It may not be perfectly uniform, but it is perfectly mine. And it *is* beautiful."

"How do you now feel about the dark threads that border your colors?" Child asked, looking deep into Lenny's eyes.

"They are beautiful, too, because they are an intricate part in my tapestry's overall pattern," Lenny answered. "Awareness of my ignorance has actually been my salvation from fear and pain and from staying stuck in the past. I have been sick in my heart and mind. And does not wisdom begin with the awareness of one's own not knowing? I've spent a long time asking myself where I was going and where my path to greater self-realization could be found. So many questions are wordlessly being answered as I merge into this richly colored tapestry of both bright and dark places where I've lived.

Emotion suddenly overcame Lenny and she could no longer speak. Child patted Lenny's hand in understanding, and Lenny reached out to hold Child's hands in hers. But she did not hold them for long. Child soon jumped up and began to dance. She circled round and round Lenny, kicking up her legs. Lenny got up and joined her. They held hands and made up silly dance steps. After several minutes of spinning and kicking, Child stopped to catch her breath.

"Why did you start dancing?" Lenny asked, also panting.

"Did you not hear music?" Child asked.

Lenny had only heard laughter, thinking it was their own. But as she stood in silence, she heard what sounded like the haunting melody that Elizabeth's dancing-doll music box had been playing the night before.

"Does this melody have a name?" Lenny asked.

"Not yet. But you can give it one," Child answered.

"Then let's call it our *Dancing in Heaven* song," Lenny said with a laugh. "I like to keep things as simple as possible."

"I know!" Child said, laughing in response. Holding tight to Lenny hand, she danced her across the sand, back to the tapestry. Then Child fell to the ground, Lenny joining her.

"Let's make sand angels," Child said with a grin.

Lenny laughed. She lay back against the sand and then fanned her legs and arms back and forth, leaving the impression of a skirt and wings in the sand. Child did the same.

"We're making pictures for White Angel. See?" Child said, pointing above their heads. "She is looking down at us right now."

Lenny gazed upward, expecting to see her bargain, tree-topper angel with the cracked foot. But as before, when Child first showed her the tapestry, all Lenny could see was a flash of white light so bright it seemed to her it should have hurt her eyes. But it didn't.

"I can't see her," Lenny said with a sigh. "Her light is too bright for my eyes. Is she beautiful?"

"Yes, she is very beautiful," answered Child. "She wants me to read your life story so your grown-up eyes can see it with simple, child-eyes.

"Does my story, our story, have a happy ending?" Lenny asked.

"I hope so, but it hasn't ended yet. You are still writing it, silly!" Child responded, laughing.

Lenny kissed the top of Child's head, as she had often kissed Elizabeth's. When she did so, she smelled baby powder and thought of Color, her unicorn.

"You smell like Color," she whispered looking down on her own innocence.

"In the kingdom of heaven, all things are new," Child said with a giggle.

"I too feel renewed," Lenny said, hugging Child close to her chest.

Without saying a word, Child stood up. Tiptoeing over to the tapestry, she touched it, and then she walked back to Lenny, carrying a book with a black cover and gold lettering.

The book's binding was stitched together with long, curly, rainbow-colored ribbons. Child sat down and began twisting one of the ribbons around and around her right pointer finger. Sitting beside her, Lenny noticed an angel on the cover of the book. The drawings reminded her of Elizabeth's artwork. Lenny sat for what seemed a long time, waiting for Child to open the book.

"When I was as young as you," Lenny whispered to Child, "I twirled my hair around my index finger, just as you are twirling that ribbon."

"I know," Child said, smiling. "I was waiting for that memory. Now we can begin."

CHILD'S STORY

The human mind is not capable of grasping the Universe. We are like a little child entering a huge library. The walls are covered to the ceilings with books in many different tongues. The child knows that someone must have written these books. It does not know who or how. It does not understand the languages in which they are written. But the child notes a definite plan in the arrangement of the books... a mysterious order which it does not comprehend, but only dimly suspects.

—Albert Einstein

FIRST BEGINNINGS

Heavenly lights twinkle bright as I awaken.
How glad I am to see White Angel's smiling face.
"Smile, smile, smile!" her ivory voice exclaims.
"Today is your day to begin a new life.
"You are going on a journey, but will leave my arms not."
I take a fresh new breath of joyful air.
"You must remember this," she warns.
"Remember?" I ask, slowly opening from sleepy imaginings.
"Shhhhhhh," she whispers. Her smile warms me.
I reach up for her beautiful white hand.
"I shall go where you lead me."
"No," she whispers into my curly blonde hair.
"I shall go where *you* lead *me*."
Light and love swirl around us.
I see many faces, all friends with happy wishes.
I arrive in spring, amid roses and thorns.
Shooting Stars and Wild Columbine wave as I descend.
"What flower shall I be? I love them all!"
"You shall be a tree, dreaming of a starry blossom."
I feel wise and happy.
Soon, I will be born.
White Angel gives me a pearly white, salty tear.
"When you're frightened, stand inside its light.
"It grows big and round and ever brighter with each year."
I take it in my hand and place it in my heart.
My heart says, "This is First Mother's tear.
"It shall keep you safe from all your fears."

FORGETTING BEGINS

A black hole swallows me whole.
It squeezes me into a thousand pieces.
"Come back!" I scream.
They don't listen. I'm frightened.
Something's wrong. I need to fix it! But I don't know how.
For now, my eyes don't work.
All the smiling faces, all the shining lights—now gone!
I'm nothing more than a speck of stardust.
The spit of Great Father,
A grain of sand held in Great Mother's hand.
They help me grow. My day of birth arrives.
Something is wrong. My angel's gone!
"You've nothing to fear," she whispered in my ear.
"You are on a journey. Remember this."
I turned my head. I see a man. They call him doctor.
Doctor giggles, saying, "Looks like another baby girl."
"But I ordered a boy!" New Mother says, sighing.
I scream and kick in protest!
I search the room for White Angel.
I cry. "I'm the wrong baby!" I scream.
"New Mother ordered a boy baby!"
"Shhhhh," White Angel whispers. "You are on journey, remember?"
White Angel's face fades into a white ceiling.
I'm in New Mother's arms. She smiles at me.
"She is so beautiful! I think we'll keep her!"
She hugs me tightly. I want more hugs like that!

NEEDINESS GROWS

Mother and Daddy take me home.

It didn't look like home. But I am wise.

I remember. I am on a journey.

I felt wet, cold, hungry! I speak.

But no one listens to the words I think in my head.

I kick and cry. Then, I kick and reach and cry.

New Mother brings me warm milk, dry clothes, and hugs.

I am happy again. I must indeed be wise.

I play this game. I cry and someone picks me up.

Now I understand my angel's gift of the tear.

Tears bring good stuff.

I cry…and cry…and cry…and cry.

I get more milk and hugs.

I hear my mother's voice. She sounds unhappy.

"I'm not picking her up this time! She's spoiled already!

"It's your turn, Daddy!"

Daddy's tired. He's worked all day. "It's midnight!" he yells.

I don't get hugged. I cry myself to sleep.

I'll think of some new trick by morning!

Light! Glorious light. I see light. Is it White Angel?

No, I see it's just the sun. I'm still on my journey, far from home.

I hear Big Sister crying out to Mother and Daddy.

"Take her back to the hospital! She cries too much!" she protests.

I speak inside my head to White Angel. She just smiles back at me.

She hasn't spoken a word since my birth. I wonder why not?

Maybe because I am spoiled and loud, or even worse—a girl!

I cry and cry and cry.

GOODBYE FRIENDS, HELLO FEAR

When I am five, I have lots of friends.
Mother and I like to go shopping.
I see friendly faces as we walk. I wave hellos at them.
Some are short and some are tall.
Some are wrinkled and old. Some are younger than five.
My friends are everywhere!
Mother smiles down at me and shakes her warning finger.
"Strangers are not friends! Strangers hurt little children!"
"They do?" I say and drop my black toy pony.
Mother picks it up. "Next year, you'll go to school.
"Then you'll make friends your age, like Sissy.
"Until then, stay close to me and far away from strangers!"
I hold her hand through housewares.
She lets go to feel a soft blanket.
I see toys and skip down toward aisle number nine.
I see monkeys in pink dresses and bears in pajamas.
But no Mother! "I've lost Mother!" I scream.
A tall gray-haired stranger in brown shoes appears.
She's wearing a strange badge on her collar.
"What's your mother's name, little girl?" she asks.
"Mother! Just Mother!" I cry.
Fear gallops with me back to housewares.
Mother, still lost in linens, grabs my trembling hand.
Her hand makes me feel safe. Fear gallops away.
A scary gray-haired stranger smiles and waves at me.
I hide my head in the folds of Mother's cotton skirt.

SIBLING RIVALRY

I am seven. I love school.
I have a best friend named Kathrin. She is an only child.
I like her long, raven black hair and freckled nose.
She has lots of paper dolls and pretty dresses.
Easter's coming soon. Mother gets busy sewing.
She makes Sissy and me matching dresses.
They are yellow with purple ribbons that tie in a bow.
The Easter Bunny brings painted eggs, yellow chicks, and chocolate...
And a baby brother!
He's red with a lumpy head. He cries and cries.
He gets lots of hugs. Sister says she likes him more than me.
I hit her. She tells me I look like my new stuffed monkey.
I yell dislikes for both of them all over the living room.
"I hate you and our matching yellow dresses!
"And I hate Baby Brother for stealing my attention!"
A strong arm swats me on the bottom.
"You love everybody!" Mother scolds pointing her warning finger.
"I don't!" I scream. I'm sent to bed without my supper.
I'm angry, full of sin and hate. It feels like it's growing.
I swallow hard. It goes away for now.
As Baby Brother steals my needed hugs, I peep out a window.
I see a star to wish upon.
My wish tonight is to be an only child like my friend,
The one with long raven hair, and freckles on her nose,
And fancy paper dolls and pretty dresses."
Sister orders me to breakfast in the morning. I try to swallow my anger.
It feels lumpy in my throat. I squish my eyes and look mean.
She sticks out her tongue at me and kisses Baby Brother.
I'm mad, I'm spoiled, and no one is listening to me.

DIVORCE, A CHILD'S VIEW

I am ten. I love to ride my bike and feel the wind.
It kisses my face and gently strokes my hair.
The temperatures outside are hot, as well as those as in my home.
During the day, I pick daisies and make long chains.
I wear them on my neck and atop my head.
Green meadow grass tickles my back as I search each cloud.
I see elephants and rabbits but none no smiling angels with knowing eyes.
Daddy packed a suitcase on his way to work.
He's not going on a trip. My parents are getting divorced.
We had Cream of Wheat, burnt toast, and yells for breakfast.
If I saw my angel's face beyond a cloud, she'd tell me why.
For now, I'm not allowed to ask.
I ride my bike, as salty tears fall from my eyes.
The hot and heavy wind burns my face.
I raise my fist. I yell at the wind.
My daisy chain tumbles slowly to the ground.
"I hate daisy chains!" I scream. "They never stay together!"
I ride faster and faster. But I can't outrun my thoughts.
Soon more tears catch up with me.
"What will we do without two hands to hold?" I ask of no one.
No one hears me.
I am frightened, and I feel very much alone.

BODY BEAUTIFUL

I'm thirteen years old today. It's my birthday.
I paint flowers on my ceiling. I put my baby doll Alice into a box.
I have a slumber party. Four girls and I light bananas like cigars.
They won't stay lit!
I paint my light bulbs blue to match our moods.
The paint smokes up my bedroom. It smells terrible!
Mother's screams fill up the rest of the house.
I pray my feet will stop growing. I've outgrown my training bra.
It didn't train me well. I pray the boys will stop looking at my chest.
I long to be thin like Twiggy. She's my idol!
I get my hair cut short to look like her.
But then I look like a boy. It made my ears and nose grow too large.
I tell my friends I'm saving money for a nose job.
They giggle and we whisper for hours about boys.
Next morning, my friends look pretty as they wave goodbye.
I go to my room, stare at the mirror…and cry.
I pull my hair to make it grow fast. It gives me a headache!
"Pretty is as pretty does," Granny scolds with her finger.
"Soon your hair will grow, and your nose will stop."
I don't believe her. She tells me to stop being vain.
"I'm ugly!" I scream. "Can't you see I'm a mess?"
I stare at flowers on my ceiling and ponder wonder-whys with my friends.
Now, I'll never be able to marry a Beatle.
Where is my guardian angel when I needed her most?
Is she white and fluffy like a dove in the park?
Or does she wear paisley bellbottoms and daisies in her hair?
Couldn't she, at least, change my stinky blue feelings?

FIRST LOVE

I am fifteen and happy! I've fallen in love.
He is handsome and wise. He loves my crooked tooth.
He laughs at everything I say.
And he thinks I'm smarter than I think I am.
I mask my fear that he'll find out I'm not as he thinks I am.
His kiss is sloppy, but French. I'd been anxious for that!
It makes me feel like a woman. All grown up and tasted.
He names a song our song.
It is full of shadows, smiles, and the light at dawn.
I play it over and over until the record skips a lot of beats.
He graduates the summer I turn sixteen.
At college, he finds prettier smiles to light his dawn.
I know my heart will never mend again.
I vow I'll never love another quite the same.
I'd dreamed of white dresses and wedding bells.
He'd wanted lots of smiles and honeymoons.
But I'm not cool! And I have braces on my teeth.
I smash our record upon the floor.
I hate boys! If only my parents weren't Baptists,
I'd join a Catholic convent and become a nun!

YOUNG MATRIMONY

I am eighteen. My heart's no longer wide open.
But it's slowly mended. I have a gang of girlfriends.
We're all going off in new directions. I get a summer job.
My braces are off now.
And I've slowly grown into my nose. Or maybe it's grown into me.
My boss thinks I'm cute and funny. He asks me out on a secret date.
No one's to know, it's not allowed at the Air Force BX.
He looks like Roy Rodgers. He's handsome and wise.
He can read a book, then recite it backwards.
So he says. I don't believe him.
On our first date, he catches a wild bird with his bare hands.
I'm so impressed! We kiss and hold hands.
In our secret moments, we share our hopes and dreams.
They don't exactly match, but they're close enough for me.
Before long, we have our special song. It isn't romantic, but it fits.
He tells me he'll soon be going places in life. Would I join him?
I hurry home and plan my dream wedding.
Everyone in my family is either shocked or disappointed.
"No art career?" they ask me.
I tell them he's leaving. I don't want to be left behind.
On our honeymoon, he tells me I am beautiful in the mornings.
I tell him he is silly. We save pennies in a jar for special things.
When it is full, we feel as rich as kings.
Children in our neighborhood sing songs about our love.
First love, then marriage. Oh no! Too soon! A baby carriage!
Time has woven a new spell over my heart,
And it grows three sizes overnight!

DIVORCE - A WOMAN'S VIEW

For three years, my husband's work takes us many places.
Soon a baby girl joins our toddler son.
I promise my babies no daisy-chain marriage for their parents.
But I am wrong. A seven-year itch does us in.
We go to bed mad, pretending we aren't.
Our living room is full of icy stares and unkind words.
When he works past midnight, I stare at the stars.
I ask them questions, whys of every kind.
I stare at our penny jar. It is full, but we are empty.
I go shopping. I fill up shopping bags with everything but love.
I wear pretty clothes. But I no longer feel beautiful in the morning.
And so it happens, exactly as I'd long ago feared.
Our daisy-chain marriage falls apart at my feet.
We cry good-bye. I pack up our two children.
We fight our way through our penny jar.
I walk into my beautiful new home, but I see only broken promises.
They stare back at me in the watery eyes of my children.
If God is love, what cut of cloth am I?
I pray to be a tiny bird, as on my long-ago first date.
I pray for His hands to hold me,
A fallen sparrow, too sad to fly.
And way too far from home.

SINGLE PARENTHOOD

I walk lonely in the shadows of my life.
By day, by night, my spirit makes feeble attempts to conceal my guilt.
Like shattered crystal, my broken heart feels useless.
Each morning, I throw back the covers, sling on clothes.
I make the breakfast, dress my kids, and pray.
At night I shiver and dream terrible things—
Like being naked at church! And going to work without my shoes!
I listen to country music on the radio.
Seems everybody knows my life story.
I join a church and pray for a new hand to hold.
I search the pews for him. But he is not found.
All my friends seem happy and married.
I stop going out. A year flies past.
And once again, I find delight in being single.
My pen and brush catch my fancies and my dreams.
I am almost happy when fate comes knocking at my door.
It is a man needing a woman. I am a woman needing a man.
What a mess we are, but we fall in love.
On our second date, we go to church.
That's a good sign, isn't it?
By our third date, my friends say he is not for me.
"Fools rush in where angels fear to tread," they warn.
I don't listen. My new love wants to marry right away.
I cry when I say "yes."
I think this must be a good sign!

SECOND MARRIAGE

We marry among azalea bushes.
A weeping willow blows wildly in the wind.
It begs me listen to my heart. But it isn't open, so I cannot hear it.
It rains on our heads before the ceremony is over.
Isn't this a good sign? Not a single wild bird takes wing.
Can my new husband catch birds with his bare hands?
I never believe he can. He never believes I love him.
From our first steps, we try hard to walk in love.
But never once do we have a special song or a special memory.
New signs begin to surface. I see my friends as wise.
I am the fool. I desired not to be alone at such a heavy price.
For now, each day, I grow more lonely as his wife.
This gradual separation fills our house with chaos.
I'd rushed headlong down a path no angel would have followed.
My children don't like their new dad.
Four cannot pretend to be a family when they're not.
I step on his pride as I ask him to leave.
He steps on my heart as he walks out the door.
My heart shatters upon my kitchen floor.
And I leave it there in pieces.

WOMB OF DREAMTIME

I dream of realms where angels fly.

And visit loved ones long after our last goodbye.

Words captured in my journal haunt me like dark truth unopened.

I hold a serpent in my hand and fear I'll die of fright.

I fall into deep darkness with images that haunt me ever after.

My thoughts keep scattering like bubbles in my sink.

They're hard to hold, but they are my only trophy.

My fear wears a mask, as does my pain inside my brain.

What seeds have my thoughts planted today?

Have they planted a future like the glitter atop my candy cane apron?

I scour my dishes and my thoughts for hopeful possibilities.

Can a Desert Rose grow in such poor soil?

The sands beneath my roots are full of tears and limitations.

As I watch dirty water drain, I journey back from my looking-within place.

Oh, how cruel and careless I have been to me.

The house grows long, dark shadows as does my heart and mind..

I carry armloads of presents down the hall.

Are there unseen gifts of dancing stillness awaiting me?

Can a Desert Rose grow in such poor soil?

GUILTY & SINGLE AGAIN

I am thirty-something, strangled by unkind beliefs of who I am.

The kids are fed, all warm in bed.

My thoughts fall into my television set and I imagine I'm Scrooge wearing red snake skin shoes.

My own greed feels like love withheld from self and others.

Ghosts of the past tumble 'round in my head.

I see in my hand a paper rose.

It's thin and tears easy like my heart.

Can I ever love again?

Will I ever be happy?

A dark hole in my heart remains,

Where a child's wish once long ago called…home.

A Christmas tree, a crown of stars,

I wish upon a fractured angel to become a blossom of delight in someone's eyes, including mine.

I stop looking out and drift within, as my angel whispers in my ear, "Arise!"

A CHILD'S WISDOM

A child, as I have said, possesses a sense of completeness, but only before the initial emergence of his ego-consciousness. In the case of an adult, a sense of completeness is achieved through a union of the consciousness with the unconscious contents of the mind.

—Joseph L. Henderson

Child carefully closed the book and looked up. Lenny was aware Child had finished, but she couldn't quite speak. She felt as if she were drifting up and away from where she had moments ago been sitting, absorbing a light-hearted version of her life. Then she felt a small hand patting her arm, and she was back with Child.

Lenny went to put her hand on Child's, where it was patting her arm, and she was quite surprised to see their clothing had been transformed. She and Child were both wearing beautiful gowns that matched the description of how the Nursery Magic Fairy from *The Velveteen Rabbit* was dressed. The fabric appeared to be made of white cotton candy covered in pearl-like dewdrops.

"Oh, how beautiful!" Lenny exclaimed in delight. "I only wish Elizabeth could see me now."

"She's dreaming of her own Nursery Magic Fairy," Child said with a smile.

"Dear Child, my tapestry and your storybook tale of my life have made me see the power of my words," Lenny said. "I understand now how the words I took to heart as truth created my life. I cannot tell you how often I wanted to blame certain happenings on God—too many times to count! I admit I'm a little ashamed of trying to cast the blame for my unhappiness, when I alone am the only person to blame.

"When more sad lines to our story, spin threads inside your head, remember me," Child said. "I am your joy."

"Yes, you are," Lenny said. "Now I know *exactly* how the tattered bunny felt when he became real. All he wanted to do was play. That's how light my heart now feels."

"Do you love who you are, Lenny?" Child asked.

"I really *do* love me," Lenny answered, beaming. " But I can see now that the love I gave myself and everybody else was the love of a paper rose. It may have looked pretty, but it was only an imitation of the real thing—just like Marie Osmond's song! But the love of a Desert Rose...now *that* isn't like paper that can dissolve in the rain, is it? The love of a Desert Rose is unconditional. And it's solid, solid as a rock!"

"A Desert Rose is also a rose without thorns," Child pointed out, smiling brightly.

"Oh, my goodness," Lenny said with a sigh. "You're right! I see that now, too. I see so clearly how this name represents so many ways in which to grow my soul power.

"Yes!" Child said, delighted. "And remember, the symbol of the Desert Rose is both who you are *and* who you can become. Your garden has been tilled. Creator has planted your seed. And now, you must become the guardian of unwanted weeds. It is now your job, dear Lenny, to water and nurture new ideas, new seed thoughts that will make you happy. When you call yourself unhappy, you will grow unhappy."

"Child," Lenny whispered, barely able to speak. "I feel released as if I have unwittingly held myself captive in an unseen prison. The bars on my prison were like the black outlines I used to draw around my colors, and like the black threads in my tapestry. But now, I see I'm responsible for both the webs of illusion I spin *and* the glorious light and love I bring into all of my relationships.

Child nodded, her eyes filling with what appeared to be watery tears. But they did not roll down her cheeks. They remained like diamonds strung across her blue-green eyes—innocent eyes.

"How is my dear Desert Rose?" Granny whispered in Lenny's left ear.

"Granny!" Lenny cried out in surprise, turning around and falling into her warm embrace in a single fluid motion. Lenny curled her face against her grandmother's neck. She felt as if their hearts had become one. After a long while, Lenny spoke.

"I've missed you so much!" Lenny said. "I'm sorry for all the rebellious things I did as a teen. And I'm sorry I talked back and slammed doors when you made me mind rules I hated."

"There's nothing I can think of that needs an apology, Lenny," Granny said in a comforting tone. "The body you chose and the personality you developed over time is exactly what your Self needed. Never doubt this! You are *far* more than your thoughts. You are *beyond* thought, and this is something you must never forget."

"Granny, I know this time, I'm dreaming. The first time I saw you in my dream-walking, I felt confused for days. Can you help me remember all the magic I have witnessed tonight when I awake?"

"It is the same as telling yourself you will remember your dreams when you wake up. Believe you will remember, Lenny, and you will."

"I *will* remember, then, Granny. *I will!*" Lenny declared without a trace of doubt.

"Remember when you first read the quote by Kahlil Gibran on your dishtowel calendar? You sat and wept because you knew your dreams outshined your deeds."

"I do remember it, but I had to throw the dishtowel away recently. It was faded and covered in mildew."

"Yes, I remember trying to kick it without success," Granny said, laughing. "Do you remember Gibran's words written at the top of the towel?"

"Of course," Lenny said. "I know the quote by heart: *I would not measure thee by thy deeds but by thy vastest dreams.*"

"In all of heaven, not a soul is measured by deed alone," Granny said, patting Lenny on the back.

"Child's story has shown this much tonight," Lenny said. "Her story put me in touch with the shadow side of my own confusion and misperceptions. Granny, I had no idea how lost I had become in my head."

"Now that you've seen who you really are with clear eyes, you will never forget. But the shifting sands of time may someday catch you unaware and you will feel lost and alone again. Walking in the flesh, there are many barriers filled with silent longings to embrace and heal. If you stay centered and continue to grow in spiritual power, you can stand strong. Remember the spiritual warrior's quest is often a journey of struggling to become what he already is. And if you truly know this in your heart and mind, you will not struggle. You'll just let it be."

"I knew you would say that!" Lenny laughed. . "Thank you for my Christmas present, Granny. My candy-cane gift card with your message will always remind me of who I am, and it will encourage me to grow every time I read it."

Suddenly, the tapestry and the black book with the gold lettering vanished. Lenny's inner peace and joy were so great it felt as if her body could not contain them. A sudden powerful life force exploded throughout her body with a rush of tingling sensations. All three of them—Lenny, Child, and Granny—shot upward into an inviting black velvet sky. Lenny felt like a bullet of light, headed straight for a distant ball of light— the only star in heaven. She could not help but wonder where all the other stars had gone. Perhaps, she thought, as the sensation of upward movement grew more intense, she was headed straight into the sun!

As soon as this thought crossed her mind, she feared bodily harm. And as soon as fear hit her heart, Lenny and her companions came to an abrupt stop. Then, in the time it took Lenny to catch her breath, the sun she had been heading for came into sharp focus.

Instead of a mad swirl of flaming gasses, this sun looked like a sparkling crystal planet, webbed with a million strands of vibrating lights. At the core of each cluster of light strands was a round, star-like circle. Lenny laughed; thinking how it looked like the star-circles were all holding hands with lightning-bolt arms and legs. It was brilliantly beautiful, vibrant and alive. All traces of fear and panic that gripped her heart moments ago vanished completely, as wonder and awe took their place.

"I see, Granny! I see my light!" she exclaimed, her arm trembling as she pointed to a Light she knew herself to be. It was formless, identical to all the other lights, but Lenny knew this one star belonged only to her. Each star embodied the joy of being and loving. All were vibrations of pure understanding, linked one to each other. There were no barriers, only blazing embraces. Was she witnessing each and every spirit's highest potential in the Mind of God? She didn't know. But it didn't matter. This image of Oneness filled her with bliss. Once again, as if wrapped inside the protective, nurturing arms of an unseen Mother, Lenny knew there was nothing to fear in the energy of this beautiful black velvet space in which her spirit body traveled.

"I understand! I understand *everything*! *I understand EVERYTHING!*" Lenny cried out over and over with such intense joy it seemed to her she would burst.

24
NEAR AND FAR

When to the new eyes of thee
All things by immortal power,
Near or far,
Hiddenly
To each other linked are,
That thou canst not stir a flower
Without troubling of a star.

—Francis Thompson

Granny kissed Lenny on her cheek. Only it wasn't Granny—it was Lassie. Lenny must have been making strange sounds while she was dreaming that Lassie didn't understand. Although, Lenny had just a moment ago been trying to say she understood everything, she seemed to know less in this one minute than she'd ever known in her entire life. All she knew for sure was that she was lying in her bed, remembering vivid details of the most lucid dream she had ever had.

In the living room, the grandfather clock chimed six times. This seemed utterly impossible. Lenny had been asleep for less than an hour since she had left the living room couch and fallen back to sleep in her bed. But her dream seemed to last so much longer than an hour. *Did anything in life make sense?* Lenny wondered. But she no longer cared. She was just going to let it be.

A new freedom flooded her from head to toe. She'd once thought herself to be broken beyond compare. But just like the white angel tree-topper, this had not made her unlovable. In her mind, she had been given a second chance at life. She felt as new as a newborn babe. And if this is how living in center felt, she did *not* want to leave. An unchangeable point of Love and Light were now fixed in her mind and heart. All barriers that kept her from loving others as herself had melted away.

Lassie barked as she tumbled out of Lenny's bed. She ran down the hall toward the front door, turning once to see if Lenny was following her.

"Just a minute, girl," Lenny whispered. "First, let's honor Christmas in our hearts," she added, remembering Ebenezer Scrooge's comment when he, like Lenny, had awakened on Christmas morning from a life-changing dream. Lenny didn't have the money to buy anyone a prize turkey, as Scrooge had, but she had plenty of other goodies in her kitchen. As she walked down the hallway, Lassie followed. She opened her Santa Claus cookie jar and pulled out a handful of sprinkle-topped sugar cookies. She picked out the very best ones and placed them in an oversized bell jar. Then she found a red bow on the floor in the living room and taped it to the jar's lid.

"Perfect!" she exclaimed. She bent down and patted Lassie on top of the head. "Lassie," she whispered, "I'll bet Ms. Tallulah won't even notice the crispy brown edges."

Then, not wanting to wake her children, she tiptoed down the hall to her bedroom. She dug deep in her shoebox and pulled out the last candy cane gift tag and taped it to the side of the jar. Then she wrote "Love, Santa," on the tag. Lassie whined, sensing Lenny was delaying her urgent need to go outside.

"Shhhh," Lenny whispered. "We have a little work to do before the children wake up. Coffee first, then *out*."

"Out" was Lassie's favorite word, and the dog responded by running excitedly to stand in front of the living room door.

Lenny's avocado green coffee pot plopped and gurgled as she and Lassie prepared to make their exit. A new fluffy white terry robe lay on the floor near its box. She picked it up and put it on, thinking it was the softest robe she had ever felt. The robe had been a surprise gift from Lenny's mother, who usually only gave money. Lenny sniffed a sleeve and discovered the blanket-soft terrycloth smelled vaguely like baby powder. Then she remembered a dream within a dream.

"Hi, Color," she whispered, petting the robe's sleeve. She'd never wear it again without thinking of her beautiful unicorn.

Lenny slipped on a matching pair of fluffy slippers and headed out the door. A cold breeze blew her hair as she stepped onto her concrete front porch, which was covered in a blanket of fresh snow. It looked pristine and divine, and Lenny marveled at the sight. Her children were going to be overjoyed when they awoke.

With the cookie jar held tightly in her hands, Lenny leapt into the snow, toward her neighbor's house. She took long leaping jumps into the air trying to keep her slippers as dry as possible. As she passed Ms. Tallulah's dead azalea bush, she brushed the snow off its bare limbs.

"Now *grow!*" she whispered to the bush. "If I can do it, so can you. I know you feel dead. I, too, have felt this way. But please try to live! I've been told plants love to be talked to. If that's true, please don't let me down. Ms. Tallulah loves you—of this I am sure."

The tiny branch she held gently in her bare hands seemed to be holding on to a couple of dead leaves. One fell off as Lenny released the branch. She watched it drift downward, making a tiny dent in the snow.

Well, you have to let go of some things in order to grow, she thought as she bent down low to the ground and whispered, "While I'm thinking about it, I love you, too."

Lenny laughed at her own foolishness with each step she took toward Ms. Tallulah's front door. A light was on in her neighbor's kitchen, and Lenny figured Ms. Tallulah had probably been up for hours. She carefully placed the cookie jar on the porch next to the door, pressed the doorbell, and ran back down the hill. Her new slippers were starting to feel soggy. Lassie barked and tried to nip Lenny's feet as she often did to the children when they were running around the yard.

"Shhh," Lenny whispered. "You'll ruin our surprise."

As she hurried behind the house, she felt the urge to sing.

"O little town of Bethlehem, how still I see thee lie," she began to croon. "Above thy deep and dreamless sleep, my silent star does shine!" Lenny loved making up her own words to familiar songs, and this time her lyrics expressed a new sense of oneness with the world.

She looked up at a fading dark sky and thought about the sky she had just witnessed in her dream. Was her crystal planet located above her head or within her own inner universe? It didn't really seem to matter. She knew what she had seen and it had changed her. That was enough.

She didn't see Ms. Tallulah, but she heard her open her front door and then close it again. She hurried toward her door and tried to blink falling snowflakes off of her lashes as she walked. She opened her mouth wide to try to catch some, imagining she looked just like her red and yellow killer snake. Snow laced her face with feathery kisses, but Lenny tasted nothing.

Feeling properly frosted, she hurried back into her warm house. Her new slippers looked as if they'd gone for a morning swim. She took them off and warmed her reddened feet on the floor heater. When she felt sufficiently thawed out, she decided she simply couldn't feel this happy without someone to share it with. She hurried down the hallway with Lassie fast on her heels. She stopped long enough to smile at the family portraits hanging on the wall and to kiss the baby portraits of her children. Being a single mother was one of the most challenging roles of her life, but right now, she wouldn't have her life any other way.

She stopped right before reaching Elizabeth's and Mack's bedrooms. Then she yelled as loud as she could, "SNOW!"

She ran into Elizabeth's room and without restraint jumped atop her daughter's small bed, pulling off her covers and tickling her awake.

"Merry Christmas, sleepy head!" she whispered. Elizabeth woke up in giggles.

"Did Santa come?" she asked eagerly, squirming loose of her mother's hugs and kisses.

"Yes! And there's a ton of snow outside! Let's go tell your brother."

"Mom," Mack said in a sleepy voice from the open doorway. "I'm awake! Your screaming scared me half to death. Did it really snow?"

"Look out your window," Lenny said as she and Elizabeth ran into his room.

He did. The ear-to-ear smile that broke out across his little-boy face warmed Lenny's heart all the way through. Lenny gathered both her children into her arms, and all three stuck their faces to the frosty windowpane. It was a deep snow, deeper than Lenny had seen for years. She felt just as much a child as Mack and Elizabeth.

"Let's go see what Santa brought!" Lenny exclaimed.

"Okay," Mack said in an innocent tone of voice that she hadn't heard him use in years. "Come on, Elizabeth, I'll race you!"

They all three hit the narrow doorway at the same time. They shouldered into the family photographs hung on the wall, and a few of them turned sideways. But none fell.

Soon the living room became a mountain of opened boxes and shredded wrapping paper. Mack loved his baseball and glove. He quickly discarded a blue sweater, probably hoping he wouldn't have to wear it anytime soon. Lenny let him ride his skateboard across the kitchen floor. It rattled the dishes in the cabinets, but as with the portraits in the hallway, nothing broke.

She wasn't broken. She was alive and growing. She'd just returned from the most incredible soul journey of her life. She was filled with understanding of the power of love. She silently thanked God, her inner teachers, her Granny, and all the angels and stars that watched over her. She'd found her Center, and forever changed by the extraordinary energy of Divine Oneness.

Sitting in her kitchen, Lenny poured coffee into a cup covered with red and pink roses. She watched as Elizabeth's new dolls toured the house in a pink convertible. Elizabeth parked the car only long enough for a bowl of Cheerios and a piece of buttered toast Lenny didn't eat.

Elizabeth wanted to take Steve, her mouse, for a ride in her doll car. Much to her surprise, Lenny agreed. Steve curled up in Barbie's lap and seemed to like his new wheels. He didn't even seem to mind Elizabeth pushing him back and forth. Perhaps he was just petrified with fear, Lenny thought, or maybe Elizabeth played with him like this when Lenny wasn't around. Lenny couldn't help but laugh at how silly he looked, as she swung her legs high off the floor and into an empty chair just in case Steve made a dash out of the car.

Then suddenly, as if he had read her mind, the mouse jumped out of the car. Lenny screamed as he scampered toward her. She jumped atop the kitchen table, almost spilling her coffee. The open box of cereal scattered all over, and Lassie ran over and started licking it off the floor. Without needing to be told, Elizabeth giggled as she scooped Steve up, took him down the hallway to her room, and put him back in his screen-covered tank.

Breathing deeply to calm herself, Lenny climbed down off the table and poured another cup of coffee. She then waded into the living room, stepping on empty boxes and shredded papers as she went. As she sat down on the couch, the phone rang. Lenny picked it up on the second ring.

"It's snowing!" Dawn said, chuckling. "And my Joseph has a Jeep! Do you and the children want to take a ride to the mountains later on today?"

"Yes, absolutely!" Lenny answered. "I don't even have to ask the kids. What time will you be over?"

"Let's try for sometime after lunch. I'll bring some baked goodies and hot apple cider."

"I love you," Lenny whispered to her friend and began to cry.

"What's wrong, girlfriend?" Dawn asked, hearing Lenny sniffle.

"I love you," Lenny said, choking on her words. "I just love you. Really, that's all it is."

"Well… okay. That's good," Dawn replied. "Just keep it up! And Lenny, I love you too! See you soon."

"Okay," Lenny said, wiping tears off her cheeks.

"Mom, why are you sad?" Elizabeth asked as she walked into the room.

"These are happy tears," Lenny answered. She stood up and took hold of Elizabeth's hands. She danced her around the room and kicked at the boxes and papers. Elizabeth let go of Lenny's hands, bent over, and grabbed a handful of ribbons and shredded paper. They both began slinging them into the air.

"Now you've *both* gone crazy!" Mack exclaimed, walking into the living room. He jumped up and quickly closed the drapes. Then he danced along with them.

"We're not crazy, Mack," Lenny said, kicking like Mack's karate dance stomps. "This is how happy people act."

"I like you better this way, Mom," Elizabeth said, laughing and tossing her doll into the air. "I'm glad you're not in a bad mood."

"So am I, Elizabeth. So am I," Lenny said, feeling almost breathless. Mack karate chopped the doll and it flopped against the wall. Elizabeth screamed in horror. Her high-fashion doll landed quite unfashionably in the Christmas tree upside down. Elizabeth quickly rescued her, and they all romped merrily through the house, wearing box hats and tying ribbons around their heads and necks.

When they reached utter exhaustion, they all collapsed upon the floor. Lenny told them about Dawn's invitation, and Mack and Elizabeth squealed with delight.

"Before we go, we have to build a fort for a snowball fight," Mack said, pulling back the drapes to see if it was still snowing. It was.

"No, I want to build a snowman!" Elizabeth said.

"There's tons of snow, so we can build them both," Lenny said with a laugh. "So go get your clothes on, you two, and let's get to rolling snow balls."

"This was fun, Mom," Elizabeth said, after finally catching her breath.

Mack stretched his arms back and put his hands behind his head. He was lying beside his mother on the floor. He looked deep into his mother's eyes.

"Mom," he said in his serious voice. "I'm glad you're crazy. I think it's kind of cool having a crazy artist for a mom."

"Then I'm glad I'm crazy," Lenny said, smiling back at him. "I really *must* be crazy because before you guys got up, I took Ms. Tallulah a surprise Christmas present. I put a jar of sugar cookies on her porch with a tag that said they were from Santa."

"Do you think Santa forgot to give her a present?" Elizabeth asked.

"Well, he probably marked her name on the naughty list," Mack said, laughing.

"Giving Ms. Tallulah something for Christmas made me happy," Lenny said. "I hope she likes the thought behind my gift. I don't think she will ever allow me the opportunity to get to know her better. But that's okay, too. She doesn't have to match my idea of what a good neighbor should be. Today it felt more important for me to try to be a good neighbor to her. And I must have succeeded because I feel very good about myself right now."

"What brought all this generosity on, Mom?" Mack asked with a puzzled look on his face.

"I had a dream!" Lenny exclaimed. "I can't even begin to explain it. I don't even understand it. All I know is that it changed me. It helped me feel loving, more connected to the best in me and the best in other people. Now, let's get dressed so we can make your fort and Elizabeth's snowman before Dawn gets here!"

25

I HAD A DREAM

I... had an experience.... I can't prove it, I can't even explain it, but everything that I know as a human being, everything that I am tells me that it was real. I was given something wonderful, something that changed me forever.... A vision of the universe, that tells us, undeniably, how tiny, and insignificant and how... rare, and precious we all are! A vision that tells us that we belong to something that is greater than ourselves, that we are not, that none of us are alone.

—the character of Dr. Eleanor Arroway in the movie *Contact*

The grandfather clock was chiming nine, and the sky was still salting the earth as Lenny and her children stepped into their front yard. The flakes were large, almost as if they'd married other flakes on their way down from the sky before they landed on hats and overcoats. Within minutes, Lenny, Mack, and Elizabeth all looked as if they were coated in sugary white frosting.

Elizabeth's new red and yellow stocking cap hung so low Lassie tried to bite the tassel off the tip as Elizabeth ran. The color of the stripes reminded Lenny of her anger snake. It seemed her outside world often mirrored her inside world. And this was good because it reminded her of the importance of mindful presence.

After the bottom ball of a snowman was finished, Lenny sat on the ground and looked up. It had stopped snowing, and the morning was whisper quiet. Lenny was watching Mack stack up a mountain of small snowballs for his glorious war game when another movement caught her eye. It was Ms. Tallulah's curtains being pushed aside. Lenny saw her neighbor's head pressed against her windowpane. Lenny waved. The curtain closed.

She helped Elizabeth make a smaller ball for the snowman's middle section. They lifted it into place and then patted it with more snow to make it stick. Mack announced he already had a great snowman head. He walked over and stuck one of his little snowballs on top of their creation.

"No!" Elizabeth screamed. "That head is too small!"

"No, it isn't, Elizabeth," Mack answered. "He's a *pinhead* snowman!"

The siblings chased each other in circles, throwing snowballs and falling on the ground. As the children rolled in the snow, Lenny decided to give Ms. Tallulah one more call. She walked up the steep incline to her neighbor's house, noticing when she got to the door the jar of cookies was nowhere in sight. Lenny rang the doorbell.

"Who's there?" Ms. Tallulah demanded in a frightened voice.

"It's Lenny, your neighbor, Ms. Tallulah. I wondered if you might like to come out and play in the snow with my children and me. We're having so much fun!"

The door opened with a rattle. To Lenny, is sounded as if Ms. Tallulah had several security latches on her door. The older woman's dark hair was twisted up and held in place by crisscross bobby pins. She was wearing a dark purple chenille bathrobe that made her purplish roots look even brighter. Lenny tried not to stare at them.

"I know you're my Santa, Lenny," Ms. Tallulah said in a not-so-friendly tone of voice. "How could I not? You were dancing and singing about as if you'd lost your mind. *Well*, have you?"

"No!" Lenny responded with a laugh. "Well, actually, Ms. Tallulah, I'm sure I lost it years ago. But the best thing I've lost recently is my anger toward you. You see, I had this snake dream. And then I fell into a deep well. And…it's a little too complicated to explain, actually. My Granny, had she lived, might have been about your age. She always told me to stop spilling my guts to strangers. But you're not really a stranger."

"A *what* kind of dream?" Ms. Tallulah asked, looking more than a little startled.

"A snake dream, but that's not all. Just think of it as a breakthrough. Then, I had an even *more* amazing dream last night. You see, Ms. Tallulah, I dream wondrously. I really do. And I really feel we might someday become better neighbors. I'm going to do much better keeping Lassie out of your yard. And you were right—female dogs as beautiful as my Lassie are bound to attract a yard full of male dogs. You have the prettiest azalea bushes in the neighborhood, and it's such a shame your one bush died. Come spring, I will buy you a new bush. Just tell me the variety you would like, and I'll even come over and plant it for you. I promise!"

"That is very considerate, Lenny," Ms. Tallulah said, still sounding a bit formal, but not quite as unfriendly. "I accept your gift and your offer."

Lenny's neighbor moved away from the door and had almost closed it when Lenny screamed, "Wait!"

"Yes? What is it?" Ms Tallulah asked impatiently. "I can't stand here jabbing away all day with the door open. I've no desire to heat up the whole neighborhood."

"Will you come out and play?" Lenny asked with a smile. "You didn't answer my question."

"Come out and *play*? Lenny, don't be ridiculous! I'm an old woman!"

"Does one ever get too old to play?" Lenny asked, using her most serious tone of voice. "I don't think so! And besides, how long has it been since you saw snow on Christmas Day in East Tennessee?"

"Well, that's true, and I can't say I recall when that might have been. But it's freezing outside, and besides, you are acting mighty queer. I hope you're not some kind of druggy or something like that. And why did you bring me a gift? We hardly know each other. We don't even *like* each other for that matter."

"Because of late, I have been thinking a lot of mean thoughts about you. And I fear you have similar thoughts about me. I know you hate dogs and my children annoy you when they run and yell outside your windows. But you were once a child, Ms. Tallulah, and this is why I want you to come and play. The child in you wants to play with my child. I know she does."

"*Nonsense*, Lenny! I grew up with dogs," she huffed. "I don't hate dogs. I simply hate *crowds* and I don't like endless chitchat, either. If you call this mean, then I *am* mean."

"No, I don't call that mean," Lenny said. "I call what we are doing right now getting to know each other better."

"Well, have your play Lenny. I wish to decline and that's that."

"Yes ma'am," Lenny said, taking off her glove and extending her hand. "I'm sorry to have bothered you. I hope you have a very merry Christmas, Ms. Tallulah. Goodbye."

When Lenny held Ms. Tallulah's hand in hers, it felt as cold as ice. Perhaps it was the silliest thing to ask someone her age to come out and play in the snow. Had she asked her own Granny, she would probably have stayed inside, too. But then she would have baked a cake and simmered hot cocoa on the stove. This is what Lenny knew of childhood. Perhaps she couldn't gift her children with a home life complete with a father and a mother, but she could warm them with her love. This would have to be enough because it was all she had to give. As she ran down the hill toward Mack, she picked up a handful of snow and threw it at his back.

"Snowball fight!" he yelled with glee. "The enemy has attacked! And remember, Mom, no crying like a sissy if I hit you with a snowball."

Soft snow exploded across Lenny's face and down her neck. Soon balls were flying all over the yard and everyone's cheeks and noses turned bright red. Lenny's gloves were so crunchy with ice she could hardly form a round ball. They chased each other around the yard. A headless half-finished snowman served as their silent referee and marked a free zone. All three took turns resting there.

Lenny declared Mack the winner after Elizabeth said she didn't want to play anymore. Mack threw one last snowball at Elizabeth and she chased after him, throwing a few punches as she ran. Lassie didn't follow. She was running up the hill. Lenny looked up to see Ms. Tallulah walking toward them with something in her hands. Lenny couldn't tell what it was.

The old woman was bundled from head to toe. Her hat was bright green with long fur-covered earflaps. It looked like a man's cap and was certainly too large for her small head. Her pants looked like rubber waders a fisherman might wear. As Ms. Tallulah drew closer, Lenny saw what she was carrying. In each hand, she held branches from her dead azalea bush. *Oh, no!* Lenny worried. *Is she going to berate me for killing the bush again?* But as Ms. Tallulah approached, Lenny could see she looked more shy than angry.

"Does your snowman need arms?" Ms. Tallulah asked when she reached Lenny.

"Yes, I believe he does," Lenny said, choking back hot tears.

Mack's mouth dropped open as he looked over at his mother. She gave him a quick be-kind-to-our-neighbor look, and he nodded. He walked over to Ms. Tallulah and took the branches from her hands.

"Thanks, Ms. Tallulah. These will work just great!" he said. Then he walked over to where Lenny was standing by the snowman, and together they pushed them into place. Elizabeth finished rolling a proper head and set it on top. Then she took Ms. Tallulah's hand.

"Can you help me find some good eyeballs?" she asked, looking up hopefully at her neighbor's face.

"Well, I have a carrot in my pocket if you need a nose. Maybe we can find rocks in the street for the eyes and mouth. When I was your age, that's how my brother and I made snowmen."

"I know!" Mack exclaimed. "I'll go get my bag of marbles."

He was back in a flash, and Ms. Tallulah and Elizabeth searched the bag until they found two matching marbles. They were black with long white streaks. Once the eyes were attached, their snowman looked very distinguished.

"Well," Ms. Tallulah said, brushing snow off of her gloves. "This has been rather fun, but it's time for me to go home."

"Wait, Ms. Tallulah," Elizabeth begged. "Before you go, would you like to make snow angels with me?"

"*Me?* Well...." she said tentatively, looking over at Lenny. Then she surprised all three of them by saying, "Why not?"

Elizabeth was on the ground in seconds, swishing her arms and legs against the snow. Ms. Tallulah walked over, hesitated for a moment, and then lowered her body slowly to the ground. She stretched out with her back against a blanket of thick white snow. Lenny and Mack joined in, too.

All four of them lay silently fanning their legs and arms into the snow. The sun was shining as the cotton-ball snow clouds moved off toward the Smoky Mountains. Lassie nipped at their feet, fearing something was wrong with her family. Lenny had to sit up and clap her hands to make the dog stop nipping their snow-covered boots.

Lassie stopped nipping, but still feeling left out, she jumped up and stole one of the snowman's arms. She ran it back to Lenny as if they were playing a game of fetch. But no one could toss the branch for her to retrieve because they were all laughing too hard.

A bright blue jeep honked its horn as Joseph and Dawn pulled into Lenny's driveway. Dawn jumped out of the car wearing a heavy parka and a worried look upon her face.

"Come play!" Lenny yelled, waving the snowman's arm in the air.

Dawn looked at Ms. Tallulah and her mouth dropped open. At first, she'd thought they were wrestling. She knew Lenny had been having a bit of a war with her neighbor, and when she saw them all thrashing around on the ground, she had feared the worst. She'd told Joseph to honk his horn to break it up. Seeing the snow angels, Dawn threw back her head and laughed as only Dawn could laugh.

Lenny invited everyone, including Ms. Tallulah, in for hot cider and homemade cakes and pies. Ms. Tallulah accepted Lenny's offer. Lenny smiled and brushed away another tear as they entered the house together, and no one seemed to mind the messy floor. Mack and Elizabeth busied themselves cleaning up all the paper they had thrown about earlier while Lenny was in the kitchen preparing their snacks. When everyone was settled with something to eat and drink, Dawn grabbed hold of Lenny's arm.

"Excuse us," Dawn said to Joseph and Ms. Tallulah. "Lenny wanted my advice about a problem with her…drapes. She hates them. I promised to share some great ideas I have for them."

"Yes," Lenny lied. "I'm thinking about doing something completely different with them." Of course this was the first time she'd heard Dawn had such plans for her window treatments.

"Take your time," Joseph said. He and Mack were reading the instructions for a football game Dawn had given Mack. Ms. Tallulah didn't even look up as they exited the room. She seemed captivated by Elizabeth's chatter concerning her latest fashion dolls wearing designer jeans. Lassie was curled up beneath the Christmas tree, sound asleep.

Lenny and Dawn walked down the hall to Lenny's bedroom. "What is going on?" Dawn whispered once they got there. "I still can't believe my eyes! When I saw Ms. Tallulah laying in your front yard, I thought you had punched her lights out. *What gives?*"

"I know," Lenny whispered. "I can hardly explain it to myself. Last night, I had another dream, Dawn. This one was as wondrous as the other one was frightening. But even that one doesn't scare me anymore, not after the experience I had. I feel transformed by the truth of Love that I now see in all beings. I feel clean, free and, empty of what is not true within me. And it's carried over into how I feel about my neighbor, Ms. Tallulah."

"Wow," Dawn said, shaking her head. "Your whole face is lit up like a light. Happy looks very good on you," she giggled.

"Dawn, I've spent my entire life engrossed with form and outer influences. I've wasted half my life in a mental prison, obsessing over my history of failed relationships. Granny's message has shown me I could never be happy permanently living amid such destructive mind patterns. Granny was simply saying what Jesus said: *Be perfect, therefore, as your heavenly Father is perfect.* And perfect *is* my center, and your center, and Ms. Tallulah's center. And I cannot express how easy it is to love my neighbor from this new 'center' point of view."

"Oh my gosh, girlfriend," Dawn said, laughing. "I *love* it. I *love* to hear you talk like your old self again. And those tears rolling down your face are not sad tears. I know those all too well! I can't help but be reminded what you just said is the greatest of God's commandments. Loving yourself and all others with your whole heart and soul and mind *is* living from center. I get it! Like your Granny said, a center stays where it is. If you don't live from center, focused on the supremacy of love, whatever happens in your life wreaks havoc, inside and out."

"I know," Lenny said. "Center is so clear to me now."

"I love life according to Lenny!" Dawn exclaimed. "If you fell into mud you'd come out smelling like a rose," she giggled.

"That's so sweet of you to say," Lenny said, laughing.

"Lenny, it's true. Please be kind to Lenny. You are a beautiful, blossoming rose and a treasured friend," Dawn said, reaching out and embracing her friend. You know, Carl Jung, used similar imagery of the soul's journey in his autobiography, *Memory, Dreams, Reflections*. He saw the soul as a perennial bulb possessing many seasons of death and rebirth."

"Except in my case I'm not a bulb, I'm a tiny seed that grows into a tree," Lenny said. "At different stages of growth, I've been rock hard and prickly. And another thing I learned about the Desert Rose, it cannot grow without proper drainage. And last night," she giggled, I got drained."

"Just seeing you happy has made my day," Dawn smiled, handing Lenny a tissue from the dressing table by her bed.. "Now dry your eyes and let's get our party face on."

Lenny nodded in agreement as Dawn whispered, "Welcome back" They walked arm-in-arm down the hallway. The aroma of hot cider greeted them as they walked into the kitchen. Joseph handed Dawn a cup, looking at her with adoring eyes. She blew him a kiss.

Ms. Tallulah visited for almost an hour. She even allowed Lenny to hug her before she walked back up the steep hillside to her house. The hour-long jeep ride to the mountains was simply a joy ride. Once there, they had another snowball fight and took a long walk along a snowy mountain stream outside the national park. After a couple of hours, they agreed it was time to go home and get warm and dry again.

Before long, Lenny was standing by her front door, waving goodbye to her friends. That evening, she read Elizabeth a chapter from *Alice in Wonderland*. Then Mack read the "Ali Baba and the Forty Thieves" chapter from *The Arabian Nights*. All three went to bed with their heads full of magic.

In the still of the night, before sleep, Lenny drew pictures and recorded new symbols into her dream journal. Then she opened her gift from Dawn and read the first chapter of *The Secret Door to Success*. Each sentence confirmed her newly acquired belief that one's thoughts and words indeed created one's outer reality. And to become aware of these seeds is divine indeed. Lenny closed her eyes and thought of Ali Baba. He had opened a door just by saying, "Open Sesame." Last night she had opened an inner door, although she hadn't spoken any magic words. All she had to do was surrender. Struggling against a problem made it stay. Not seeing a problem, it vanished.

As Lenny's eyes grew too heavy to stay open, she began to dream. The sound of rushing water filled her with peace. She slowly walked toward the sound and saw the same beautiful fountain where she'd earlier met Atlas. He still supported a marble globe, but this time, his world was not too heavy for his strong shoulders. Steams of crystal clear water rippled down his muscular forearms. As Lenny smiled up at him, he smiled back. He was a perfection to behold.

In the distance, she heard a crowd of people approaching. They circled Atlas, and his fountain, their voices sounding like humming birds in search of a bright red blossom. Every man, woman, and child wore white, sparkling, dewdrop clothing. Lenny looked down at her clothes and saw she was wearing a similar radiant garment.

Her dark-haired stranger stepped forward from the crowd. It was the man who'd been sitting at the Parisian café a few nights before. But he was no longer ignoring Lenny. He was reaching out for her hand, and Lenny saw not a trace of bad behind his knowing grin. Lenny took his hand in hers, and then they both reached out for the hands of countless others.

Soon, the crowd increased both in brilliance and in size. And as all the people circled around the glowing statue of Atlas and his world, Lenny felt as if she knew the best in all of them. Perhaps, long ago, they were all Divine star-seeds in a distant galaxy, one that was merely a heartbeat away.

> That which oppressed me has been slain
> that which encircled me has vanished;
> my craving has faded,
> And I am freed from my ignorance.
> —a chant of victory from the *Gospel of Mary Magdalene*

AUTHOR BIOGRAPHY

Deborah's paintings, as a visionary artist, display her love of nature and always incorporate a touch of the divine feminine. Her lifetime body of work includes oils, watercolor, pen & ink and commercial illustration. At an early age, Deborah often experienced lucid states of dreaming, conversing with deceased loved ones and electrifying archetypal figures. Upon awaking she often felt confused about what was real and what was unreal. From this fertile ground her inner author awoke. Her heart's desire is to paint with words, from a Southern woman's perspective, a rich and beautiful dimension of life just beyond the five senses.

www.ingramcontent.com/pod-product-compliance
Lightning Source LLC
Chambersburg PA
CBHW020834260626
47169CB00003B/988